HEARTWARMING

A Single Dad in Amish Country

Patricia Johns

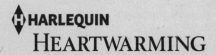

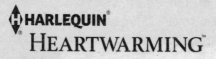

ISBN-13: 978-1-335-58503-5

Recycling programs for this product may not exist in your area.

A Single Dad in Amish Country

Copyright © 2023 by Patricia Johns

For questions and comments about the quality of this book, please contact us at CustomerService@Harlequin.com.

Harlequin Enterprises ULC
22 Adelaide St. West, 41st Floor
Toronto, Ontario M5H 4E3, Canada
www.Harlequin.com

Printed in U.S.A.

Patricia Johns is a *Publishers Weekly* bestselling author who writes from Alberta, Canada, where she lives with her husband and son. She writes Amish romances that will leave you yearning for a simpler life. You can find her at patriciajohns.com and on social media, where she loves to connect with her readers. Drop by her website and you might find your next read!

To my husband and son—
you're the happiest part of my life!

CHAPTER ONE

JOE CARTER HOISTED a bag of soil off the back of his pickup truck and carried it over to the garden plot in front of Butternut Bed and Breakfast. It was a popular little place in the Amish community of Danke, Pennsylvania. He dropped the bag of soil onto the grass and glanced over at his four-year-old daughter, who was crouching nearby, a few blond curls falling free from her ponytail to dangle in front of her eyes.

"What do you have there, Lottie?" he asked.

"A bug." She didn't look up, but she did poke at something with the wing of her die-cast metal airplane.

Joe smiled to himself and headed back over to grab the last bag of soil. He'd been hired by Belinda Wickey, the Amish owner of this bed-and-breakfast, to take care of the gardens and the lawn, since she was too old now to do it herself. He was glad to get the contract—

he'd done this job for her before, and she always offered fresh baking as part of the deal.

Lottie had to come to work with Joe for the next week since her day care was temporarily closed, and it was rather nice to have his daughter around while he worked...so far. Eventually, she'd get bored, and then he'd be in trouble. But he was banking on a great big Amish yard being wildly entertaining.

This being the last day of May, Joe was putting the flowers into their beds. He'd brought a wide array of petunias, zinnias and some brown-eyed Susans for around the edge of the house.

"Hello!" Lottie called, and he looked up to see his daughter trotting over to a woman who'd emerged from the front door of the two-story house. She had on a white sundress and a pair of strappy leather sandals, and her sun-bleached blond hair tumbled in tousled waves around her shoulders. She looked to be about his age—late thirties.

"Hello," the woman said.

"I'm not in day care," Lottie announced. "Do you want to see my plane?"

"Sure, I'll see your plane." She smiled and held her hand out for it. Lottie handed it over and planted her little hands on her hips.

"Do you want to know why I'm not in day care?" Lottie asked.

"Lottie!" Joe called out in warning.

"It's because we all got lice," Lottie went on, ignoring him. "*Somebody* got it first and spread it all around to the whole class. And there was lice everywhere! *Somebody* did it."

"Oh, my." The woman didn't look shocked or horrified, which was the response that would please Lottie most, and Joe could only be thankful for that.

"The somebody in that story isn't my daughter," Joe called.

A smile split over the woman's face. "Well, that's a relief."

"No, it was my friend Julie," Lottie went on. "She got lice from her big brother, who goes to big-kid school, and then she brought it to day care, and those bugs are everywhere! They're in the toy bin, and in the curtains, and the carpet… Our teachers had to shut the whole place down!"

"For a few days," Joe said, rolling his eyes. "This isn't permanent."

"But Daddy says you can't just say who started it because then nobody would want to play with them, and that would be mean.

Daddy says it wasn't Julie's fault she had lice," Lottie said.

Joe grimaced. "This is a very exciting thing in her world."

"I can tell." The woman chuckled.

"And my daddy had to comb my hair very carefully with a tiny comb, and he had to wash all my clothes, and he threw my shoes in the garbage and got me new ones. See?"

She poked a foot out to be inspected.

"Thorough." The woman looked up and met Joe's gaze with an amused look of her own. "I get it. My daughter starts college in the fall, but we went through all of this, too."

She looked too young for a college-age daughter, but a lot of people started their families a whole lot sooner than he had.

"So I get to come to work with my daddy!" Lottie exclaimed with a proud smile.

"Lucky you," the woman said to Lottie.

Joe brushed some soil off his gloves and ambled over to where the woman stood on the step. The broad veranda was set up for comfort—there was a swing with cushions on it, and a little table arranged with some unopened cans of pop.

"My name's Lottie," his daughter said. "And I was named after my grandma."

"That's a lovely name," the woman replied.

"What's your name?" Lottie asked.

"I'm Hazel Dobbs."

"Hazel Dobbs..." Lottie said thoughtfully. "If you went to my day care, I'd just call you Dobby. I like that. He's an elf."

"She's Hogwarts waiting to happen," Joe said with a laugh. "I'm Joe Carter—Carter Landscaping."

"Hazel." She held out her hand, and he pulled off a glove and shook it. She didn't say what she did, but if she was here at the bed-and-breakfast, she was likely on vacation. She looked down at the airplane in her hand. "Do you know what kind of plane this is, Lottie?"

Lottie shook her head.

"It's a Boeing seven fifty-seven," she said, handing the toy back to Lottie. "That's a very big plane for carrying passengers."

"Oh... It's a what?" Lottie frowned, fixing her gaze on Hazel's face.

"Boe-ing...seven fifty-seven," Hazel said slowly.

"Boeing..." Lottie nodded. "How'd you know that?"

"I'm a pilot," Hazel replied.

Joe looked at her in surprise. "Really?" he asked.

"And I'm this close to being employed, too." She held up her thumb and index finger spread about half an inch apart and grinned.

"That's pretty neat," Joe said. "Where are you going to work?"

"I've been hired by a Pennsylvania regional airline. I start in two weeks. This is my chance to relax before the pressure starts."

He noticed a couple of official-looking books behind her on the swing. The hefty-looking one on top was called *American Aviation Protocols: Updated Edition*.

"She flies planes, Lottie," Joe explained.

"You're a plane driver!" Lottie exclaimed. "Really and truly?"

"Yep." Hazel laughed. "You like planes, do you?"

"I love planes!" Lottie said. "My favorite show is *Miley and Buster's Airport*, and when I grow up, I'm going to be a plane driver, too!"

The screen door opened, and Belinda came out onto the porch. She had a little wicker basket in one hand, and she passed it to Lottie.

"Lottie, dear, I need you to look around the yard and gather all the little purple things you can find," Belinda said.

"Little and purple?" Lottie knew this game already from earlier.

"Little and purple," Belinda said. "Can you do it?"

"I can do it!"

Lottie took off with the basket, and Joe called after her, "Not in the garden, though, Lottie!"

"Oh, it's not a problem. Gardens are for enjoying for little people, too," Belinda said with a wave of her hand.

"Maybe for Amish kids," Joe said with a laugh. Lottie had been raised in a day care, and she wasn't overflowing with the common sense that farm kids had. Lottie was an imaginative chatterbox who'd demolish an entire garden for one purple bloom.

Joe headed back to the garden plot and got to work spreading a nice thick layer of topsoil. He used a hand cultivator to mix it into the dirt below. Every once in a while, he'd glance up to see where his daughter was searching for her small purple treasures, and his gaze would pass that front porch.

Hazel had settled onto the swing with a can of pop and that thick book. The swing creaked softly, and he found his gaze drawn back to the slim woman. She had a quiet, sure way about her, and he couldn't help but notice that tumble of thick blond waves… She was gorgeous…and he was grubby today. But that wasn't what was on his mind. She'd mentioned having a college-age daughter—she had parenting experience that he didn't have.

How weird would it be to ask her a few questions?

Joe had been raising Lottie alone since her birth, and while he was determined to do right by his daughter, he knew he'd come up against a lot of things he wouldn't know how to handle. And girls were a different world. What he needed was some tried-and-true advice from someone who *knew*.

"Daddy!" Lottie called. "Did you know there's a donkey over there?"

"Yeah, I know," Joe said. "If you're really good, maybe Miss Belinda will let you feed him a carrot later."

"Can I feed him now?" Lottie asked.

"No!"

"Why not?"

"It's not safe, Lottie," he replied.

"Will he bite my hand off?" Lottie hollered back.

"Yes. Definitely. That's why you have to wait."

"Okay!"

Joe heard a stifled laugh from the porch and looked over to see Hazel had put her book down onto her lap.

"That's a fun age," she said.

"Yeah…a tiring one, too."

"This is the sweet spot. After this is school, and separation anxiety, and emails from the teacher…"

"Your daughter was a handful, was she?" he asked.

"No more than any kid," she replied. "But there's always something. Is Lottie an only child?"

"Yep."

Hazel just nodded.

"I've heard about only children needing extra socializing and stuff." He headed over to the porch again. She'd brought it up, hadn't she? "Do you just have the one daughter?"

"Yes. Madison," Hazel replied. "And don't listen to what they tell you. Kids learn from their experiences. Some kids experience brothers and sisters, and other kids experience a whole lot more adult interaction. They all grow up. Madison is great. She's smart, caring, a superhard worker… I couldn't be prouder."

"Any advice for this age?" He leaned against the railing.

"You seem like you're doing just fine."

"Anything coming up soon I should be keeping an eye out for?"

"A thousand things." She chuckled. "But you'll tackle them all one at a time and figure them out."

"I was hoping for something more concrete."

She shrugged. "Sorry. Just enjoy this age. I think that's the secret, looking back on it. Enjoy her being little and all the funny things she says. Because soon enough she'll be fourteen and she'll know absolutely everything."

Joe laughed. "Yeah, I guess, right? So how long are you in Danke for?"

"A little over a week. I arrived from Pittsburgh today." She looked down at the book on her lap, then closed it. "My daughter got on the plane for England yesterday. She's meeting her father's family for the first time."

"Wow... How tough is that for you?"

"Harder than I thought," she said. "I'm distracting myself with work. Maddie wouldn't approve, but she isn't here to roll her eyes at me, either."

He chuckled. "I can sympathize—with missing her, I mean. My daughter hasn't reached the eye-rolling stage yet."

"That comes faster than you think." Her blue eyes sparkled with humor, then her smile faded. "After this trip, she's going to college. So this is it. I've got an empty nest."

"And a great kid," he said.

"Yes, and a really great daughter." She smiled. "I'm not saying this stage is easy, but I've been looking forward to it, too. After making being a mom my top priority for nineteen years, it's my turn now."

"What'll you do?" he asked, but his gaze slid down to that book on her lap.

"I'm taking the job of my dreams." A smile touched her lips. "And for the next week, I'm reviewing all sorts of protocols and some airplane specs of the machine I'll be flying. I was supposed to relax for a week, but I'm just... I'm not used to all this quiet and solitude anymore."

"Well, with us around, I'm not sure you'll get the quiet."

She chuckled. "My point is, enjoy this. It passes so much faster than you think it will. And when you have your turn to live your life and do whatever you want to again...you'll miss her a lot."

Joe couldn't imagine a time when Lottie

would be that grown up. It felt like this little-kid stage would last forever, and he just felt like a wild success when he managed to lie on the couch and catch a catnap on the weekend while Lottie watched TV. But she was right. Lottie would grow up.

"Sage advice," he said.

"Thank you. It was hard-won." She smiled again.

"If you think of any parenting hacks for this age, let me know," he said with a laugh. "You know, like how to get her to tell fewer embarrassing stories to strangers, that kind of thing."

"Where's the fun in that?"

"I'm still looking." He grinned. "I'd better get back to work."

Joe headed back to the garden and picked up his hand cultivator. Some guys hated it when strangers gave advice, but he lapped it up. He didn't have a wife to figure things out with, and while he wouldn't take every piece of advice, there was always a nugget in there somewhere that worked wonders with Lottie.

And one of these days, someone would tell him the secret to getting his daughter to stop telling overly revealing stories. He was sure of it.

HAZEL WATCHED THE tall man's forearms flex as he worked the soil, then she sighed and looked back down at her book. He was a good-looking guy, with dark brown hair that shone just a little bit auburn in the sunlight, and dark eyes. Traditionally handsome— that's how she'd describe him to Madison later on. Imagining this vacation had been a whole lot different than the reality of actually slowing down. And she missed Maddie something fierce. Somehow knowing that there was a whole ocean between them made this trip harder.

And maybe it was also knowing that when Maddie came back, she was heading straight to college. Maddie was moving into her adult years…and at thirty-eight, Hazel was ready to finally do the stuff she'd missed out on as a single mom for the last nineteen years.

Hazel's parents, a lawyer and a dentist, had raised her for "better things," and they'd been deeply disappointed when she had ended up pregnant at eighteen. Almost as old as Maddie was now, and the thought of her daughter stopping to have a baby at this age was a little heartbreaking for her, too. Maddie deserved some freedom, and a chance to build her life on her own terms. But Hazel was lucky—

she had supportive parents who'd helped pay for both her private and commercial pilot's licenses, and those didn't come cheap. And they'd been enthusiastic grandparents who'd taken great joy in spoiling Maddie rotten whenever they got the chance. Maddie might not have had her dad in her daily life, but she hadn't suffered like some kids did. Hazel got to fly, and Maddie was going to college—her parents had made sure of it.

Hazel could hear the chatter of the little girl behind her, a running commentary of what she was doing that suddenly changed tone from searching for her treasures to playing with her plane. Then she was chattering about some art at day care—at least that's what it sounded like.

"And you put your hand in the paint, and put it on the paper," Lottie said. "And then it will go on the wall, and we can go see it!" There was a pause. "Daddy! Daddy!"

"Yes, Lottie?"

"We're making a handprint art to go on the wall and everyone can walk past and see it!" she hollered.

"That's great, Lottie."

"Will we go see it on the wall?"

"Sure thing."

Hazel couldn't help but smile. Back when Maddie was little, she hadn't had any interest in airplanes. She'd been polite about it, but she'd been much more interested in her plastic ponies. Hazel could still remember trying to explain it to Maddie when she got her private pilot's license.

"Your mom flies planes, Maddie. Your mom can fly a plane all by herself! That's a big deal, you know. I bet you don't know anyone else whose mom can do that, do you?"

Maddie had just shrugged. "Nope. That's very nice, Mommy. Very nice. You want to smell my scented marker?"

Hazel read the next few pages of her book, murmuring aloud to herself as she went over the pertinent information, and she looked up when Lottie came up the steps and leaned against the railing, looking at her. Her hands were dirty now, and there was a streak of soil down the front of her T-shirt.

"What are you doing?" Lottie asked.

"I'm reading."

"Why?"

"Because I have to study so I don't make a mistake."

"Oh." The little girl looked down at her airplane.

Maybe that had been a little too heavy for a child that age. Preschoolers didn't need to know that mistakes could cost lives during a takeoff and landing.

"Where did you get that airplane?" Hazel asked.

"Santa gave it to me."

"You must have been very good," Hazel said with a smile.

"Oh, yes. I'm always good. But I didn't ask Santa for an airplane. I asked him to find me my mommy."

Lottie looked down at her toy, her lips pursed in a thoughtful little pout. Hazel's heart gave a squeeze. What could she say?

"Santa specializes in toys," Hazel said after a beat of silence. "He does his best, but toys are really where he shines."

"I know…" Lottie came up to the swing and looked up hopefully. "Can I sit on here, too?"

Hazel moved over and Lottie climbed up. Then Hazel started them gently swinging again. Lottie leaned back and heaved a sigh.

"My mommy left when I was a little baby," she said. "She went away, and she never came back."

"I'm sorry, sweetie," Hazel said.

"Yeah… My daddy says it's okay and that we're just fine the two of us, but my friends have mommies."

"Every family looks different," Hazel said.

She'd told Maddie something similar when she was young. They'd sort out life, just the two of them. There was nothing to worry about… But Maddie had missed having her dad around more often, and Hazel knew it. But what could Hazel do? She couldn't wave a wand and give her daughter that fairy-tale family. So she'd said exactly what Joe had told Lottie—that they'd be just fine.

"When I grow up, I'm going to be an airplane driver, and I'm going to find my mommy," Lottie said. "I'll look out the windows until I spot her. She might have gotten lost, or something. I think she'd be very happy to see me. I think she must miss me by now, don't you think? Don't you think she misses me?"

What could Hazel say to this little girl? She knew nothing about the situation. Kids often got an idea about what had happened that was filled in with their own guesses. It sounded like Lottie had come to the conclusion that her mother had just wandered off and gotten lost. And Hazel didn't dare say the wrong thing.

"Oh, Lottie…" she said softly.

"Charlotte!" Joe called. Hazel felt a wave of relief.

Lottie straightened, and her expression turned alert. "What, Daddy?" she hollered.

"There you are." Joe came over to the porch, the cultivator tool over one shoulder. He cast Hazel an apologetic look. "Sorry about that." Then he hooked a finger at his daughter. "Come on, you. This lady wants to read her book on the porch, and you need to let her do that. We're here to work, not bug Miss Belinda's guests."

"You can call me Hazel," she said with a small smile.

"Sorry. Hazel." Joe shot her a boyish smile, and the way his dark gaze caught hers for just a moment made her breath catch. Wow… He was charming when he put in some effort, wasn't he? She forced herself to look down at her book again, the information swimming across the page. But she wasn't here to flirt with landscapers.

Belinda pushed open the screen door and looked out at them. She was an older woman, portly, and neatly dressed in a pink Amish cape dress. Her hair was white, and her *kapp* was a shade whiter than her hair. She wore a pair of rimless glasses that made her blue eyes sparkle.

"Did you find your purple treasures?" Belinda asked, leaning against the railing.

"Let me get my basket!" Lottie ran off around the house and returned breathless a moment later. "I only found one purple thing."

"What is it?" Belinda asked.

"A flower."

"How wonderful," Belinda said thoughtfully. "I know of another purple thing you might like. It's a thing with purple in the center of it. I have doughnuts."

"Doughnuts?" Lottie asked softly, then her eyes brightened. "What's in the middle that's purple?"

"Blackberry jam," Belinda said. "Why don't you come inside and have one, Lottie? Is that okay with your *daet*?"

Lottie looked over at Joe. "Can I, Daddy?"

"Sure," Joe said. "Go on inside."

Lottie followed Belinda into the house, her clattering footsteps echoing.

"Save one for me!" Joe called after her, and he smiled, shaking his head. "It's harder than I thought to get anything done with her here, but what can you do, right? I don't think any timing would be great for the day care to shut down for a week, so it might as well be in the summer. This would be a whole lot harder if I was plowing snow."

"She really loves planes, doesn't she?" Hazel asked.

"She really does."

Hazel eyed the man for a moment. Was she overstepping if she told him what his daughter had said? It wasn't the easy thing to do, but it was probably the right thing.

"She told me that she wants to use a plane to look for her mom." Hazel winced. "She said she thinks she's lost and misses her. I'm only telling you because I'm a parent, too, and I thought you might want to know."

"She said that?" Joe pressed his lips together, his gaze moving toward the house.

"Yeah."

"Shoot…" He sighed.

And now he might feel like he'd failed or messed something up. She knew that feeling all too well.

"My daughter told her entire second-grade class that her father was a duke who had a castle in England," Hazel said. "Kids make things up about their missing parent sometimes. It's normal!"

"No castle?" Joe asked with a short laugh.

"No dukedom, either, although he does live in England. She just…made up a story she preferred. It sounds to me like Lottie is doing the same thing."

"Thanks." Joe rubbed a hand through his hair. "She's been obsessed with her mom recently."

"That does happen," Hazel said.

"She's never met her mother, though."

"That might make her more mysterious, more intriguing."

"Yeah, that and she's just figured out that other kids have moms and she feels the lack," he said.

"I'm sorry."

"It is what it is," he said with a shrug.

"I raised my daughter without her father for the most part. I mean, he did visit her sometimes, but the day-to-day was just the two of us. So I get it. I had to go through all of the why-doesn't-my-dad-live-with-us questions, too."

Joe nodded. "Does it get easier?"

"Not really," Hazel admitted. "As soon as you think they've made peace with one level, they start asking more complicated questions."

"I was afraid of that." He brushed some dirt off his forearm. "How did your daughter deal with it all?"

"She's done pretty well," Hazel said. "She's nervous to meet her half siblings for the first time, but I'm glad that Todd stayed in her life. And to his credit, he never missed a child-support payment."

Todd's family had been very well off, and Todd had never seriously considered a future with Hazel. That had been a rude awakening—that he'd sleep with her, whisper sweet nothings and have no intention of committing. They'd broken up while Hazel was still pregnant, and Todd had gone to England shortly after Maddie's birth and started his life there. He worked in the family business—sportswear. It wasn't glamorous, but it was lucrative.

"That's good he kept up his responsibility there," Joe said.

"Do you mind if I ask what happened to Lottie's mom?" Hazel asked.

"She…" Joe sighed. "She didn't want to be a mother. It was a fling. We fell fast, and she got pregnant, and only then did she make it clear she didn't want kids. Ever. But she was willing to have Lottie…and give her up for adoption. I wanted to raise Lottie myself. So we came to an agreement."

"I guess it's a similar story—a fling that made a baby. Never simple, is it?"

"Never."

Hazel let her gaze move over the large green lawn. Some apple trees lined one side of the lawn, and in the other direction she could see an Amish farm. All was quiet. Then a susurration of birds swung up like a flapping sheet from a copse of trees, circled around and then settled back into the branches. Hazel had chosen Butternut Bed and Breakfast for the solitude and quiet, but now that she was here, she wondered how much peace and quiet she could actually tolerate. Even thick technical books couldn't fill up all this silence.

"I'm planning on visiting a local airplane hangar tomorrow," Hazel said. "It's a historic site—the original structure was used in World War II. But, full confession? I just want to check out the planes."

Joe laughed. "Good for you. Make the most of your visit."

"I bet your Lottie would love it," Hazel

said. "A lot of times you can get tours of the planes and the hangar. The guys who work there aren't always busy, and they enjoy talking about anything aviation."

"I might do that," he said. "But I'm just a guy with a four-year-old who likes planes. I don't know anything about it myself, so I can't talk shop with them. I'm not sure I could just waltz in there and ask to let my preschooler look around an airplane."

True. Flyboys could be a territorial lot— she knew that from experience.

"I don't know if you could…but I could." Hazel met his gaze.

"Yeah, but you're one of them," he said.

"Then come with me," she suggested. "I don't have much else to do around here besides reviewing protocols, and I'd like the company. Besides, it's nice to light a passion for aviation in little girls. I feel like I'm doing something for our future."

Joe looked toward the house, thoughtful. "She'd really love it…"

Hazel waited, watching him as he thought it through. He turned back to her and a smile touched his lips.

"Sure. Yeah. Let's do it. As long as you're

sure we won't be in the way. You don't have a car here, do you?"

She shook her head. "I'd take a taxi."

"Forget that," Joe said. "You get us in for that tour, and I'll drive you. A way of evening the score a bit. Besides, Lottie will get to tour the hangar with a pilot. She won't know how lucky she is."

"They never do," Hazel said with a grin. "And thank you. I'll take you up on that offer."

Joe angled his head back toward the garden plot.

"I need to get back at it," he said.

"Of course." She picked up her book and tried not to let him see her as she watched him saunter back to his truck, where a flat of flowers was waiting.

She might regret making friends with the landscaper, but right now it was better than facing all that peace and quiet on her own. This was her fresh start, her chance to do the one thing she'd dreamed of as Maddie had grown up... And she was afraid to stop and feel it, because if she did, she might start getting scared and start second-guessing if she was good enough to step into the role of regional airline pilot.

Focusing on her material to make sure she was successful from day one was key. She'd do what she did best—jump in and prove herself.

CHAPTER TWO

THE NEXT AFTERNOON, after bringing Lottie home for lunch and to get changed, he buckled her into her car seat and headed back down the highway toward Butternut Bed and Breakfast. He liked this drive—it was relaxing with the stretches of leafy trees that banked the road interspersed with pasture and grazing cattle. Tufts of clouds surfed the blue sky overhead, leaving splotches of shadow on the rolling farmland below, and the scent of fresh grass came in through the cracked window.

When Lottie was a baby, Joe had moved away from Scranton and out to Danke— partly to stay true to his word to Jessica about not letting Lottie know who her mother was until she was eighteen, and partly for his own personal reasons… He'd been adopted, and he knew one thing about the woman who gave birth to him—she was an Amish girl from this area. When he moved out here, it wasn't to find her or contact her. It had just felt like a connection to the people he came from. And now? Now, he'd been starting to think he might want to find the family who had given him up, after all. If he could get his courage up to start looking. He hadn't even told his parents he'd been considering it, but he was sure it had occurred to them when he moved to Danke.

"We're going to see airplanes!" Lottie sang from the back seat.

"Now, you have to be quiet when we go in there," Joe said, looking at her in the rearview mirror. "And you have to walk nicely beside me. No touching anything unless I say you can. Got it?"

"I'll be good," she replied.

"And Hazel is being really nice to us by bringing us with her to the hangar, so we have to be extra nice to her, too, okay?"

"I'll be nice."

Yeah, Lottie always meant well, but she was a chatterbox, and she said whatever came into her head. As of this year, her lisp was gone, too, so she was easy to understand…to everyone within earshot. There was a reason why he preferred taking her to a kid's play center than to a restaurant. Four-year-olds were a tangle of energy, and Lottie seemed to have more than most.

But then, Hazel wasn't new to the different stages little girls went through, and that was a relief. Because some days, sweet little Lottie became an emotional wreck, and there were grocery stores where the cashiers gave him the side-eye as soon as they walked into the store. He hated that because his daughter was a good kid. But when she was tired from day care, and they still had one more trip to make to get some food in the house, the cashiers didn't get to see the sweet kid he saw when he dropped her off in the morning. And he knew that Lottie noticed the glares, and they didn't help.

"I think Hazel's hair is pretty," Lottie said.

"Uh…yeah." Hazel's shoulder-length blond hair had definitely caught his eye, too. She was a beautiful woman—no argument there.

"I wish I had pretty hair like Hazel's," Lottie said.

"You have very pretty hair," Joe said.

"Do you think Hazel's hair is pretty?" Lottie asked.

"Sure I do. It's pretty, too." Maybe Lottie was noticing how a woman did her hair… Joe was capable of doing Lottie's hair in a ponytail, and that was about it. The older his daughter got, the more he realized he was out of his depth when it came to feminine things.

Butternut Drive was at the corner of a prominent four-way stop along the narrow highway. He turned down the shade-dappled road and slowed for an Amish buggy that came down the road toward him. The driver had a bushy, gray-streaked beard, and Joe lifted two fingers in response to the older man's nod of greeting.

The Butternut Bed and Breakfast sign was a little faded—a white wooden background with green lettering.

"That's the sign with all the *B*s!" Lottie said. "See, Daddy? The *B*s!"

Pretty hair had apparently been forgotten.

"What other letters do you see on there?" he asked as he turned into the drive.

"Just *B*s," Lottie said, and Joe chuckled. They'd been learning some of the alphabet at day care. He really should practice with her at home so she'd be ready for kindergarten next year, but he hadn't had the energy to try and make her sit still and stare at flash cards. He'd played *Sesame Street* in the background at home, though, hoping something might stick.

"I wish my name had a *B* in it," Lottie said.

"Why?" he asked. "You have a *C* for Charlotte. And an *L* for Lottie…"

"But *B*s are so pretty," Lottie said softly, and he almost felt like he'd done her a disservice in naming her.

He pulled up next to the house. Belinda stood by the front door chatting with Eli Lapp, who lived next door. Eli's black dog sat at their feet. They turned as he came to a stop. Behind them, in the corral, the donkey looked up from the watering trough, water dripping from his muzzle.

"Hello, Joe!" Belinda called.

"Hi!" Joe called out his open window.

"Daddy, can I go see the donkey?" Lottie asked.

"No, you stay put," he replied. "We're leaving right away."

"It won't take me long!" she pleaded.

"Lottie, I said no. Stay put." Joe left the truck running, and Hazel came outside wearing a pair of blue jeans and a light blouse, and carrying a purse over one shoulder.

"Are you off somewhere?" Belinda asked.

"Hazel is going to help me get Lottie a tour of the local hangar."

"Well, isn't that a perfect idea?" Belinda

said. "Lottie does seem taken with planes. And you're really a pilot, dear?"

"Sure am," Hazel said.

"You don't look like a pilot," Eli said.

"What do pilots look like?" Joe asked with a laugh.

"Maybe—" Eli mimed being taller, bigger and having a beard.

"That's very old-fashioned," Hazel said with a chuckle.

Eli and Belinda just looked at her, expressions blank. *Old-fashioned* didn't have the same connotation for the Amish—it was just their way of life.

"How's the herd, Eli?" Joe asked, mostly to break the awkward moment.

"Well, it's a herd of five right now. Not much of a herd," Eli replied. "But I'm renting out my western pasture, and I've got someone else renting out some crop fields… It's a patchwork quilt, but it's a living."

"You ready to hire someone to mow that lawn of yours?" Joe asked with a grin.

"Nope," Eli said. "I do it myself. It might take me half the day, but at least I know when I look at my lawn, I mowed it myself. I offered to take care of Belinda's lawn, too."

"Eli, you don't have the time for that!" Belinda said. "I'd be a terrible neighbor if I let you do that. I can pay to have a company come."

Eli muttered something in Pennsylvania Dutch, but it seemed clear to Joe that Eli's male pride had been wounded.

"Well, you keep me in mind when you're ready to hire someone," Joe replied.

Eli just shook his head. He was a stubborn old guy, and he'd probably die propped up against his push mower before he caved in and hired an *Englisher* to mow his grass. Amish farmers were a tough lot, and Eli was probably the toughest Joe had come across.

Hazel hoisted herself into the passenger side of his truck, and Joe got into the driver's seat. He gave Belinda and Eli a wave, then put the truck in Reverse.

"The Amish world has really strong gender roles," Joe said as he turned around and headed back up the drive. "There's men's work, and there's women's work. Women work in the house with the kids, and men work in the fields. Period."

"Yeah, I know about that," Hazel said. "Don't worry, I'm not offended. Makes you wonder how many of their girls wish they could do something else, though, doesn't it?"

"That could be the same for boys, too. But if they want it badly enough, they leave," Joe replied.

"True, but that's sad, too," Hazel said softly.

"They leave?" Lottie echoed from the back seat, and Joe grimaced. "What do you mean, they leave? Where do they go?"

"They, um—" Joe hadn't meant to say something like that in front of Lottie. "When they're grown up, sometimes they decide to go live somewhere else."

Hazel glanced over at him. It was a lie. When Amish girls left home to try out a new way of life, they were teenagers and certainly not grown. But Lottie might take that to heart once she dug in on the idea.

"Do they have mommies and daddies?" Lottie asked.

"Of course."

"Do their mommies and daddies live in the same house?" she persisted.

"Sure," Joe said, trying to stay casual.

"And they don't want to stay with their mommies and daddies?" Lottie asked, her voice starting to rise.

"Lottie, you're going to stay with me forever, right?" Joe asked, glancing over his shoulder and shooting her a grin. "You're never getting married. You'll hang out with me, and we'll make french fries on Saturdays and go out for ice cream on Sundays, and the rest of the week we'll eat broccoli!"

"Ew!" Lottie moaned. "Not broccoli!"

"I like broccoli," Joe said. This was a familiar game. "Lots of it. Heaps of broccoli on Monday, and Tuesday, and Wednesday..."

"No!" Lottie laughed.

There—he'd successfully gotten her derailed off a much scarier thought.

"I agree with Lottie," Hazel said. "No broccoli."

"See, Daddy?" Lottie laughed. "She agrees!"

"I think you should have brussels sprouts!" Hazel said.

"Ew!" Lottie groaned from the back seat.

Joe laughed and met Hazel's gaze just for a moment. This was nice—for once he wasn't feeling outnumbered by a single four-year-old. He stopped at the large stop sign and turned onto the highway.

The drive to Danke Hangar was quite direct. There were a few prominent signs along the highway for some tourist locations like Lehmann's Family Fun Farm, which had mini golf, a corn maze in season and crafts for sale. He'd been curious about that place for a while now and kept thinking he should bring his daughter to check it out.

The hangar, however, was located just outside of town on a side road. The sign that pointed in its direction was small and subtle, and if Joe hadn't known where it was, he might have missed it. The hangar was a large, low building with two crisscrossing runways and an ample tarmac attached. It was a traditional hangar—all made of wood that had been painted and repainted over the years. Currently, it was painted white with dark blue trim. This was the place for hobby pilots to house their planes and get flight lessons.

There were a few vehicles parked in a line in front of the hangar, and Joe pulled in next to a rusty Ford pickup. A small plane buzzed down a runway, the engine whining, and then it wobbled up into the air and started to climb. Joe looked into the back seat to see his daughter's gaze locked on the window as she watched the plane take off. He couldn't explain her love of airplanes, aside from the fact that it had started with *Miley and Buster's Airport*. The other girls her age liked ponies and princesses. But his daughter had locked on to airplanes with a passion so fierce that it left him amazed.

Would it last? Who knew?

"Can we do that today?" Lottie asked, her voice low and eager, her eyes still fixed on the little airplane climbing into the sky.

"No, kiddo," Joe said. "We're just here to look today."

"You sure?" Lottie asked, looking up at him.

"I'm positive. But come on, let's get you unbuckled."

When they all got out, Lottie stood where she could see the plane's ascent. Joe looked over at Hazel to see her watching Lottie with a smile.

"How old were you when you discovered planes?" Joe asked.

"I was a teenager," she replied. "But that look—I recognize it. She's hooked."

"Should I be afraid?" he asked with a chuckle.

"That depends," Hazel teased. "Are you saving for her flight lessons yet? They're pricey."

Joe rubbed a hand over his eyes. That was a legitimate worry. He wasn't a rich man, and he knew a couple of single fathers right now battling their exes about horse-riding lessons for their daughters. Some hobbies were expensive, but his soft spot was that look on Lottie's face when she saw planes.

"Not yet." Then he ruffled Lottie's hair. "Come on. Let's go see if they'll give us a tour." He noticed Hazel eyeing him thoughtfully, and he shot her a grin. "Hazel is going to sweet-talk them for us."

IT DIDN'T ACTUALLY take that much sweet-talking, Hazel thought as she chatted with the hangar manager for a few minutes. His name was Miles, and he was in his seventies. He had an air force background and one amputated leg—from diabetes, not the Vietnam War. He'd told her that in a tone that suggested there were better ways to lose a leg, in his opinion. She showed both her commercial and private pilot's licenses, which she kept in a little blue folder inside her purse. Miles nodded enthusiastically.

"Nice to see some women in the field these days," Miles said. "The air force was pretty male-dominated in my day. I hear it's a bit better nowadays, but I imagine you get a pretty girl with her wings, and she'd have a hundred fighter pilots at her beck and call."

"It's more competitive, at least in the commercial classes," Hazel said. "No one wants to be beaten by the pretty girl with her wings."

Miles barked out a laugh. "Yeah, I could see that, too. I was more of a lover than a fighter myself, though. In my day, I wouldn't have been intimidated. If I'd met you, I'd have charmed you senseless."

She chuckled. "I believe you, Miles."

"All the same…" He looked toward the window, where Joe was looking outside at the runway, Lottie next to him. They both had their heads cocked at the exact same angle, Lottie not even coming up to his waist.

"That your daughter?" Miles asked.

"No, she's my friend's daughter," Hazel replied. "But she loves planes."

"Well, as long as you don't let her touch anything too important," Miles said. "And we've got a Cessna for sale right now. You don't happen to be interested in buying a plane?"

"Not today," Hazel said.

"Because if you were, you could take a look inside," Miles said with a shrug. "Wouldn't hurt anything."

"Then, maybe I am," Hazel said with a chuckle. That would be convenient to be able to show this little airplane enthusiast some controls. "Thanks, I appreciate that."

"Just leave it like you found it," Miles said. "And if you want to rent a plane one of these days, just go up for the fun of it, I've got reasonable prices."

"I will definitely take you up on that." Getting into the sky again would be a relief, and she loved the feeling of bouncing along the air currents in a small plane. It wasn't the same as a passenger plane, though. The larger the plane, the bigger the thrill. It was like the difference between going down a hill in a semi versus on a bike. The bike might have more bumps, but the semi had that feeling of gathering momentum and power growling in the engine that rumbled under the seat.

The hangar was a low, sparse, echoing building with four planes parked inside. The walls that sloped up into a curving ceiling were all pristine white, and the floor, marked with paint to show where planes belonged, was concrete. She noticed some old WWII photos on the wall in Miles's office. Those were well before his day, and there were more WWII photos by the main doors, above which a big propeller was fixed to the wall. Something was holding Joe and Lottie's attention at that window, though, and it wasn't the pictures on the walls beside it. Hazel headed over to where they were standing and looked out over Lottie's head. A young man in a set of green rubber overalls was washing a plane, and Lottie was entranced.

Joe glanced over at her and raised his eyebrows.

"Yep, permission to poke around granted," Hazel said.

"Great," Joe said. "Come on, Lottie, let's take a look."

"We can start outside, if you want." Hazel looked over her shoulder at Miles and pointed to the side door. Miles gave her a thumbs-up.

They headed out the door and Hazel gave the young man a nod. He nodded back and continued his work. Lottie pulled out her toy plane, and her gaze moved over to the bucket of soapy water. It looked to Hazel like she wanted to wash her plane, too, and the thought made her smile.

"No," Joe said firmly, and he and his daughter exchanged a look, and then Lottie pulled her plane back against her chest.

"Do you want to see what the runways look like?" Hazel asked. "You see how there are two?"

"Is one for going away? And one for coming home?" Lottie asked.

"Not really. They're numbered, though, so the guy on the ground can tell the pilot which one to use. Really, it's just helpful for pilots coming in from a different direction. But a big airport would have more runways. Do you see that little road that leads up to the big runway?"

Lottie nodded.

"That's called a taxiway. The plane can drive on it to get to the runway."

Hazel pointed out the features around them, and they strolled slowly along. Joe fell in next to her, close enough that his arm brushed hers sometimes. Hazel wasn't sure how much of her commentary Lottie was really listening to. The little girl sometimes flew her toy airplane out at arm's length as they walked, and then landed it on her father's arm.

"My friend Carrie went on an airplane," Lottie said. "She went to Disneyland, and she flew on a plane, and she cried because her ears hurt, so she got to chew gum."

"That helps," Hazel replied.

"And my friend Nelson's daddy went on an airplane and never came back." Lottie announced this with the same matter-of-fact tone as she'd used for the Disneyland story.

"Oh…" Hazel said.

"Sorry," Joe interjected. "Lottie, maybe that's not a story we tell…"

"It's okay," Hazel replied. "I'm sorry Nelson's daddy didn't come back."

"So my daddy said he'll never go on an airplane without me, not ever ever," Lottie said.

"My daughter went on an airplane without me," Hazel said. "And I know she'll come back."

"Hmm." Lottie didn't look convinced of this, and Hazel watched her as she flew her plane in little buzzing circles.

"What happened with this Nelson kid?" Hazel asked.

"The dad left the family. Four kids, too." Joe shook his head. "I don't understand that. To just walk away from them…? I was willing to turn everything upside down to make sure I got Lottie. But he left the family for some other woman, and they hardly hear from him. They're all wrecks about it."

"Wow…" Hazel murmured.

"And Michelle's mommy wanted my daddy to be her boyfriend!" Lottie went on. "Right,

Daddy? She brought my daddy cookies, and she asked him to go with her to a movie. A movie!"

"A movie!" Hazel shot Joe a grin, and his face colored a little bit. Was this embarrassing him?

"But my daddy doesn't want to be Michelle's mommy's boyfriend," Lottie said. "Because she's not pretty enough."

Hazel eyed Joe, and his face grew pinker. Kids didn't miss much, and she could just imagine the single moms at the park developing crushes on Joe. He was good-looking, and a really good dad to his little girl. That would be a hard combination for a young mom to resist, especially if she was hoping to find a stepdad for her own child. Maybe Joe knew exactly how attractive he was.

"It's not exactly like that," Joe said.

"You said you didn't think she was pretty," Lottie said defensively.

"What I said was that when you're someone's boyfriend, you have to think of them that way," Joe said. "Like when a guy thinks a lady is really pretty. And I didn't think that way about Michelle's mom."

"Yeah…" Lottie shrugged. "Because you don't think Michelle's mom is pretty."

"No!" Joe rubbed his hands over his face. "It isn't that. I'm sure lots of people think she's just great."

"But Hazel is pretty, right?" Lottie asked. "And I'm pretty. And my teacher, Miss Pinch, is pretty."

"I—" Joe seemed to be at a loss for words. "Miss Pinch?"

"I think she's pretty," Lottie said. "Miss Pinch has pretty fingernails. And she has pretty sweaters that always match her running shoes."

"Right…" Joe frowned.

"Daddy said you were pretty in the truck," Lottie said, looking up at Hazel.

Joe stared down at his daughter, then his gaze whipped up to Hazel. Hazel tried not to laugh as she watched the embarrassment flood over Joe's face. Had he really said that? It had been a long time since she'd been complimented on her looks.

"I tend to give off the busy-mom vibe," Hazel said, attempting to dispel the discomfort. "Men run from it."

"We were talking about hair," Joe said

feebly. "And... Okay, so, yes. I think Hazel is pretty. Alright? We're all okay with this? Hazel is pretty, Lottie is pretty, and I am, apparently, a huge idiot."

Hazel started to laugh. "I'll take the compliment, Joe."

"It's yours." Joe shook his head.

"And Miss Pinch has the loveliest running shoes!" Lottie sang out happily, trotting on ahead of them.

Hazel chuckled. "It's okay," she said. "I know how kids are."

Joe didn't look down at her, but a smile did toy at the corners of his lips.

"I'm actually really bad at flirting," he said. "And at the dating scene. With a daughter to raise, I've been pretty focused on her. I mean, it's a lot more complicated. I can't just start up with someone unless I know they'd be good for Lottie. And you don't just pick up a single mom and see where it goes... It's... complicated."

"Oh, I know," Hazel said. "I did the same."

"Did you date at all?" he asked.

"A little bit. There were exactly three guys. Once every five years was my pace—pathetic as that might sound. One was very sweet, would have made a great stepdad, but I just didn't feel what I should. Another had a really complicated relationship with his kids' mom, and I couldn't handle that level of drama. The last one…" Her mind went back to the last man she'd gotten her hopes up for. "The last one broke up with me. I was too busy with working, flight school and all that. And he didn't want that."

He didn't want the combination that made up the best of her. That one still stung.

"Now your daughter is grown, though…" Joe glanced down at her. "Will you find someone?"

"I might." She shrugged. "I'm more focused on this pilot job, honestly. When you've got a child at home, everything is about parenting…as it should be. But I've always dreamed of flying for a commercial airline, and I have the chance. It's a whole new world out there for me now."

Boyfriends and their unrealistic hopes could kick rocks, for all she cared.

They headed back into the hangar, and for the next few minutes, Hazel pointed out parts of the planes and then showed Lottie on her own little toy. Joe seemed to be standing back more as Hazel gave Lottie an external tour of a gorgeous new Beechcraft Bonanza plane. Farther back in the hangar, a little Cessna sat unobtrusively to one side. A For Sale sign was taped on one window. Hazel looked toward the office window, where she could see Miles watching. She pointed over her head toward the Cessna, and the man gave her another thumbs-up.

"You want to see inside a plane?" Hazel asked.

"Really?" Lottie's eyes widened.

"But you can't touch anything without my permission," Hazel said. "Can you promise that?"

Lottie put her hands behind her back and nodded vigorously.

Hazel looked over at Joe, and she felt that old familiar tug of longing… A good-looking guy, a heart of gold—yep, that was hard to resist for any woman, not just Michelle's mom. But Hazel had a little more life experience under her belt. She knew how this went.

"Okay, Lottie," Joe said, coming forward. "We're going to look with our eyes, not our fingers."

"I know!" Lottie said.

Hazel opened the door and leaned inside to take a quick look around. The cockpit was in good shape—whoever owned this plane had taken care of it. There was a plastic sleeve with the plane's details inside, and she pulled it out, glancing over it. If she was in the market for a plane of her own, this one looked like it had been well cared for.

"You can come sit in the pilot's seat," Hazel said, and she laughed as Lottie just about bounced up there by herself. Hazel got Lottie settled so that she could look around—although from her height there wasn't much to see, aside from a dashboard full of controls. Lottie was true to her word and didn't touch any of them.

"You see, you don't have to be worried about where an airplane is going or who it's taking when you're the one flying it," Hazel said.

And that went for life, too. So much could go wrong. So much could break a heart—Hazel knew that all too well. But when a woman took control of her life and got into the driver's seat, it was a whole lot less scary.

That was a lesson Hazel was taking to heart right now as she moved forward with her life. It was a bit scary because she had a whole lot of hope and ambition tied up in this new job, but it was a choice she'd made for her own future.

She was in control.

CHAPTER THREE

THAT EVENING, Hazel stood outside by the corral fence, her phone held up in front of her so that Maddie could see the donkey on their video call. Eeyore came ambling over, and Hazel gave him a handful of clover when he poked his velvety nose at the phone.

"He's so cute!" Maddie laughed.

"He's really affectionate," Hazel said. "His name is Eeyore. This bed-and-breakfast is just so peaceful. It's all lazy afternoons and good Amish cooking. I'm going to gain ten pounds, guaranteed."

"Sounds amazing. Are you actually resting?"

"Yes, I'm resting."

"Are you?" Maddie didn't sound fully convinced.

"I'm reviewing a few things for the job, but that's relaxing for me. Judge away, little miss, but I'm excited."

"Alright. I forgive you. But have some fun,

too. I hate for you to leave Amish country without actually seeing Amish country."

"I'm going for a flight one of these days. And today I checked out a local hangar. I'll see Amish country in my own way." But it was time to change the subject from her own inability to relax. "So...you haven't told me about your dinner with Dad."

"You want to hear about this?" Maddie asked, her tone softening.

"Of course I do. How did it go? Did you meet your half brother and sister?"

"Sophie and Stephane," she said. "And yes, I met them. They're fourteen and fifteen, so pretty young."

"And?" Hazel tried not to sound like she was prodding.

"And...." Maddie sighed. "They aren't crazy about me. Let's put it that way."

Hazel's heart sank. "What happened?"

"Anything I said was just so American," Maddie said, using one hand to add air quotes on the screen. "And not in a good way. They spent half the dinner bashing American international politics, and the other half chattering away in French so I couldn't understand a word."

"French?" Hazel frowned. "They're in England."

"But Dad's wife is half-French, don't you know. And they were raised with a French nanny." Maddie rolled her eyes. "Dad tried to smooth things over, but it didn't work."

"And Adel?" That was Todd's wife—the woman he'd married two years after breaking Hazel's heart.

"Adel didn't come. She had a headache."

"So it's dramatic over there," Hazel confirmed.

"Like you wouldn't believe." Maddie sighed. "Dad wants to take me shopping tomorrow. I guess I look a little too American for their taste."

"I'm sure he just wants to buy you some gifts," Hazel said.

"Yeah…" Maddie sighed again. "This isn't the happy family meeting I was hoping for. Stephane openly loathes me. Sophie is a little warmer, but I can tell that she thinks liking me is a betrayal to her mother."

Hazel's first instinct was to think they were spoiled brats, but maybe it was more complicated than that. She couldn't expect adult-level maturity from a couple of teens.

"Sweetie, they're teenagers," Hazel said.

"And young ones to boot. They're meeting their half sister, and obviously that's tough for their mother. Maybe they'll be better the next trip. Kids don't always deal with things as gracefully as we'd like them to."

"Well, I have more reason to complain. I saw my father once every couple of years," Maddie said. "They had him every day of their lives."

That stung just a bit, because Maddie had had Hazel every day of her life…to the point that Hazel had sidelined her own goals and ambitions just to be there.

"Your dad paid child support faithfully every month of your life," Hazel said. "And not many kids with split-up parents can say that. Your dad called, too, and sent gifts. You weren't exactly abandoned, Maddie."

Plus, Todd's family, who were now in New Hampshire, had invited Maddie to visit and had sent gifts, called her on the phone and even come to Pittsburgh a few times to see her.

"I'm just saying, Dad's kids have no reason to whine," she said.

"I agree with you," Hazel said. "But you're an exceptionally decent and sweet young woman, Madison. I wouldn't expect them to have your maturity."

Maddie smiled then. "Thanks, Mom."

Hazel heard the sound of hooves behind her and turned to see a black Amish buggy turning into the drive.

"Wait—you have to see this." Hazel turned the camera around again, and the tranquil scene popped onto the screen. Leafy green trees rustling in the wind, a gravel drive and a tall, glossy copper-colored horse pulling a buggy up to a stop next to the house.

"Mom, they don't like pictures," Maddie said softly.

"Right." Hazel flipped the screen again and smiled down at her daughter's image. "But it's gorgeous, isn't it?"

"It is," Maddie said. "I wish I was in Amish country with you instead of England right now."

The driver of the buggy was a young man with a clean-shaven face and an earnest expression. He hopped down and headed for the side door. The screen opened before he got to it, and Belinda's voice said, "Obadiah! You come at last. I have apple crisp—I hope you're hungry."

The young man murmured something in

response, and the screen door clapped shut behind him. Hazel looked down at her daughter's tired face. England was five hours ahead, so it was late for Maddie.

"Hang in there," Hazel said. "You'll be glad you met your siblings, at least. And in a few years, they might be really ashamed of their behavior. They're intimidated, and scared, and don't know how to react. This, too, shall pass, okay?"

"Yeah…"

"Do you really want to come home early?" Hazel asked. Because she'd send her daughter the money in a heartbeat.

"No, no, not really," Madison replied. "A few more days with Dad, and then I'm going to see some castles and Stonehenge, and all the touristy stuff for a few days. It'll be fun."

"You be careful," Hazel said. "Keep your wallet under your clothes, and keep an eye out for weird-looking people."

"Mom, I'm the weird-looking person here." Maddie laughed.

"You are not. Don't let them get to you. But you know what I mean. Safety first. When do you meet up with Heidi?"

Heidi was a friend who was going to travel England with Madison for the summer.

"Day after tomorrow, Dad will come with me to get her from the airport."

Right. She did have a father there, and he seemed to be putting in the proper care and attention.

"Okay," Hazel said. "That's good. So…how is your dad doing?"

"Dad is incredibly stressed out," Maddie said. "His kids are embarrassing him, and I don't think he knows how to relate to me. I'm not a kid anymore. I also suspect Adel is putting him through the wringer."

"He'll figure it out," Hazel said with a low laugh. Todd had chosen Adel, after all.

"Okay, well, I'm going to get going. It's late here," Maddie said. "I'll talk to you later, okay?"

"Okay, love you. Be safe."

The screen blipped out, and Hazel tucked her phone back into her pocket. This was one of those situations that Hazel couldn't fix for her daughter. Maddie would have to figure out those relationships on her own, as hard as that could be for a mom to accept.

Hazel walked to the house and headed up the steps into the mudroom. It was a bright little room with a sink for handwashing after chores and a row of pegs with some light jackets hanging on them. When Hazel emerged into the kitchen, she found the young man sitting at the kitchen table, a frown on his face.

"Oh, hello, Hazel," Belinda said with a smile. "Can I get you some apple crisp? It's fresh from the oven."

"Thanks, that would be great," Hazel replied.

She gave the young Amish man a nod in greeting.

"Obadiah, this my guest, Hazel. Hazel, this is a friend, Obadiah."

"Pleasure," Hazel said.

Obadiah gave her a silent nod in return. Belinda came back with the plate of crisp, handed it to her with a warm smile, then without missing a beat, Belinda turned back to the Amish man and said something lengthy and passionate in Pennsylvania Dutch. Obadiah looked irritated.

Something was going on here, but it wasn't Hazel's business, so she headed toward the sitting room to give them a bit more privacy.

"No, no, no!" Obadiah said once Hazel was out of sight. "Belinda, I came to you for a reason. You can't change my mind."

Belinda's reply was in Pennsylvania Dutch again, and the man responded in kind, their voices low and intense. Obviously, they were disagreeing about something.

Hazel took a bite of crisp—tart apples and carmelized brown sugar—and looked out the front window at the newly planted flower garden. Small plants were surrounded by moist black earth. They wouldn't stay small for long. The visitor's buggy and horse were visible from this vantage point in the golden evening sunlight. It was like time stood still out here, except for a fly buzzing and the swishing of the horse's tail. She felt like she could almost watch the plants grow if she just settled herself down on that front step... Everything seemed simpler here—everyone had their feet firmly on the ground.

But she didn't want her feet on the ground. She wanted to be in a plane, soaring above the earth and getting to that sweet spot at about ten thousand feet. She smiled faintly at the thought.

The voices in the kitchen subsided. She heard the door open, and then watched as Obadiah hoisted himself back into his buggy and untied his reins. He looked worried, and he didn't seem to notice Hazel watching him from the window. Or perhaps he just didn't care. Hazel was an outsider here. She wasn't local, and she wasn't Amish.

"Sorry about that, dear," Belinda said behind her, and Hazel turned to see the older woman standing in the doorway.

"What was that about?" Hazel asked. "It looked dramatic."

"Well, it wouldn't be dramatic at all if he listened to me," Belinda said.

Hazel shot her a curious look.

"Maybe I should explain. I'm a matchmaker."

"Like, from *Fiddler on the Roof*?" she asked. She hummed a bar of the familiar song.

"I don't know what that is," Belinda said with a confused frown. "But I'm a matchmaker, and I find spouses for people looking for one." She paused and then added, "In our Amish community."

"Of course." Hazel smiled at the pointed clarification. "I know this is probably wildly inappropriate of me to even ask, but are you finding him a wife?"

"*Yah*. That's the idea," Belinda said. "But he's stubborn. He has his eyes on one particular woman, and he doesn't have a chance with her!"

"Why not?"

"Because Miriam Yoder is beautiful and funny, and she can make a strudel that melts in your mouth. She's the girl all the single men are angling for, and Obadiah is—is..."

Hazel waited.

"Obadiah is an old man in a young man's body. He's serious and pious and wouldn't even ask a girl home from singing. And now he's twenty-five, and instead of asking me for an appropriate girl who'd be grateful to have him, he's asking for the one woman he can't have. Miriam might be able to make a perfect strudel, but her father has money, and their kitchen is stocked to the rafters. She's used to a certain amount of freedom and comfort, and Obadiah can only afford to rent a *dawdie hus* on someone else's land. He needs a wife who can stretch out the resources and make a solid loaf of bread. He doesn't need to be bothering with strudel." Belinda shook her head, a tendril of white hair falling loose. "Obadiah is good and honest and pure. But those two are not meant to be!"

"So what do you do when your client refuses to see sense?" Hazel asked.

"I'll let him sleep on it, to start," Belinda said. "And then I will introduce him to some more appropriate women and see if he can't imagine himself married to one of them."

"He seemed very determined," Hazel admitted softly.

"Very. I have my work cut out for me with Obadiah." Belinda sighed. "Are *Englisher* men that stubborn?"

"I think all men are," Hazel said with a chuckle. "I work in a male-dominated industry, and I haven't come across a man yet who listens to sense the first time he hears it. At least not from me."

Belinda laughed, her blue eyes sparkling behind her rimless glasses. "I do have some *Englisher* family members, so I know there are great similarities in men from both sides of the fence."

"Why do you call us *Englishers*?" Hazel asked.

"Because your mother tongue is English," Belinda replied.

"That's it?"

"*Yah.*"

Hazel shrugged. "Makes sense, I guess."

"And speaking of stubborn men," Belinda said, "that Joe Carter is another example."

"Really?" Hazel shot her a look of surprise.

"Now, I normally keep my nose out of *En-*

glisher business, but we know Joe around here, and there have been plenty of sweet *Englisher* women who have set their sights on him. But he just won't be tethered, that one. He's got his little girl, and he's a good *daet*. That's it."

"Have there been that many?" Hazel asked.

"I hired him last year to do the garden, and he had a woman working with him who was obviously smitten. Nice-looking woman, too. And they got along very well when they were working on my yard. But he was just blind to her. The woman complained to me about it, so I probably heard more than was my business."

Hazel pondered that for a moment. He had a little girl who needed him, and he was concerned about choosing someone who'd be good for both of them. She could sympathize with that. "Maybe it's just as well."

"Maybe," Belinda agreed, then she smoothed her hands down the front of her apron. "Well, let's not let that ruin a perfectly lovely evening. We do like to help others, but it's wise to remember when it's someone else's choice, and not ours to lose sleep over. Right?"

"Very wise," Hazel said with a smile.

Amish wisdom and Amish cooking—this was why Hazel had come out here for the week. They used to drive through Amish country on family car trips when she was young, and her affinity for the area had remained. But with some Amish wisdom added in, who knew? Maybe she'd head to her new job understanding men just a little bit better, too.

"Eat up." Belinda gestured to the plate of crisp. "There's more where that came from."

JOE ARRIVED AT the bed-and-breakfast the next morning with a very tired little girl in her car seat behind him. She'd been awake in her room until almost eleven the night before, and he could hear her talking to her stuffed animals and making the engine noise of her airplane. Just wired up.

This morning, they were both paying for it. Lottie had dragged around all morning, refused to eat breakfast and then had a complete meltdown when they were already in the truck and ready to leave. She'd remembered her airplane but had forgotten her purple crayon.

Now, as he undid the car-seat straps, he wondered how the day was going to go. If he could drop her off at day care, he'd be relatively certain the professionals there would get her interested in something and everything would be okay. But today, it was on him again…and he had his regular job to do at the same time.

Not for the first time, he wondered how much easier life would be if he had a wife in the trenches with him. In his imagination, she'd be the one to stay home with Lottie, to help her learn her alphabet, and help her manage her huge emotions. In the morning, he'd help Lottie with her breakfast and brushing her teeth, and then he'd kiss his lovely wife goodbye. And when he got home at night, he could gather his daughter into his arms and read to her. And when Lottie went to bed, he'd have that wife with him to talk about their days, and plan a little family vacation together—like his parents used to do… Maybe he needed a bit of nurturing, too.

But more than that, Lottie needed it. She was in this whole new phase of searching for her mother, and if she had a mom at home with her to fill all those aching needs, he knew she'd be okay. She could stop her fruitless search then, stop obsessing over where her mother might be. Joe's adoptive mom had been at home with him, providing routine, comfort, stability and just her reassuring presence. That was one thing he couldn't give to his own daughter—she went to day care, and somehow she'd been agonizing a lot about her mother. He'd come to the conclusion that Lottie needed more. He couldn't reassure her, try as he might. So Joe might like the idea of a more traditional relationship, but Lottie needed it.

But the face of that woman who'd join their family was blurry in his daydreams, and it hardly seemed fair to long for a wife just to love Lottie and him. He'd better bring more to the table than a pile of work for her to do! Unless that wife would like being at home. Some women appreciated a big garden and the flexibility to fill their day any way they chose. Maybe what he had to offer could be enough for the right woman.

Joe slammed the truck door shut, and Lottie walked slowly toward the house. The side door opened, and Belinda appeared with a smile.

"Hello, Lottie," she said cheerily. "Oh, my, you look tired."

"Yeah…" Lottie said and heaved a shaky sigh.

"I know what you need," Belinda said. "A great big cup of coffee should do the trick."

Joe gaped at Belinda, and the older woman burst out laughing.

"That was a joke, Joe," she said, waggling her finger at him. "No coffee for you, Lottie. But your *daet* can have a mug if he likes. How would you like a boiled egg, Lottie?"

"Thank you, Belinda," he said. "It's been one of those mornings."

Belinda shot him a smile and ushered Lottie into the house. The cup of coffee would be nice, but when he looked up, he saw Hazel walking down the gravel drive toward him.

The morning was still cool, and she was dressed in a pair of jeans and a pink top that looked kind of frilly and pretty on her. He paused at his truck, waiting until she reached him.

"It's beautiful out this morning," she said, tucking her fingers into her back pockets.

"For sure." He dropped his gaze, a little embarrassed that she'd noticed him noticing her. She was definitely pretty—that had been the honest truth yesterday.

"Did Lottie like the hangar?" she asked.

"She loved it. She was wired right up until eleven last night," he said with a grin.

"Ouch," Hazel said. "I remember those days. Did you pay for it yet?"

"I'll pay for it all day," he said. "So how are you?"

"Not bad. Determined to relax a bit before I hit the books again." She nodded in the direction of the nearby farm. "That dog was following me most of my walk. He kept trying to herd me down the drive to the farm next door."

Joe looked toward the fence, and noticed the large black dog watching them. It squeezed through the rails and came trotting toward them.

"That's Eli's dog, Hund," he said. "Eli's the old guy on that farm."

The dog came bounding up and barked twice, the sound sharp and loud. Belinda appeared at the door again.

"Hund!" she said. "What's wrong with you?"

The dog barked again.

"Go home, Hund!" Belinda said. "I have no meat for you. No! Go home!" Belinda sighed. "Eli adopted him, but Hund will come out here as often as not and try to get some food from me. Or a pet." She eyed the dog uncertainly. "But this is different, isn't it?"

"Maybe I should go check on Eli," Joe said. "Make sure he's okay."

"That might be a good idea," Belinda said with a frown. "I haven't seen him yet this morning... And if Eli's just fine, I want you to tell him from me that if he doesn't buy some proper dog treats for this animal, I will not be serving him any more pie. No treats for the dog, no treats for Eli. And that's final."

Joe chuckled. "I'll pass it along."

The dog came forward again and barked, and Joe spotted his daughter behind Belinda in the doorway.

"Can I come, Daddy?" Lottie asked.

"Eli's place isn't for *kinner*," Belinda said. "Trust me there. He's a confirmed bachelor, and it just wouldn't be safe. But she can stay with me. That's no problem."

Right. He knew a little bit about Eli Lapp. He was a friendly old guy who'd never married, and apparently he was quite the eccentric, not to be tamed by a woman or the community.

"I'll be back, Lottie," Joe said. "I won't be long. I'm just going to see if the old man next door is okay."

Lottie sighed but didn't push the issue.

"I'll come with you," Hazel said, and she fell in beside him as he headed toward the farm next door. The dog ran eagerly ahead, looking back at them every few steps to make sure they were following.

"Something's up," Joe said.

"Yeah, I think so," Hazel agreed. "But I wasn't going down to some farm on foot by myself."

"Eli's a harmless old guy," Joe said. "He'd mostly just compliment you, but I get the concern."

Besides, Joe kind of liked being the protector here—the man to keep her safe—even though there wasn't much to protect her from on Eli Lapp's property. He slowed his pace a little when he heard Hazel breathing hard, and he shortened his strides, too.

"This is nice—neighbors who look out for each other," Hazel said.

"Yeah, Belinda and Eli are some old-timers who have been out here for like fifty or sixty years. We all kind of know that they're out here and keep an eye out."

"Even though you aren't Amish?" she asked.

He was more Amish than people guessed, but he hadn't clued anyone in.

"I know enough Amish people," he said. "Especially in this industry. Pretty much all my competition out here are Amish companies. You get to know people."

"That's something similar to what Belinda said," she replied. "She knows more about you than you might realize, too."

"Oh, yeah?" He looked down at Hazel in surprise. "Like what?"

"Apparently you were clueless to a coworker who had a major crush on you." She grinned.

"Who? Lois?"

Hazel shrugged.

"Lois." He nodded. "I wasn't clueless. I just wasn't interested. She was great in a lot of ways, but… I've got a more complicated situation here. She was working for the summer, taking a break from her master's degree, and I hired her. We were headed in different directions."

"So you aren't quite so clueless as you appear," she said, then laughed to show she was joking.

"Apparently, I come off dumber than I am." He grinned back. "But, yeah, out here, Amish or *Englisher*, it's a small enough community that you get to know people. So I guess I shouldn't be surprised."

Hund squeezed through the fence rails, and

Joe climbed over. Hazel climbed the fence after him, and he caught her hand as she jumped down. Her hand was soft in his grip, and she slipped her hand free as quickly as she landed.

"Eli's a unique guy," Joe said as they followed Hund toward the house. The dog loped up to the front door and nosed it open. "Just so you know…"

"Yeah, I met him before," she said.

"You'll understand what I mean when you see inside," he said. They came up to the front door of the house, and Joe called inside. "Eli? You home?"

The dog barked in response, and Joe led the way in. The front room was crammed full of canned food, some bags of dog food and what looked like hunting and fishing supplies. Joe led the way through the clutter toward the kitchen.

"Eli?" he called again.

The house looked deserted, but then he saw a flash of white and spotted Eli on the floor next to the cupboards. He was sitting up, his face ashen.

"Oh…" The old man sighed when he spotted them. "I hurt myself."

"What did you do?" Hazel pushed past Joe,

not even sparing a glance for the state of the kitchen. There was a large cage on the kitchen table with three hens inside.

Hazel kneeled down next to Eli, and she put a hand over his forehead.

"My ankle," Eli said. "I don't know how, but I fell, and it twisted."

Joe could see the swollen joint, and he grimaced. It looked incredibly painful, and at Eli's age, that wouldn't heal easily.

"When did this happen?" Joe asked.

"This morning. When I got up for chores," Eli said.

That was a good five hours ago, and Joe's stomach churned at the thought.

"You can't stay here, Eli," Joe said. "We're going to bring you next door to Belinda."

"Oh, she won't be liking that," Eli said.

"I'm sure she'd like seeing you on the floor a whole lot less," Joe replied. "Okay... Hazel, if you could find something to wrap his ankle, I'm going to get these hens outside into the chicken coop."

"They're my best layers," Eli said, sounding defensive.

"Maybe so, but you're not going to be here to

take care of them, are you?" Joe said. "They're better off in the coop for now."

"Yah, yah..." Eli agreed with a sigh. "But be gentle. They're sensitive."

Joe carried the heavy cage outside, glad to get that door open to let in some fresh air. The house smelled of chickens and dog. Hund followed Joe for a few feet and then stopped, unwilling to go farther. He was a loyal dog.

The chickens slid out of the cage and into the coop with some squawks and fluttering, and Joe tossed more feed into the coop before locking it up. He left the cage at the side of the house and headed back inside. When he got there, Hazel had found a sheet, and she'd torn a strip off and was wrapping up the old man's ankle.

"You have a good dog," Hazel said. "He tried to get me to come look in on you on my walk, and then he came over to the bed-and-breakfast and wouldn't stop until he got Joe here to come on over."

"And Belinda?" Eli asked.

"She was worried, too," Hazel said.

"But if you weren't hurt, she was going to have some choice words for you," Joe said, trying to joke. "Good thing you've got a certifiable injury there."

"Good thing," Eli agreed soberly. He held up his arms. "Okay, give me a boost, Joe."

Between them, they got the old man to his feet, and he gestured wildly toward the table.

"My hat!" Eli said. "I need my hat."

"Does it matter?" Hazel asked.

Eli shot her a scandalized look. "Any man worth his salt keeps his hat on his head when he calls on a woman. I need my hat, young lady."

Joe scooped the straw hat off the table and dropped it on Eli's head before winding the old man's arm around his own neck to help support him. Eli had on the traditional broadfall pants with a pair of suspenders, and his white shirt looked clean, albeit wrinkled.

Joe whistled in Hund's direction. "Come on, boy. Let's go. You're coming, too."

"How bad do I look?" Eli asked.

"Bad enough for Belinda's sympathy," Joe said.

"But still very ruggedly handsome," Hazel added, her expression sober.

Eli nodded and heaved a sigh. *"Danke."*

That was "thank you" in Pennsylvania Dutch. "It'll have to do."

And between them, they helped Eli hop out of the house and into the fresh air. It was time to get back to Belinda's clean, orderly home, where he could get some proper care.

CHAPTER FOUR

ONCE THEY GOT close to the side door of Butternut Bed and Breakfast, Hazel hurried ahead to open it. It swung back, and she propped open the screen with a bucket of dirt that seemed to be placed there for that purpose. Then she went back to where the men were waiting and slipped Eli's arm over her shoulders again.

"You okay, Eli?" she asked.

"I will be," he murmured, but she could hear the pain in his voice. There wasn't anything she could do, though, besides help get him inside.

Hazel's arm was just under Joe's, and she could feel that he was doing most of the lifting. Belinda appeared in the doorway, drying her hands on a dishcloth, and her eyebrows shot up.

"Eli!" Belinda exclaimed. "What happened to you?"

"Oh, just a little sprain. They're being dramatic for nothing," he replied. His hat slipped then, going down over his eyes, and Hazel reached over and righted it for him.

"Danke," he said.

"All of this is not for nothing," Hazel said. "We found him on the floor in the kitchen, and he's been there since early morning. He's nowhere near fine, and we're nowhere near dramatic."

"On the floor!" Belinda gasped. "Eli!"

"I'm trying to keep some dignity here, young lady," Eli said, shooting Hazel an annoyed look.

"You're throwing us under the bus, Eli," Hazel retorted. "And I'm not lying to Belinda. You need some help."

Belinda made way for them to come in and pulled out a kitchen chair. Lottie stood by the table staring in silence. She held her toy plane against her chest, eyes wide.

"Is he hurt, Daddy?" Lottie asked soberly.

"Oh, I'm alright," Eli said. "It's just my foot. Nothing important like my head."

The old man winked at Lottie, and a smile tickled her lips in response. Hazel and Joe eased Eli into the seat. The dog had followed them inside and stayed at Eli's side, his tail thumping the floor. The dog whined and sidled closer to Eli.

"You are a good *hund*," Belinda said to the dog seriously. She grabbed a muffin from the table, tore it in half and gave half to the dog, who swallowed it in one gulp. Then she turned to Eli. "Eli, what happened?"

"I don't even know…" He looked toward Hazel and Joe uncomfortably. "My ankle just rolled, and…it hurt really bad, and I remember the kitchen spinning and then waking up on the floor. My ankle hurt too much to stand again. So I thought I'd just wait a bit." He seemed to realize Lottie was still listening because he grimaced and looked over at the girl, then pretended to knock on his head. "But see? The head is fine. Nothing to worry about."

"It was hours!" Belinda muttered.

"I sent Hund," Eli said defensively.

"*Yah, yah*, you did." Belinda gave the last half of the muffin to the dog, who gulped it back. Belinda looked sheepish then. "I apologize, Eli. I thought Hund just wanted a treat. I didn't know he was coming for help. I can't stand here and lie to you."

"You—you sent him away?" Eli asked feebly.

"I tried to," Belinda said, and her cheeks pinked. "But he refused to be sent. He's a good dog. And I'm sorry, Eli. I thought the worst of you, and I was wrong. I ask your forgiveness."

Eli blinked, then looked over at Hazel and Joe. A teasing glint shone in his blue eyes.

"Belinda Wickey does not apologize," Eli said. "I did hear that right, didn't I?"

"Oh, you!" Belinda's expression turned baleful, and she stomped from the room, returning a moment later with a throw pillow. She leaned heavily on a kitchen chair and then kneeled on the floor in front of him. Belinda winced as she unwound the makeshift bandage from his bruised and swollen ankle. "You should be nicer to the one who's going to patch you up, Eli Lapp!"

"She has a point, Eli," Joe said with a low laugh.

"I'm always nice," Eli said, turning back to Belinda. "And I appreciate the help, Belinda. I truly do."

"Can I do anything?" Hazel asked.

"There is some ice in the icebox. If you could grab that and put it in a kitchen towel," Belinda said, but she didn't look mollified yet.

Hazel grabbed a towel from a drawer, and Joe opened the icebox and scooped chipped ice into the towel Hazel held. She looked up at him and he caught her eye.

"Wow..." he murmured. "Some morning, huh?"

"I know!" She closed the towel over the ice, and for a moment, neither of them moved.

"What would have happened if we hadn't gone over there?" she said.

He shook his head. "Neighbors are even more important for the Amish. We have phones in the house. They don't. If someone hadn't checked on him, anything could have happened."

It was an entirely different way of life. As Hazel made her way back over with the ice pack, Lottie went to Eli and held out her model plane.

"Do you want to see my plane?" Lottie asked.

"Very nice," Eli said.

Hazel handed the ice pack to Belinda.

"I'm going to be a plane driver when I grow up," Lottie said.

"Oh, no," Eli replied. "You don't want to do that. If *Gott* intended us to fly, he'd have given us wings like ducks. You should get married and have babies."

Eli grimaced as Belinda placed the ice pack

onto his injured joint, and Hazel couldn't help the surge of annoyance she felt at that kind of advice. Little girls had their ambitions put off all the time, and she hated it. But before Hazel could think of a response, Belinda cut in.

"Don't listen to him, dear," Belinda said to Lottie with a smile. "You can fly planes if you want to. Hazel does it, doesn't she?"

"That's true," Lottie agreed, although some of the excitement had gone out of her voice.

"And it's lots of fun," Hazel added.

"It's not the way we do things!" Eli retorted, giving Belinda a stern look that was ruined by the fact that his foot was sitting in the old woman's lap.

"None of these people are Amish, Eli," Belinda said softly.

"Eli, it's different for us," Joe said. "If a girl wants to fly a plane, she can do it. No reason she can't."

"I'm not singling out girls," Eli said. "I'm saying everyone. A horse and buggy keeps you close to home and close to your community. An airplane? It flies off…I don't even know where! And what about your community? What about your people?"

Belinda gestured toward the mudroom.

"Joe, would you grab me a winter scarf from one of the crates above the coat hooks?"

"Sure thing," Joe said, and he cast a concerned look toward his daughter before he disappeared into the mudroom.

"I will make a deal with you," Belinda said to Eli. "I won't fly any planes, and neither will you. And that's as far as *our* advice can go. These are not Amish people. Your conscience and mine can govern only us. Not them."

"You are a brazenly liberal woman, Belinda," Eli said.

Belinda looked up at Hazel, and the old woman chuckled. "Liberal is in the eye of the beholder, you see."

Hazel couldn't help but laugh, and when Lottie came over to where she stood, Hazel put a hand on the top of her head. How much of this would Lottie remember later in life? Maddie remembered all sorts of things Hazel had hoped she'd forget. Kids were like that.

"That's a joke?" Eli asked, looking offended.

"It's a fact, Eli," Belinda replied. "To Hazel here, I'm an absolute relic! I'm as old-fashioned as she can imagine, and then some. Take it from me. I know! I have *Englisher* family, so

I know how they see me, in particular. But to you, you think I'm flapping in the wind with the laundry, liberal and unanchored."

Eli muttered something in Pennsylvania Dutch, but Belinda seemed to think her point was made, because she nodded a couple of times and gave Eli a pointed look. Joe returned with a scarf. Belinda accepted it with a nod of thanks and proceeded to wrap up Joe's ankle with expert folds and tucks to keep the cloth tight.

"There…" Belinda said, gently setting Eli's foot back onto the floor. She reached for the chair, and Joe stepped forward, taking her hand to help boost her back to her feet. "Thank you, Joe. You're a gentleman."

"You know, I was curious, Belinda," Joe said. "I know the Amish community has its ways, but what happens if you do go too far…? Will you get in trouble?"

That was a good question, and Hazel looked over at the old woman, waiting for her answer.

"Me?" Belinda batted a hand through the air. "Don't worry about me, Joe. I follow all of the *Ordnung*. That's our set of rules. And when I'm not sure, I ask the bishop. That's the safest way. I was just pointing out that our rules for our way of life don't apply to anyone else. How on earth would I run a bed-and-breakfast for *Englishers* if I expected them to act like Amish? It would be impossible."

"Hmm." He nodded. "So…if someone is born Amish, but doesn't join the church, they don't have to obey the rules, either?"

"That's trickier," Belinda said. "If you're raised Amish, we have a few expectations of you. If you aren't…" She looked over at Eli. "See what you've done, Eli? You've upset the *Englishers*."

"I didn't mean to," Eli said, sounding remorseful.

Joe's expression hadn't changed, though. "What if someone, I don't know…had a baby outside of wedlock?"

"Joe, no one is judging you here," Belinda said gently. "I promise you that. I'm sorry to have upset you. We don't expect our rules to apply to you, dear."

"Yeah, I know," Joe said. "I'm not upset, I'm just curious. What if an unmarried Amish girl had a baby?"

"Well," Belinda began slowly, "that would be complicated. It does happen very rarely, and each situation is dealt with differently, depending on the people and the circumstances."

"They'd be required to get married, that's what!" Eli interjected. "That baby would be born to married parents, I can assure you of that!"

"Would you even know about a baby born, uh, unexpectedly?" Joe asked. "Or would that be a secret?"

"That entirely depends upon the people involved," Belinda replied, and she frowned. "I might. Why do you ask, Joe?"

Hazel was wondering the same thing. Why was he going down this rabbit hole of questions?

Joe shook his head. "Curiosity. A guy gets to thinking." He looked toward the window. "I'd better get some work done for you, Miss Belinda."

Hazel stayed silent, and she watched as Joe ushered his daughter outside with him. He glanced back, meeting her gaze just once before he and Lottie disappeared into the mudroom, and then the screen door slammed shut.

"I wonder why he's asking about that," Belinda said thoughtfully. She looked over at Hazel. "Any idea?"

Hazel shook her head. "No, none."

"Well…" Belinda put her hands on her hips. "It'll remain a mystery, then. Eli, I'd best feed you. You must be half-starved."

"A bowl of oatmeal would do nicely," Eli said, his eyes lighting up. "And maybe a coffee. I never did get breakfast."

"You'll have a fried-egg sandwich," Belinda replied. "And I'll start the coffee."

"Okay," Eli said with a shrug. "That sounds good, too."

Hazel couldn't help but smile as she watched Belinda bustle off into the kitchen. And then she looked out the window toward Joe as he pulled some tools out of the bed of his truck. Joe was a man who seemed to like the Amish community and their way of life. He also seemed to have more of a personal connection to the culture than Hazel herself did. She sensed there was more to his pointed questioning…

Was it possible that Lottie's mother had been Amish?

JOE PULLED A bag of fertilizer out of the back of his truck and carried it over to the far garden Belinda had designated for vegetables. He'd wanted to ask a few questions, but he felt like maybe he'd asked one too many. He'd seen the way they all looked at him—he was sparking a little too much curiosity for his own comfort. He wanted to find his mother, not invite closer scrutiny.

Lottie ambled over in the direction of the pasture. There was a solid wooden fence between her and the field, and the horse and donkey grazed a few yards off.

"Lottie, you stay on this side of the fence," Joe called.

"I know!" Lottie hollered back.

He rolled his eyes. Lottie did not know, but this was her most recent acquisition from day care. Now she declared she knew absolutely everything. But she did seem to be obeying, and more importantly, both donkey and quarter horse were utterly disinterested in her.

The front door opened, and he heard the squeak of the porch swing. He tore open the bag and started spreading fertilizer over the garden patch. Once he finished with the bag, he looked over and saw Hazel settled on the swing again. The swinging stopped and she turned around to look at him.

"You have the right idea," he said, raising his voice so she could hear him. "It's a nice day."

Hazel stood up and came down the steps,

heading in his direction. She was awfully pretty.

"I don't have a garden at home," she said.

"No? If you have the space, you can rent a rototiller and turn up some soil." Was she a woman who'd appreciate a big garden? He hadn't put in a vegetable garden in his backyard yet, but he'd been thinking about it.

"I live in an apartment."

"Oh. Well, that won't work then, will it?"

She smiled. "Not very well, but I follow some gardening pages on social media. It looks relaxing."

"Do you want to try it out?" He shot her a grin. "I mean, your sandals won't stay clean, but you can get the experience of actual dirt. You'll either love it or hate it. There's no in-between."

She looked over her shoulder back toward the porch. Right. She was busy reviewing her books to get ready for that new job.

"I mean, no pressure," he added. "Feel free to go do your work. I don't mean to hold you back."

She seemed to pause, considering for a moment. Then she shrugged, and a smile touched her lips. "I could take a break, I suppose. Love it or hate it, you say?"

"In my experience, at least," he said.

"That sounds like a challenge to me. What do I do?"

"Here—I'm spreading fertilizer before planting. I spread, you use this cultivator to work it into the soil. Lean on it hard. You want those blades to go as deep into the soil as you can make them."

Hazel accepted the tool from his hands and looked down at it with a mildly curious look on her face. She hefted it in her hand a couple of times, seeming to test its weight.

Joe broke open a new bag of fertilizer on one end and started to spread it. Hazel did as he'd instructed, and started working the soil behind him, leaning all of her weight onto the cultivator, and then turning the soil. Her golden waves fell in front of her face. She was beautiful. More beautiful than was safe for him to be noticing. He brought his attention back to the bag of fertilizer.

"You're a natural," he said.

"You'll say that until I have blisters," she joked.

Maybe he was halfway hoping this gardening thing would grow on her.

"Joe, I was curious…" Hazel said, leaning on the handle of the cultivator again and then twisting up the loosened dirt. "Is Lottie's mom Amish?"

Jessica? Joe shook his head and frowned. "No. Why would you ask that?"

"You were asking questions about babies born to Amish girls out of wedlock, and I put two and two together," she said.

Right. He hadn't thought that anyone would jump to that conclusion, but he could see why she had. He shook out a little more fertilizer, then straightened.

"It's not Lottie," he said. "I'm the baby born to an Amish girl."

"What?"

He smiled faintly. "I was adopted by my parents when I was a few days old. The only thing they knew about my biological mother was that she was Amish and from this area, she'd gotten pregnant and she gave me up."

"Oh…Joe…"

"It's nothing to be sorry for," he said. "It is what it is. I mean, if you're adopted, your biological parents came from somewhere, didn't they?"

"And you're wanting to connect with your roots?" she asked.

"I—" Was he wanting to? "I've been considering it. I mean, I don't have a lot of information to go on, but it's been nagging at me lately. Maybe because Lottie has been so fixated on her own mother... So, yeah, I've been considering it. But finding her would be another problem."

Hazel was silent, and Joe put down the bag and held out his hand for the cultivator. He was being paid for this. She wasn't. She handed it over, and he started to work the fertilizer into the soil, pushing his frustration into the moist earth along with the sharp tines. He didn't know why he was even getting into this with Hazel.

"I know it's hypocritical," he went on. "My daughter is longing to know about her mother, and I won't tell her a thing. My mother gave me up, too, and I want to find her. It's hardly fair."

"But understandable," Hazel said.

Was it? Joe wasn't so sure.

"Does Lottie know you were adopted?" Hazel asked.

"No." He looked in his daughter's direction again. She was leaning over the rail. "Lottie! Stay on this side!"

"Okay!" She pulled back and put her hands behind her back as if to prove her good intentions. He shook his head.

"It just seemed, I don't know...complicated for a four-year-old."

"It doesn't have to be," Hazel said.

"It's a conversation I'll have to have with her soon, especially if I find my mom." Joe sighed. "Look, I'm not the perfect father. I try really hard, but I'm sure I'll mess up a lot of stuff. I'm just doing my best."

"And I'm not judging you any more than Belinda is," she said.

"Maybe I'm judging myself a bit," he conceded, because he'd been wondering lately if he should just drop this. He wasn't telling his daughter about her mother, and he should keep this fair and drop his own search. What was good for his daughter should be good for him. Right? Except he hadn't been able to just brush it aside.

"I can guess why she gave me up," he said, continuing his cultivating. "From what I've learned, if an Amish girl has a baby before she's married, it's just about impossible for her to find a husband and have a family of her own. She probably wanted to have that chance."

He came to the end of the spread fertilizer with the cultivating tool, and Hazel picked up the bag. Dirt smudged her pale feet, and her sandals, as he'd predicted, were attracting soil. She shook out more fertilizer, as he'd done, but he could tell the bag was heavy for her.

"Here, trade me—" He held out the cultivator, and she passed over the bag with a rueful smile.

Her fingers brushed over his as they made the exchange, and he tried not to notice how soft they were compared to his own calloused hands. Maybe she had a point about getting blisters. He'd feel bad if she did. He hoisted the bag into his arms.

"I wouldn't want to ruin anything for my mother," he went on. "Except that I started to worry lately that maybe she didn't get married after all. I mean, not everyone gets married, right? What if she gave me up and didn't get that family of her own? What if she's—" He stopped there. He was talking too much.

"What if she's what?" Hazel asked, continuing to work the soil.

He shook out the last of the fertilizer and looked over at her, the empty bag hanging limply at his side.

"What if she's lonely?" Joe said.

It sounded silly saying it out loud. He dropped his gaze and tossed the bag to the side. But he had this nagging worry that his mother might be a woman in her fifties, without kids, without a husband and with an aching hole in her heart from the son she'd given up. What if her plans hadn't panned out?

"What do you know about her?" Hazel asked, stopping the cultivating and leaning on the handle instead. She rubbed a hand down her hip.

"Not a lot. I know her first name is Rebecca. There's probably a lot of Rebeccas in every community. I know she was sixteen when she gave birth to me. My mom told me that she had her mother with her when she talked to them. So she had family support." Joe shrugged. "That's about it. A Rebecca who gave birth at the age of sixteen, thirty-seven years ago. Not much to go on, is it?"

"But a matchmaker might have more community information at her fingertips than other people do," Hazel said slowly. "It's Belinda's job to know people, to know their history and background...isn't it?"

"Yeah. Right?" Joe looked momentarily in the direction of the house. "That's why I was asking some questions in there."

He reached for the cultivator, and Hazel handed it over, then put her fingers into her back jeans pockets, watching him. He plunged the tines into the soil again. It was nice having her here—like teamwork. He pressed his lips together as he twisted the blades in the earth. "I'm still trying to decide if looking for my biological mother makes me a bad dad or not."

And that was the problem, wasn't it? Because one day, he'd have to explain himself to his daughter. Why was it good for him to find his biological mom and not good for her? Eighteen was a long way away, and a lot of resentment could grow in that amount of time.

Hazel looked down at her palm, and he stepped closer and caught her hand. He smoothed her fingers back and ran his thumb over a reddened spot on her palm. Hazel stilled, and he stood there, a breath away from her, suddenly realizing what he'd done.

"You need gloves," he said.

She smelled nice—her perfume mingling with the smell of freshly turned soil—and he realized this close to her that she was the perfect height. Not that it should matter.

"I probably do." She looked up at him, then she licked her lips and stepped back.

Yeah, that was probably wise.

Lottie came ambling back in their direction, and Hazel brushed a tangle of blond hair away from her face.

"Can we keep that talk about my biological mother between us?" Joe asked. It was a little late to be asking now, but somehow Hazel felt like a safe person to confide in.

"Of course, Joe," she said. "It's the parent pact."

He smiled. "Thanks."

He wasn't sure why he'd even told her all of that, except that it had been stewing around inside of him for so long now, and Hazel was that odd mix of experience and compassion that he seemed to need right now.

"Daddy, do you think Eeyore would let me ride him?" Lottie asked as she arrived at the garden plot.

"No," he said, shaking his head.

"I think he would," Lottie said. "I'm a nice girl. And I like him a lot. I think he'd let me."

Joe rubbed a hand over his forehead. "Lottie, you can't try and ride the donkey. It's dangerous. Okay? If you're coming to work with me, you've got to obey."

"Or what?" Lottie asked. Her expression was perfectly sweet, perfectly curious.

"Or you'll get hurt!" he said. "And I might have to just take the week off and teach you how to scrub the baseboards instead of play-ing outside."

He was only halfway joking. If he had to take a week off work, he'd have to make the most of it. In fact, he'd probably sit her down with those alphabet flash cards. But she'd react better to scrubbing baseboards.

"I don't want to scrub." She made a face.

"Good. I don't want to teach you how. So you'd better listen then, right?"

"Yeah. I better." Lottie nodded soberly.

Hazel brushed off her hands and stepped out of the garden plot. Suddenly, she felt very far away. For a moment, her focus was on her sandals as she took them off and shook them out.

"I'd better get back to that reviewing," she said. "But thank you for letting me experience some real gardening. Maddie would approve."

"So what do you say, love it or hate it?" he asked.

"I'm still deciding." She shot him a grin, and he smiled ruefully. She was a woman who refused to be put into a box, wasn't she?

Hazel walked back toward the covered porch, and he turned back to the work in front of him. There was something about Hazel that tugged at him. But he'd made that mistake with Jessica—hoped that she was a different kind of woman than she really was.

There was a middle-aged Amish woman out there who had an inexplicable piece of his heart, even though he'd never met her before. At the age of sixteen, he doubted that any choice would have been completely her own. Was there a Rebecca somewhere in Danke wondering about the son she hadn't raised?

And would it be wrong of him to find her?

CHAPTER FIVE

JOE FINISHED UP the cultivating, then planted three rows of carrots and two rows of green beans before he took a break. He put the empty seed packages onto sticks and stuck them into the ground at the start of each row so Belinda would know what he'd done.

"Lottie?" he called.

His daughter appeared at the side door of the house. "Hi, Daddy! I've got a carrot now!"

She held up a large carrot in one fist as proof. Belinda must have given her one inside. Joe glanced toward the front of the house, and the porch swing was still. He'd been thinking about how much he should reveal to Belinda in order to get more information, and he'd decided to err on the side of caution. If his mother had given him up to secure an Amish future for herself, then blabbing about it to the Amish seemed unnecessarily cruel. But he could still ask a few more questions.

He deposited the wheelbarrow beside the stable and headed over to the house.

"That's quite the carrot," he said, putting a hand on Lottie's warm curls as he headed inside. She followed him in. He'd left a piece of some weed in her hair, and he picked it back out. "Sorry, Lottie. Let me wash my hands."

"Did you put junk in my hair?" Lottie asked, feeling her head, and he laughed, turning to the mudroom sink.

"I said I was sorry," Joe said.

He washed up with a thick bar of soap and dried his hands with a fluffy towel. Then he headed into the kitchen, his daughter at his heels. Belinda sat at the kitchen table with some knitting in her hands, and Eli was across from her, a copy of an Amish newspaper in front of him. They looked up as Joe and Lottie came inside together.

"How's the ankle?" Joe asked.

"Getting better, I think," Eli replied. "I won't be bothering Belinda for long, I'm sure."

"When you can walk across that yard without help, you're free to go," Belinda said. "If I let you go before that, people will think I'm being uncharitable."

"Belinda, I will pay you back for your

kindness," Eli said. "You'll see. I'll take care of you properly, the way a woman should be cared for."

The words were oddly tender coming from the old man, and Joe almost felt like he should cover his daughter's ears for the intimacy of the moment. Belinda froze, and her gaze was locked on Eli, her knitting still in her hands. The older man met her gaze easily enough. It seemed like they both forgot that he and Lottie were there for a moment, and then Belinda shook herself free of it.

"Can I get you a drink, Joe?" Belinda asked, setting down her knitting and rising to her feet. "Some lemonade?"

"Yes, please, that would be really nice." Joe looked down at Lottie. "Do you want some juice?"

"She had some already," Belinda said. "Do you want more, Lottie?"

Lottie shook her head. "Nope. This is a great carrot, isn't it? It's huge. I never knew you could get carrots this big."

Belinda chuckled and went to the counter. She poured a tall glass from a waiting pitcher. Her gaze moved from Joe down to his daughter thoughtfully.

"If you're okay with it, Joe, Lottie could

go throw that great carrot past the fence for Eeyore."

Joe looked down at Lottie. "Do you want to do that?"

"I can feed Eeyore?" she asked, her eyes lighting up.

"You can throw the carrot *past* the fence," Belinda said with emphasis. "You are not to hold the carrot out to him. You have to throw it. Do you promise?"

Lottie nodded eagerly.

"Okay, then," Joe said. "Go on."

Lottie clattered out of the house, and Joe followed her outside. He watched as his daughter hurled the carrot overhand past the fence. It was a good throw, too. Eeyore plodded over and picked it up between his big teeth. Joe had been hoping to ask Belinda some questions, but he'd forgotten that Eli would be there, too, and he'd wanted to keep this private.

When he went back inside, Belinda was sinking back into the chair in front of her knitting. Eli's lips were pursed as he perused the paper.

"Belinda, I was hoping to ask you a few questions," Joe said. "I can't tell you who I'm talking about for privacy reasons, but…" He looked toward Eli again.

"Do you want me to leave the room?" Eli asked, and he made a show of trying to stand up without putting any weight on his injured foot.

"No, of course not," Joe said quickly. He couldn't be the meanie who made a hurt old man hobble out of the room. If he wanted advice, he'd need to get it here, with Eli present.

"If you're sure," Eli said, resettling.

"I'm sure," Joe replied. "It's just…delicate. I hope I can count on your discretion."

"Mine?" Eli shrugged. "Of course. I don't gossip, and if I did, I don't have anyone to tell besides Belinda. You're safe enough."

Joe smiled faintly. "Okay, well, I was hoping you could give me some insight, Belinda. If you don't mind."

"I'd be happy to," Belinda said, and she handed him the lemonade. "What do you need to know?"

Here went nothing. He glanced over at Eli, who looked up in open curiosity.

"I know of a young Amish woman who had a baby out of wedlock," Joe said slowly. "Her family helped her to give that child up. What reasons would they have for doing that?"

"Oh…" Belinda ran her hands down her apron and exchanged a look with Eli. "A few, I suppose. How young was the girl?"

"Sixteen."

"So…young enough." Belinda nodded a couple of times. "Well, I do know of a few situations like that over the years. Sometimes the family will help the girl raise her child. Other times, if the pregnancy was a secret, they'll send her away to have the baby so no one local need know about it."

"And then give the child up for adoption," he said.

"Yah," Belinda said. "It doesn't happen often."

"Normally, the father would be made to marry her," Eli added. "I think I mentioned that last time."

Which added a new question to his personal list—who was his father that wouldn't marry his mother when she was pregnant?

"So the father might have been someone shocking?" Joe asked with a frown.

"My dear, my people are easy to shock." Belinda shot him a smile. "He could have simply been not Amish."

"That is shocking enough," Eli said soberly.

Belinda batted a hand in his direction to make him quiet.

"You see, there are always a lot of girls looking to get married. More boys seem to leave our communities than girls do, and that leaves an imbalance. So a girl who had a child already but wanted to get married would have a harder time finding a husband. Presuming the father of that child wasn't Amish—because Eli is right, if he was Amish, the bishop and the elders would take care of the rest."

"So if she gave the baby up, she probably would have had an *Englisher* boyfriend," he said.

"That's what I would guess," Belinda said. "What do you think, Eli?"

"Me, too," the older man confirmed.

Joe smiled faintly. "Okay, so if that girl gave up her child and ended up married with more kids with her husband later, what would happen if that first child wanted to meet her?"

Eli huffed out a long sigh, and Joe looked at him uncertainly. Would it be that bad? The older man didn't say anything, though.

"Oh…well, it depends, doesn't it?" Belinda said. "Would her husband know about the child? Would it be painful for her to see that child, or a relief? That's a very personal question."

"Would it ruin her reputation in the community?" Joe asked. "If people found out that she'd had a child before her marriage, would her husband leave her?"

"What?" Belinda shook her head. "Of course not. Marriage is for life—for better or for worse. Her husband wouldn't leave. There is no divorce for the Amish."

"But there may be some big problems behind closed doors," Eli added.

"Well, that's true," Belinda agreed.

"Would she end up with people talking behind her back and would she lose her standing in the community?" Joe asked.

"Gossip happens everywhere," Belinda replied. "And I can't pretend that she wouldn't face her own fair share. Plus, once the story was out, it would reflect on her children, too. It would be embarrassing. But embarrassment never killed anyone, did it?"

Eli widened his eyes as if in disagreement, but he didn't say anything else.

"Is this someone I know?" Belinda asked, softening her tone.

Joe shrugged. "I'm not sure, honestly."

"If you told me her name, I could be discreet," Belinda said.

Joe shook his head. "No, I don't think I want to do that. Not yet. I only have a first name, anyway, and this might not be the right community."

"So...this isn't Lottie's *mamm*?" Belinda asked.

He supposed it was understandable that people jumped to that conclusion. "No, it's nothing to do with Lottie."

Belinda pressed her lips together.

"Dear, I'm going to give some Amish advice," Belinda said. "You can use it or discard it...whatever works for your situation. But I think it might be useful."

"Okay..." Joe said cautiously.

"We Amish often say that *Gott* doesn't make mistakes," Belinda said, and she turned thoughtfully toward the window.

"Mmm-hmm," Eli murmured in agreement, his gaze back on the paper.

Belinda slowly turned back toward him. "There is a story about a man who wanted to raise horses. He loved horses, and he wanted nothing else than to raise them and sell them. It would be his way of providing for his family." Belinda put down her knitting needles. "And so he asked his father to help him start up."

"And his father said he didn't have an extra horse, so he gave him what he did have, and that was a cow," Eli said. Obviously this was a well-known tale.

"Yes." Belinda exchanged a look with the old man. "A cow. The man was upset. He didn't want a cow. So he went to his uncle and told him he wanted to raise horses."

"His uncle said he didn't have an extra horse, and he gave him some chickens," Eli said.

"And he was very upset again," Belinda said. "So he went to another uncle, told him he wanted to raise horses. His uncle said he'd give him what he had, and he gave him some wood. But what good was wood?"

"No good at all," Eli said, shaking his head.

"So he went to his aunt, and he told her he wanted to raise horses," Belinda said.

"And she gave him some seeds for his garden," Eli said.

Belinda nodded. "That she did. So the man took the seeds home, and he put them on the table, and he told his wife how angry he was.

He said that he could never raise horses now. He didn't have what he needed to do it. And he was angry enough to die." Belinda looked over at Joe and met his gaze. "Do you know what the wife said?"

"What did she say?" Joe asked.

"She said, 'We now have a cow, and we have chickens, and we have wood to build a coop. We even have seeds to plant our garden. Dear husband, we're going to have plenty to eat this winter. Let's be thankful.'"

Joe eyed her for a moment, and Belinda simply looked back at him, her blue eyes shining from behind those rimless glasses she always wore. Was that it? It seemed to be, but he wasn't sure what she meant by it all. That story was a little vague. He wasn't looking for a career change. But it seemed like a discouraging story for a guy who had a mission…

"Daddy!" Lottie called, her footsteps coming up to the side door. It opened, and Lottie came dashing out of the mudroom. "Daddy!"

"Yeah? What's wrong?" Joe asked, turning toward his bouncing daughter.

"I did something." She made a face.

"What did you do?" he asked.

"I wanted to pet Eeyore," she said.

"That is very dangerous. You were told to throw the carrot. That was all. Did you obey?" he asked sternly.

"I opened the gate just a little bit," she said.

"Oh, no…" Joe sighed. "Where is Eeyore now?"

"He went that way." She pointed in the direction of the road. "I'm sorry, Daddy."

"That donkey…" Belinda said with a shake of her head. "It's okay, dear. We'll find him. At least he didn't go up the mountain again."

"Maybe I can do something—" Eli started pushing himself up again, but he wasn't going anywhere on that hurt ankle.

"I'll go after him," Joe said. "He can't have gotten too far. Where do you normally find him?"

"Oh, anywhere," Belinda said. "If you hurry, you might be able to see him on the road still."

"I'll go," Joe said. "Lottie, you stay here, okay?"

Tears filled Lottie's eyes, and she looked over at Belinda, her lip quivering.

"Hey…" Joe sank down next to her. "It's okay. I'll find him."

"I'm very, very sorry," Lottie whispered. "I was bad, and I opened the gate."

"Lottie, dear," Belinda said softly, "it's okay. You're only four. Anything you do is fixable. Trust me there, little one."

"That's not what Belinda tells me when I let the donkey out," Eli muttered.

"Because you're almost eighty. You should know better!" Belinda countered. "Come along, Lottie. I'll find you a cookie."

Joe took one last look at his daughter, and his heart flooded with love. She was small and rambunctious and always into something. And maybe Lottie would grow up to be a woman always searching for her own mother, too. But she'd never have to search for her dad. Joe was right here—and he'd be her hero.

Starting today, with finding that blasted donkey.

THE WIND WAS warm enough to feel like summer, but Hazel's mind wasn't on the warm sunlight or the rippling grass in the pasture to her right. She was still turning over the airport map in her mind. She'd need to know that airport like the back of her hand— it would be her home base for the regional airline, and Hazel hadn't gotten as far as she had by not worrying about the details. Hazel had been overprepared for everything except parenting. There were other pilots who were more innately skilled or who had better connections, but they'd never find another pilot as diligently prepared as she was.

That was her edge.

Her sandals weren't really meant for long walks, but something about the day drew her on. Her books were waiting for her up in her room, but the words and diagrams had all started to blur together. It was definitely time for a break.

She reached a big stop sign at the highway, and beyond the highway was another gravel road and a hand-painted sign that read Fresh Fruit, Fresh Eggs, Fresh Bread, Free Kittens. There were no cars coming, so she crossed and continued on. Some cattle grazed in the field, one tiny calf drinking hungrily from his mother. There was still a bit of umbilical cord attached, so he must be very new. She stopped and watched for a moment, took a picture and sent it to Maddie, then kept walking.

Cute, Maddie texted back. Looks like you're relaxing!

Hazel felt a small twinge of guilt, and she just responded with a happy face. She wasn't relaxing so much as giving her brain a little break so she could get back to the books. That wasn't what Maddie meant, and she knew it.

The sound of clopping came from behind her, and Hazel turned to see Eeyore standing at the side of the highway. She stared at him in surprise. That *was* Eeyore, wasn't it? How many donkeys were there around here?

"Eeyore, is that you?" she said.

In response, the donkey plodded onto the road, and an oncoming pickup truck slowed down and maneuvered around him. The window came down.

"That your donkey?" the man called.

"Um, no," she said. "But I think I know whose he is."

"Well, good luck," the man said, and the window went back up again, and he drove off.

She may have overstated her confidence there. "Eeyore, get off the road. Come here!"

Eeyore plodded toward her and stopped a few feet away. Calling him over was probably a terrible idea, after all. What was she supposed to do with him? But he couldn't stand in the middle of the highway, either.

"Eeyore, go home," she said, looking both ways down the road. No one was coming.

She clapped her hands together loudly. "Go home!"

Nothing.

Maybe if she kept walking he'd get the idea and go back. She turned her back on him and carried on up the drive. She crested a hill and looked down at the gravel road, tumbling out like a ribbon beneath her. There was a farm below—a large red barn, a chicken coop and a white house shielded from view by a line of trees. There were several ample greenhouses, too, and beyond them what looked like stables and some grazing horses. This was a prosperous farm.

Hazel heard the clopping coming up behind her again. Whenever she stopped and looked over her shoulder, Eeyore stopped and looked away as if he'd just been standing there all day.

There was a roadside stand ahead, too, and three black buggies were sitting next to it. Hazel took out her phone and took a picture of the scene, then looked back at Eeyore.

"Go home!"

Eeyore looked away again, and she sighed. If the donkey was going to follow her, she could drop him off at this farm. They were neighbors, and at least she'd be able to tell

Belinda where her donkey was. If she tried to lead him home, she wasn't sure he'd even follow. This was one stubborn animal.

"Come on, then," Hazel sighed, and she started down the gentle slope toward that roadside stand.

Eeyore plodded after her, and after a few yards, he caught up, then passed her, picking up his pace until he was trotting at a brisk rate. She hadn't anticipated that, but she wasn't sure what else she could do. She picked up her own pace to a quick walk, and she was mildly relieved when Eeyore stopped at the fruit stand.

A young Amish woman was working at the stand, and Hazel couldn't help but admire how incredibly pretty she was. That was the gift of youth—the soft skin, the pink glow, the bright eyes... Maddie had that kind of beauty, too. It was something a girl never fully appreciated while she had it, and any man who tried to make her forget how gorgeous she was deserved to be ground into powder.

That was Hazel's perspective now.

And there were three young men all standing around that stand, looking at the girl with nothing short of worship in their eyes. There was a cardboard box beyond the men, and one of them held a little ball of fluff in his hands.

"Eeyore, what are you doing here?" the Amish girl asked with a laugh.

The young men only now seemed to notice Hazel's approach, and they all took about three large steps back to give her room. Apparently, they weren't in line to buy anything, except for perhaps the young blond man with the kitten in his palm.

The fruit stand had some baskets of ripe strawberries—a little early, if it wasn't for those greenhouses. There were blueberries, too, and cartons of eggs. Some loaves of braided bread and muffins were bagged and on display as well.

"He followed me, I'm afraid," Hazel said. "I'm not sure what to do with him."

"Oh, he does this sometimes," the girl replied. "He's a naughty donkey, and we all know him. He belongs to Belinda up the way."

"I'm staying at her bed-and-breakfast," Hazel said.

"Oh! I hope you're enjoying your stay. Belinda's bed-and-breakfast is a favorite around here. Tell her that Miriam says hi."

"I'll be sure to," Hazel said. "But about Eeyore...what do I do?"

The donkey nuzzled toward the fruit on display, and Hazel put a hand between his nose and some strawberries.

"Nothing. He's fine. Don't worry about him. He gets out all the time and wanders around. We all know where he belongs. I'll send someone to tell Belinda where he is."

Her gaze moved subtly in the direction of the three young men, who were still hanging back. Yes, she'd have errand boys to spare, Hazel was sure. Miriam took out a paring knife and grabbed an apple from inside the stall. She cut it in half and fed Eeyore from the flat of her palm. He gobbled up the apple.

"This all looks wonderful," Hazel said. "Do you make the bread yourself?"

"*Yah*, my sisters and I bake it all," Miriam said with a smile. "I'm almost sold out of the egg bread. This is the last of it. I'm sure Belinda has baking there, though. If I send you back with my bread, she might be offended."

"I was actually curious about the kittens," Hazel said. "I'm on vacation, so I can't take one. But does that work—just putting a sign out for free kittens?"

"It seems to." Miriam gestured toward the young Amish men.

Hazel chuckled. Yeah, she was pretty sure these guys weren't here for kittens. But she wasn't about to ruin anything for them, either.

"Our cat had a litter. We got her fixed, and then we got the girl kittens fixed, too. But I guess we missed one, because we've got more kittens! Come take a look."

"I can't take one," Hazel repeated, just to be sure there was no misunderstanding, "but I'd love to hold one."

"Of course," Miriam said. "Noah, you'll take a kitten home, won't you?"

The smooth-faced young man who seemed to be named Noah looked startled, and when Miriam fixed him with a glittering smile, his face reddened.

"Well, I shouldn't, but... I guess one couldn't hurt."

Hazel accepted a little ball of fur from Miriam's hand and smothered a smile. These kittens would find homes, she was sure of it. And those three Amish men were going home with a kitten each. Guaranteed.

CHAPTER SIX

HAZEL SET THE kitten back into the box. If Maddie had still been a little girl, she'd beg for a kitten. Her daughter loved animals, and she'd always wanted pets. Whenever Hazel had given in, the pet had become Hazel's responsibility. From a gerbil named Hank to a fish tank full of goldfish, to a golden retriever puppy named Edward that had become Hazel's constant companion. Edward passed away a couple of years ago. But those days were gone, and Hazel was going to be incredibly busy going forward. There wouldn't be time for pets, and there wouldn't be anyone at home to take care of one in her absence.

No, this kitten was better off with someone else.

The young Amish men had turned their attention to Eeyore, who was now munching on some grass at the side of the road. They stood there, eyeing the donkey, arms crossed, talking to each other in Pennsylvania Dutch.

"Could I get some strawberries, please?" Hazel asked.

"Of course!" Miriam smiled brightly.

Hazel pulled out her wallet, and paid for a pint of fresh, ripe strawberries. These were plumper and redder than the supermarket variety, and she could smell their sweetness already. She heard the rumble of an engine and turned to see a red pickup truck coming down the road with a billow of dust behind it. It slowed as it approached, and when it got close enough, she recognized Joe in the driver's seat. He pulled to a stop at the side of the road and hopped out, shooting Hazel a grin.

"So you have Eeyore," he called.

Joe's gaze took in the scene around her, but his smile seemed intended for her alone.

"He followed me," Hazel replied, heading in his direction. "I wasn't sure what to do."

Joe held up a halter and a lead rope. "I've got it."

"Everyone else seems to know how to deal with runaway donkeys," Hazel said. She held out the basket of strawberries, and he took one.

"Just give me a minute," he said, and he

popped the berry into his mouth, then nipped off the stem and tossed it into the grass.

Hazel leaned against the warm side of the truck and watched as Joe walked up to the group of young men. He looked older, a bit tougher, and he joked with them—something she couldn't make out, but that the younger men chuckled at—as he slipped the halter over Eeyore's muzzle. He led the donkey across the street to the grass beside his truck just as a car pulled up at the roadside stand, and Miriam turned her attention to serving new customers.

"You want to head back now, or…" Joe met her gaze.

She thought about the books and diagrams waiting for her, and then of what Maddie would say if she ever let slip that she'd given up an opportunity to enjoy some Amish ambiance with a handsome guy in exchange for her pile of books.

"We could eat some strawberries before we go," she said.

"Sure. We could do that." He secured the lead rope to a tie-down on the side of the truck. Then he came back around, dropped the tailgate and gestured toward it.

"This is the best seat on a country road," he said.

She smiled and hopped up. He scooted next to her, his arm just brushing hers. He was right about the seat. From where he was parked, they could watch the produce stand, the buggies, the Amish people chatting and the farm beyond. It was the kind of scene that lowered one's blood pressure.

"Apparently, this donkey wanders around here a lot," Hazel said.

"My daughter will feel a little better knowing that," Joe said with a half smile. "She's the one who let him out."

"Oh, no!" She laughed. "What happened?"

"I don't have all the details, but she wanted to pet him, and Eeyore had other plans."

She took a strawberry and sank her teeth into it. It was sun-warmed and sweet. She'd never eaten such a fresh berry in her life, and she rolled her eyes upward.

"Good?" he asked.

"Mmm." She swallowed. "Really good."

Hazel's phone buzzed, and she looked down at an incoming video call from Maddie.

"My daughter—" she explained and picked up the call. In the little rectangle that showed

Hazel's own face, there was half of Joe's surprised expression, too.

"Hi, Mom," Maddie said, then her eyes widened. "Oh! Am I interrupting anything?"

"No, I'm showing you proof that I'm actually relaxing," Hazel said. "This is Joe. He's a local landscaper."

There was a beat of silence, and then Joe leaned into the frame and smiled ruefully. "Hi, Maddie. I've heard a lot about you."

"Hi, Joe." Maddie grinned. "I haven't heard about you yet, *at all*."

"We've gotten to be friends," Hazel said. And she hoped she wasn't overstating things, but they felt like friends now, at least. "We've bonded over being the parents of daughters."

"Oh, nice. How old is your daughter, Joe?"

"She's four," he said.

"So you have a whole lot in common?" Maddie chuckled. "I'm not sure how to take that."

"Your mom has good advice," Joe replied. "And I'm grateful for it."

Hazel looked over at him and laughed. She had really put him on the spot here, hadn't she? Oh, well, she'd always told Maddie to make sure someone knew who she was spending time with. This could arguably be a safety measure.

"So how's it going over there?" Hazel asked. "Everything okay?"

"Yes, Mom. Everything's fine." Maddie had that tired sound to her voice that she got when she thought Hazel was being too much of a mother hen. "I just wanted to tell you that I'm mailing a package to you. I don't know how long it'll take to get from England to the US, but it's just some souvenirs I don't feel like packing around all summer."

"Smart," Hazel said. "I'm sure I'll be home again before it arrives."

"Me, too." Maddie shot her a playful smile. "Anyway…I won't keep you. 'Bye, Joe!"

Joe leaned into the frame again, and Hazel noticed his face had gone just a little bit pink.

"'Bye, Maddie."

"Talk to you later," Hazel said. "Be safe."

"Always. See you."

And Hazel hung up.

"Sorry," Hazel said. "I didn't mean to drag you into that. It's just that I hate to not answer when she calls. I miss her."

"No problem," Joe said. "So that's what nineteen looks like in a daughter, huh?"

"Sure is." Hazel looked over at him. "Intimidated?"

"Very." He chuckled. "I guess I'll be ready for it when I get there."

Over at the roadside stand, Miriam was arranging little cardboard boxes of strawberries. She looked pretty close to Maddie's age, too, but they had very different lives. Hazel sighed softly. "To be that young again…"

Joe leaned toward her, cocking his head to the side. "That young lady is pretty popular around here. Her name is Miriam Yoder."

"You know her?"

"This roadside stand is mentioned in tour books and stuff. And I've done some work with her brothers. They're a nice family, and her brothers are very concerned with keeping the wrong type of guy away from their little sister."

Miriam Yoder… It was only connecting now, but she'd heard that name before.

"Is this the Miriam that Amish man was wanting to be set up with?" she asked.

"That's my bet." Joe chuckled. "I mean, there are a lot of Yoders in these parts, and Miriam isn't an uncommon name…but probably. The Amish dating scene is pretty cut-throat around here. These people date with intent, if you know what I mean."

"They're looking for marriage," she said.

"Yup."

At least they knew what they wanted, and apparently they found their own ways of getting it. Obadiah was going to the matchmaker. These young men were coming straight to the girl.

"Obadiah seemed pretty smitten with her, but I can see that he's got a fair amount of competition," she said.

The customers headed back to their car with a full crate of fresh produce, and the young Amish men moved back in to chat with Miriam. Hazel could see an older Amish man walking up the drive from the Yoder farm, his head down and his face shaded by the brim of his straw hat.

"How's your daughter?" Joe asked.

"She's having some difficulty getting along with her father's other kids," she said. "They see her as a threat to their home, I think."

He nodded. "Isn't he doing anything to fix that?"

"I hope so." She sighed. "I don't feel like I should be launching myself into the middle. Todd has always been good to Maddie, and this is a family affair. And…it isn't my family, is it?"

"What does Maddie think?" he asked.

"She vents to me, but she's not asking for help in this. She and Todd have their own father-daughter relationship."

"I'll bet you want to do something about it, though," Joe said.

She did. She wanted to pick up the phone and let him have it. She wanted to point out what a phenomenal young woman Madison had become and tell him that he'd better be more careful with how this trip went. She was an adult now, and she'd be making her decisions about whether or not she had much to do with her dad.

Hazel shook her head. "It doesn't matter what I want to do."

"I don't know," Joe said. "If I were you, I'd just do it. What's the worst that can happen? Your ex will be annoyed with you? Who cares?"

"I agree—I don't really care if Todd is annoyed. No, the worst thing that can happen is that my daughter will think I overstepped, and she won't tell me what's going on next time, for fear I'll get involved."

Joe sobered. "Right."

"Madison is pretty independent, and I can feel her pulling away with some things. It's normal—it's good! She's growing up, and this is a whole new stage…but it gets more complicated when they get older."

"For her dad, too," Joe said.

"But he'll have to figure that out."

"You're not going to help him?" Joe arched an eyebrow.

"He hasn't asked for my help, either," she said. "And he could."

Todd would resent it if she butted in. His wife would resent it. Maddie would, too. That made it harder still to just sit here and wait for it all to shake out.

The Amish man came to the top of the drive and arrived at the stall. He was older, with a bushy beard that had a bit of gray in it. He said a few words to the young men, and they all straightened. One wiped his palms down the sides of his pants.

"Sometimes I wish things were that simple with the rest of us," Joe said, nodding in the direction of the Amish people.

"How on earth is that simple?" she asked. One beautiful girl, three young admirers… and a fourth trying to get the matchmaker on his side.

"The dad walks up, and the men interested in his daughter fall into line," Joe said. "He can protect her, and the young guys respect her dad."

"Not so simple for the girl," Hazel replied. "What about her having the chance to fall in love?"

"Not today, apparently." Joe chuckled. The young men were headed back toward their buggies. They looked resigned, as if this was to be expected. She caught the look on one young man's face, and he had that satisfied look of someone who'd furthered his cause, somehow. This was a long game.

"Wait!" Miriam called. "The kittens!"

Everybody froze. It was like she'd stopped time with that shout, and the men came back. One by one, they reached into the box and each took out a ball of fluff.

"Free kittens," Hazel murmured. "Miriam wasn't too worried about finding them good homes."

Joe laughed softly. "She knows her power."

"Good for her," Hazel said quietly. "I'm glad she does. And I hope she gets the life she wants."

It was her deepest wish for her daughter, too. Maddie had more power than she realized when it came to her father and her half siblings. They wouldn't be so intimidated by her if she didn't.

Joe picked up a berry and handed it to her. It was the last berry.

"It's yours," he said.

His voice was low, warm and deep, and it made goose bumps run up her arms. Guys like Joe didn't realize the power they wielded, either.

Hazel took the strawberry, and Joe hopped down from the tailgate.

"I'll get you another pint," he said, and he cast her a smile over his shoulder as he ambled back toward the stall. He had faint freckles on his arms she hadn't noticed before, and he had a sort of cowboy swagger that she found hard to refuse.

But Hazel's days of twining men's hearts around her finger on a whim were well in the past. And it was just as well. This was a new stage of life—empowering in its own ways. She watched him select a basket, pay for it and then head back in her direction.

"Here you are," Joe said, handing her another pint of berries. When she took it, he said, "I appreciate you giving me insights into raising a daughter."

"You'll do fine, Joe."

"Yeah…I guess I just know I'll need a mom for her sooner or later," he said. He met her gaze easily enough, his eyes holding hers.

"What about a wife for you?" she said. "Kids grow up, you know."

"Yeah." His cheeks colored slightly, and he dropped his gaze. Maybe he'd realized that he seemed like he was considering her for the role. "But it's more complicated when there is a little girl in the middle."

"It is," she agreed.

"Besides," he said, heading over to the tie-down and prying at the knotted rope, "I need to find a woman willing to be a stay-at-home mom for a daughter that isn't biologically hers. Lottie is a kid who just needs that extra reassurance. She's never even met her mother, but it's like she's grieving the loss, all the same. She's really been struggling. So for her sake, I need to give her that traditional family security. And for a woman who'd be her stepmom, that's a big ask."

Of course. He was looking for a woman willing to be at home, to make their marriage and children her world. There was nothing wrong with that, and she could see why Joe would long for it, but Hazel wasn't that woman anymore. She'd raised her daughter, and she was ready to step into her freedom at long last. She'd earned it. But she did feel a wash of disappointment that she'd be eliminated that quickly and easily. Maybe it was for the best. She couldn't be toying with romantic feelings when she was supposed to be preparing for her position as a regional pilot. It was a much-needed reality check.

Joe looked back at her. "You okay?"

"Yep." Hazel hopped down from the tailgate and slammed it shut. Then she picked up the berries from the truck bed. "How can I help here?" She paused when she realized it sounded like she was referring to his marital situation, and her face heated. "I mean with Eeyore."

Joe chuckled and shot her a warm smile. "Hold his lead rope out the window, and I'll drive really slowly. But you keep an eye on him to make sure he can keep up comfortably."

Hazel went to the passenger side of the truck to put the berries inside the open window. "I can do that."

"Come on, Eeyore," Joe said, angling his steps around the truck toward the donkey. "Time to go home."

JOE BARELY TOUCHED the gas as he crept down the gravel road. He could hear the clip-clop of Eeyore's hooves, and when he looked over, he could see the donkey's head, ears high, as he plodded along next to them. They made a good team, he and Hazel.

"This'll be a vacation to remember," Hazel said.

For Joe, too. Strangely, this woman had started to seep into the cracks around here, and he'd miss her once she was gone. He should probably do his best to curb that, but for the time being, they'd be seeing each other quite a bit, and he couldn't complain. He knew what it felt like to have women interested in him when he didn't reciprocate the feelings. But Hazel was a different story—she wasn't angling for him, and he found himself only wanting to see more of her.

"Slow down, Joe…"

He liked the sound of his name on her lips. Yeah, he'd have to rein this in. He touched the brakes and slowed down, then came to a stop at the highway. There were no cars coming.

"Are we good?" Joe asked.

"Come on, Eeyore," Hazel said, and her voice held more command. "Let's go. Come on."

She gave a tug on the lead rope, and Eeyore

started forward again. Joe touched the gas, and the donkey clopped along faster. They crossed the highway and started down Butternut Drive.

"I think he senses home," Hazel said.

"Well, I don't trust him to go back without us," Joe muttered. He'd return this donkey to his pasture and lock that gate himself. The donkey seemed to be an escape artist, and the next time he broke out, it better be someone else's fault.

When they got past Eli's property, he spotted the Butternut Bed and Breakfast sign, and then he saw the flash of pink of Lottie's dress. She'd insisted on wearing that dress this morning, despite how dirty it would get, and Joe hadn't had the energy to take on that battle.

"Daddy's coming!" Lottie's voice reached the open truck windows, and he couldn't help but smile.

Belinda stood next to her, and she held her hand firmly until Joe eased to a stop in front of the drive.

"Come here, you rascal," Belinda said, taking the lead rope and giving Eeyore a very stern look. "You are a naughty donkey, and I ought to give you a long lecture for what you did."

Maybe it was just Joe, but the donkey honestly looked abashed. Hazel pushed open the door.

"Come on, Lottie!" she called. "Hop in!"

It was just a short jaunt down the driveway, and he watched as Hazel helped to scoop up Lottie into her lap and slammed the door shut. Hazel held his daughter naturally—she settled her on her knee and tugged down her dress.

"You found Eeyore!" Lottie said. "Where did you find him? Where did he go?"

Lottie chattered nonstop, and Joe answered her where he could. When he looked over at Hazel, her cheeks were pink from the heat, and her hair was mussed up. One slim hand was lying on Lottie's leg, and no matter how much his daughter wriggled, she looked entirely comfortable. He felt an unexpected wash of tenderness, and this time, it was all about Hazel. She would be…perfect.

Joe pulled to a stop in front of the house, and Hazel pushed open the door. Lottie bounced back out, and Hazel undid her seat belt.

"Thanks for the strawberries," she said, picking up the pint that had sat between them.

"No problem. Thanks for helping me get the donkey back."

She smiled, and then she got out. She closed the door and he watched her walk—strawberries balanced in one hand—toward the house, Lottie skipping along next to her. He knew that he, Hazel and Lottie didn't actually belong together, but to anyone who might peek in on this scene from the outside, it sure looked like they did. And Joe was starting to seriously wonder what that might feel like.

THAT EVENING, Joe flicked off the light to his daughter's bedroom. She was lying snuggled in her new single bed—he'd just switched out the toddler bed last month. Now, she looked so tiny in the twin bed. She had her feet on top of a pile of pink quilt and her toy airplane in her hands as she swooped it through the air over her head.

"Daddy?" The swooping stopped.

"Yeah, Lottie?"

"I'm glad we got Eeyore back."

"Me, too," he said. "But now you understand why it's so important to follow instructions, right?"

"Yeah."

But more importantly, he now saw that he'd have to keep his daughter a lot closer while he worked. He was hoping this would be a lesson that landed for her, but he wasn't about to count on it. If anything, he'd just found out that this take-your-daughter-to-work week wasn't working as well as he'd thought.

"It might help if you stick closer to me," Joe said. "You can help me with stuff. We'll do some Dad-and-Lottie work together."

"I don't want to," she said.

"Well…" He combed through his mind for a solution to that. "What if I paid you a dollar to work with me?"

"A dollar? A real one?"

He chuckled. "Yes, a real one."

"Okay."

"Good. Now go to sleep."

"One more kiss," she said.

Joe went back into her room and bent over, giving her a kiss on her forehead. Her arms twined up around his neck, and she pressed a wet kiss against his cheek.

"Night, night, Daddy."

"Night, night."

Joe closed the door most of the way, leaving a crack open to let light from the hallway into her room the way she liked it. Then he headed down the hallway to the living room. He moved over a bucket of Barbies and dropped onto the couch with a sigh.

There were dishes on the table from supper, but he'd clean that up later before he went to bed. He had the TV on low, playing an old sitcom. He'd seen all of the reruns, but it was comforting, all the same.

He glanced over to the side table, and there was the familiar double frame. One photo was of the day his parents adopted him—a young smiling couple with a swaddled newborn in his mother's arms, and his dad looking down at him in awe. The other photo was of the day Lottie was born, and he stood alone with Lottie wrapped in a hospital blanket, snuggled in his arms. He looked tired in that photo—it had been a long wait for her delivery, and Jessica hadn't wanted him in the room with her. It was understandable—he was her ex. So he'd sat in the waiting room, anxious and worried, both for Jessica's health and for the choice she'd make. Would she let him take full custody like she'd promised? Would she change her mind?

But she'd followed through. She'd taken twenty-four hours with Lottie in the hospital, and then she'd handed her over, and his heart had grown in that moment when the nurse laid Lottie in his arms.

That was the moment he knew he'd get to raise her.

Joe looked at the pair of photos for a moment. And as he always did, he noticed the same tired, thrilled, heart-exploding expression on his father's face the moment they got him. But behind both photos had been a woman who'd given birth and made the choice to let someone else raise her baby.

Who was his biological mother?

He picked up his cell phone and called his parents' home number. It rang twice, and his mother picked up.

"Hi, son!" she said with a smile in her voice. "How are you doing? Is the day care open again?"

"Not yet," he said. "In a few days."

He chatted with his mother several minutes about her recent knee surgery, and about the adventure of taking his daughter to work with him. He turned down two sincere offers for his mother to come babysit for him. No, coming to babysit was not an option. She needed rest.

"Mom, I was actually calling because I had a few questions," he said slowly. "I was wondering about my birth mother. I know her name is Rebecca and that she lived in the Danke area."

"Yes," she replied quietly. "Have you finally decided to look for her?"

"I'm...not sure. I might."

"I've been waiting for you to ask more," she said. "I thought you would when you were ready."

"I haven't actually looked too hard yet," he said. "I wanted to talk to you about it. I wanted to make sure it wouldn't, I don't know...be a betrayal to you somehow."

"Son, you meeting your biological mom doesn't change that I raised you, loved you and would lie down and die for you. Okay? I'm your mother, and I know you better than anyone does. You have a heart that's big enough to hold both of us."

"So I won't upset you if I look for her?" he asked.

"No, son. You do what you need to do."

He exhaled a relieved sigh. "I don't know her last name, though. That might help to get started. You told me years ago that you told her my legal name. So if I did meet her, she'd recognize my name, if nothing else. But tracking her down might be harder. Do you know any more information about her? More than a first name?"

She was silent for a moment. "It was a privacy issue—I wasn't supposed to know her last name."

"Oh, right."

"But I did see it." He could hear the wince in her voice.

"You saw it? What is it?"

"I told myself I wouldn't tell you unless you were ready to find her. I don't know if that even makes it better. I felt guilty, but I saw her last name on her hospital bracelet. Her name was Rebecca Lehmann. She was sixteen, and her mother's name was Verna. We met at the hospital, so we exchanged first names. I remember that. You're thirty-seven, so that would make your biological mother...fifty-three now. And you're right. We did tell her what we were naming you—your full legal name. She knows that."

And that began the conversation where Joe heard all the information his mother had stored up about his birth mom. If he'd told her earlier that he wanted to find his birth mother, maybe she would have given him all of these details, but it was better late than never.

Would he find her? If he did, would he

talk to her or just get a look at her and let her be? He wasn't sure. Because in that bedroom down the hall, his own daughter was full of questions about her biological mom, and he was holding out on her. He would for another fourteen years. He didn't even know how he'd tell her the reason…

"Son, the Amish communities are tough to navigate. For the most part, they aren't online, and they keep to themselves. Finding her might not be so easy…"

"I'm doing some landscaping for an Amish matchmaker right now," he said. "If anyone has that kind of information, I think it would be her."

"That's…a very good idea," his mother said. "It's a place to start, at least."

"That's what I thought. I don't know how far I'm willing to dig, but we'll see."

He heard some rummaging in his daughter's room and then some footfalls on the hallway floor. Lottie was up. Private conversations were tough to come by around here.

"Well, then, good luck," his mother said. "And, son?"

"Yeah?"

"Come visit us in Scranton soon, will you? Your dad and I miss you and Lottie."

"We'll come soon," he said.

Lottie came padding down the hallway, and she stopped at the recliner.

"Mom, Lottie's back up," Joe said. "I'd better go and get her back to bed."

"Is that Grandma?" Lottie asked, her eyes lighting up.

"Yes, that's Grandma. You can say hi." He handed his daughter the phone and scooped her up in his arms. Lottie squealed and put the phone up to her ear.

"Hi, Grandma! We lost a donkey today!"

Joe carried her back to bed. None of this would be easy. It might not even be fair. But a mother mattered, and somehow, he and Lottie weren't so very different with their dreams of looking out a window and stumbling across the mother they'd lost.

CHAPTER SEVEN

JOE WORKED ON the side vegetable garden for a few hours the next morning. Lottie helped him by holding tools. When she got bored of that, he let her play on the grass with her toy plane and eat snack packs of fruit gummies. But he was determined to keep her close. There couldn't be any more mischief—the next time Eeyore got loose, he might not be able to find him. But having his daughter so close made it a lot harder to have a private conversation with Belinda.

Rebecca Lehmann.

That was all he had to say! Belinda would be discreet. He had his mom's blessing to find Rebecca…but something was holding him back. If he found her, would it make things better? Or would being faced with the truth ruin his fantasy of a sweet, Amish mother who just couldn't care for him?

Did he really want to know?

Because Lottie's fantasy of a mother who

was somehow scatterbrained and wandering around lost was completely contrary to her real mother. Jessica didn't want to have children, and he sincerely doubted that meeting her daughter would change that.

Kids were work—plain and simple. They needed constant love, attention, supervision and guidance. And even then, they had emotional days. If someone wanted to be a parent, it was worth it, but not everyone wanted that life. That reality would break his daughter's heart, and finding her mother wouldn't bring the peace she might hope for.

Would it be the same for him?

He might have been inclined to discuss it with Hazel, except she kept to herself most of the morning. He saw her hovering over those books a few times, and then around ten, she left the B&B to check out some local sights. For a moment before she left, she'd looked inclined to come over and talk to him, but then she'd just waved and hopped into the cab. Had he pushed it too far the day before? He was already feeling rather foolish for having opened up the way he had. It felt desperate on his part. He didn't need friends so badly that he'd overstep with people just visiting the area.

And yet, somehow, he had. He mentally chastised himself as he worked for the rest of the day, and those were the thoughts that fueled him as he planted row upon row of small tomato plants.

It was almost noon when Hazel's cab turned back into the drive. Joe raked the last of some hedge trimmings into a pile as she got out of the back seat and paid the driver. She was wearing a floral-patterned sundress, and her hair hung loose around her shoulders. She had a big cloth bag at her side.

"Hi, Joe!" she called.

Lottie came out of the house, and Joe watched her carrying a plate of cookies in Eli's direction on the porch. Hazel headed toward him, and he nodded down at the bag in her hand.

"Where did you end up going?" he asked.

"This is from Lehmann's Crafts," she replied. "It's a huge store, and really well stocked. I wanted to get some knitting supplies. Waiting around in airports can get boring, even if you're the pilot, and every Christmas, I give my extended family hand-knitted scarves. It's my thing."

"Lehmann's?" he said.

"Yep." She raised her eyebrows.

"Who owns it?"

"No idea." She eyed him for a moment. "What's that look on your face?"

"Nothing." He forced a smile. He'd already spilled too much the day before.

"It was something," she said, sobering. "Come on… What was that?"

"I told myself I wouldn't burden you with this stuff."

"It's not a burden. I honestly want to know." She met his gaze, and he couldn't help but soften.

"I got the full name of my biological mother." He shook his head. "It doesn't mean anything. Lehmann is an incredibly common name around here. Come to think of it now, there's Lehmann's Plumbing, Lehmann's Sports and I'm pretty sure there's even a Lehmann's Electronics."

"Lehmann's Electronics. Ironic." She smiled faintly.

"Not all Lehmanns stay Amish." He shrugged. "Not all Lehmanns are even born Amish…"

It didn't mean anything. He knew that. His mother's name was Rebecca Lehmann, and there were probably fourteen of them within a stone's throw.

"Your mother's last name was Lehmann, though?" Hazel asked.

"Yeah." He dropped his gaze. "Rebecca Lehmann. Sorry, I jumped on that, and I hadn't thought it through."

"Have you mentioned it to Belinda?" she asked.

He shook his head. "Nope."

"What's holding you back?"

That was the question, wasn't it? What was holding him back? He looked down at the bag in her hands, mostly as a distraction from this conversation. The bag was stuffed full of yarn: purple, gray, cream-colored and multicolored.

"So you make scarves, do you?" he said.

"I do." She eyed him for a moment as if deciding whether she wanted to follow his change in topic, then she hoisted the bag up.

"I'll have a lot of waiting and knitting time with this new job," she said. "I have a feeling I'll be able to start learning how to make mittens, too."

He chuckled. "Maybe one day, you can send me a scarf, if you're overflowing with them and don't know what to do with them all."

A smile broke over her face. "I'm going to

do that, Joe. A scarf for you this Christmas. And if I send you one, I'll send one for Lottie, too. Maybe they'll both be pink so you can match."

She grinned.

"Lottie would love that." He laughed. "Please don't make us match."

Somehow, the prospect of a scarf made by Hazel made everything else feel a whole lot better.

Hazel glanced over her shoulder toward the house. "I got an email while I was out. They need me to come in a few days earlier than they thought for some extra training on some new security protocols."

"Oh…" He swallowed. "Are you leaving here sooner than you thought?"

"No, but when I do leave, I won't have any extra time to get ready. I'm just going to make sure I'm prepared," she said. "Like many jobs, there's a probation period. And if I'm not up to their expectations, there's a long list of qualified pilots behind me who'd jump at the chance to take my place."

"Right." He sucked in a breath. "I have a feeling you won't let that happen."

"Not a chance." She smiled faintly. "So I'd better hit the books again."

"Understood. My daughter has some cookies on the front porch, if you're interested," Joe said. He had work to do, too. "I won't keep you."

Hazel cast him a smile and then turned her steps toward the house.

She didn't head toward the porch, though. Hazel had a life that was tugging her back, away from Amish country. He had a life, too, and obligations of his own. There were peas to plant next. He turned back to the work at hand.

"Daddy, do you want a cookie?" Lottie called from the porch.

"Save me one!" he called back, and then he laughed as he saw her squirming, looking at the last cookie on the plate. It would be torture for a four-year-old. "Alright, bring it over. We'll break it in half."

Lottie hopped down the steps and came skipping in his direction. His gaze returned to the house, where Hazel had disappeared inside.

Lehmann... It was a big family name in these parts, and he knew the chances of finding the right woman were slim, but he'd never look at those businesses the same way again, either. Even if he didn't find Rebecca, he was very likely rubbing shoulders with her family…with *his* family. But unless he found Rebecca, none of that would matter one bit.

CHAPTER EIGHT

HAZEL PUT HER things in the bedroom, tucking her purse and the bag into a space next to the bed. Everything smelled faintly of cloves and cinnamon. And although Hazel had made her bed this morning, she got the sense that it had been smoothed and straightened even further in her absence.

Maybe the Amish were like the army with hospital corners on the beds and sheets tight enough to bounce a quarter off them. At least Belinda seemed to be.

Hazel went to her window and looked out. It faced the front yard, and she could see Joe surveying the flower garden. He bent over, pulled a weed and stood back again. Then he walked away, out of her field of vision.

Her books were waiting for her on her bed, and a little white desk sat under the window. She brought them over for the natural light and pulled up a chair.

Joe was a sweet guy…more than sweet. She

didn't know him well, but she felt like she understood him in a way she didn't understand many people. If she'd met Joe under any other circumstances, she'd see more of him. It wouldn't even be a choice. He'd be the kind of guy she just kept running into until one day they'd stay up all night talking, and that would be it. They had a kind of magnetic pull toward each other that she'd never experienced before, but that somehow felt completely familiar.

She swallowed and stepped back from the window. But that would only work if he didn't need a stay-at-home mom for his little girl, or if she was willing to step back fifteen years and start all over again.

Hazel could hear Lottie's piping, chattery voice. "Does Eeyore want more animal friends?"

Eli's reply was a rumble, and Hazel couldn't make out his words. But there was something so endearing about a little girl's chatter.

"What about a…cow?" Lottie asked. "What about a…pig?"

Hazel smiled and sat down at the desk, flipping her book open to the section she'd left off at that morning.

She felt a wave of guilt even thinking about not wanting to go back to those years again. Maddie was the best part of her—her own heart existing outside of her body. But it had been hard being a single mom, and she realized that being a mom with a partner at her side was also hard. Mothering wasn't easy, no matter what package it came in, and there were so many sacrifices...

Hazel was supposed to say that it was worth it, and it was! But it was also a season. Little girls grew up, and moms got a second chance at their ambitions. Like this job. Was it so wrong to want to enjoy that?

"What about a duck?" Lottie's voice came through the window. "What about a duck friend, Mr. Eli?"

But she could enjoy the chatter of a cute little girl this week. She could listen to the laughter, and the kid logic, and remember when Maddie was little, too. And then she'd go back to her dreams, get into that cockpit and be the pilot she'd always wanted to be.

Speaking of which, she'd schedule that pleasure flight that Miles had suggested at the hangar. It would do her good and remind her where her heart lay. Somehow, she always got her balance back in the clouds.

An hour and a half later, Hazel's brain was as full of numbers and charts as she could handle, and she went downstairs for a break. She sat on the step next to Eli, her feet bare. Lottie was with her dad, helping to cart off some shrub trimmings to the burn pile, and a couple of magpies were hollering at some crows from the treetops.

"For the record, I disagree with Belinda," Eli said.

"You do?" Hazel looked over at the old man. He rubbed at his chin—the shave was a little better today than it had been in days past. Maybe that came from staying here.

"I do," he confirmed.

"Well, you seem to disagree about a lot," she said, attempting to lighten the mood. "What about?"

"About Obadiah and Miriam," Eli said. "She's making a mistake."

"I thought Miriam wasn't interested," she said.

"She doesn't seem to be."

"So why not find him a woman who is?"

Hazel asked. Personally, she sided with Belinda on this one.

"Because it won't be the right woman." Eli looked over at Hazel, his blue eyes seeming deeper today—darker, more mournful.

Here she was feeling irresponsibly tender toward Joe…and she'd never see him again after this trip. It was taking real effort on her part to focus on her studying and let the landscaper focus on his own emotional tangles. So who was she to judge Obadiah's longing for a woman he couldn't have?

"I don't think we all get that first choice," Hazel said. "That's life. Sometimes we make the best of it."

"Sometimes you know the first minute you see a woman, though," Eli said. "Sometimes, a man can look at a woman and say 'She's it.' And if Obadiah has done that, then I think he deserves a proper chance at convincing the girl. That's what I think."

"What if she breaks his heart?" Hazel asked.

"Small price to pay for having given it his best shot," Eli said. "I should know. I had my chance to tell Belinda how I felt before she married Ernie. But Ernie was a good man, and Belinda wasn't interested in me, so I let it go. But look at me now. I've lived next door to the woman for fifty-odd years, and I knew for every single one of them that she was the one for me. I knew it. But I did have one shot."

Hazel stared at him, then she swallowed. "What happened?"

"I summoned up my courage, and I went to her house one evening. I chatted with her father and ate her mother's pie, and when I found myself alone with her outside by the stable, I was about to tell her how I felt. But before I could, she asked me what I thought of Ernie. Was he as decent as he seemed?"

"And you told the truth..." Hazel said, guessing.

"I told the truth," he confirmed. "I told her that Ernie was a great guy. That he was honest and kind and decent. And then I left. I was too scared to tell her how I felt—to face her rejection. I was a fool. I should have told her then and let her choose."

That had been a long time ago, and here this man was, still pining for the same girl who'd chosen Ernie over him. That thought was a little heartbreaking.

"Why not be realistic? Why didn't you move on with some other girl?" she asked.

"I tried. The girls saw through me. I'm an

honest man, too, you see. I don't lie worth a dime."

She smiled ruefully. "There are worse character traits, Eli."

"*Yah*, I suppose."

"Why not tell her how you feel now?"

"I'm working up my courage again." He pulled off his hat and rubbed a hand through his sparse hair. "So I'm one to give advice, but not one who follows it. There you go. That's how you end up a confirmed bachelor at my age, and still hung up on the same woman."

"I'm sorry it turned out that way," she said.

Eli shrugged. "Me, too. But I feel an obligation to stand up for poor Obadiah. I'm already old. He's got a chance to do it differently, and I'm impressed by that young man. He's determined to get her, and he's even trying to get the matchmaker on his side. That takes gumption. And I think when it comes to something that matters as much as the rest of your life, that gumption is important."

"I'd have to agree with you," she said.

Joe and Lottie came back around the house, and Joe looked up and shot her a smile. Her heart skipped a beat. He was going to have to stop doing that...

But there wasn't time to worry about it because Belinda's buggy came back down the drive then, and Eli pushed himself up and hobbled over with his crutch toward the stable, where she stopped.

"Is anyone hungry?" Belinda asked, when she and Eli walked back up to the porch. "I sure am. I was thinking some sandwiches and soup would make a nice lunch."

For the next little while, there was bustle around getting a meal on the table. Joe continued working on the vegetable garden with his daughter a few yards away from him, and Hazel went inside to see if she could lend a hand. Eli sat himself down at the kitchen table to wait. It was funny, Hazel mused—knowing how the old man felt, seeing him sitting there at Belinda's kitchen table took on new meaning. Would he ever work up his courage?

"Can I help?" Hazel asked Belinda.

"No, no," Belinda replied. "You've paid good money to have food set in front of you. I won't have you working in the kitchen. That leads to bad reviews, you know."

Belinda winked and tapped the side of her nose.

"I wouldn't do that to you," Hazel said with a chuckle.

"All the same…"

When the meal was ready, Belinda went to the side door, pushed open the screen and called, "Lunch is ready!"

It didn't take long for Joe and Lottie to make their way inside. The water turned on in the mudroom, and a couple of minutes later, they both came into the kitchen.

"Sit down, sit down," Belinda said. "Anywhere will do."

Joe pulled out the chair next to Hazel, and his daughter crawled into the chair next to that one. He smelled of grass clippings and sunshine. Belinda bowed her head, as did Eli, and for a moment, everyone was silent, then Belinda raised her head and smiled.

"Eat up, everyone. Start with the soup, Joe." And the older woman reached for a plate of sandwiches and held it for Eli as he selected one.

"Give me your bowl, Lottie," Joe said.

He stretched to reach the cauldron of soup and dished up some for himself and his daughter.

"You want some?" Joe asked.

"Absolutely." Hazel passed him her bowl, and he filled it—it was a smooth and creamy tomato soup. When the plate of sandwiches came by, she chose a cheese sandwich to go with it.

"So what's going on with Obadiah's marriage mission?" Eli asked as everyone began to eat.

"I spoke with a young woman who I think would be good for him," Belinda said. "She's a hard worker, and I think she'd be a good support in his career."

"No man wants a wife like a stalk of broccoli," Eli said. "He wants a jelly doughnut."

"Well, the jelly doughnut does not want him," Belinda said firmly. "Besides, a lifetime of jelly doughnuts will kill you. Broccoli, on the other hand, will prolong your life."

"You can learn to like broccoli," Eli said. "You can appreciate it. You can even hide it in a good recipe, but you'll never love broccoli for the sake of broccoli."

Belinda and Eli eyed each other for a long, tense moment. Hazel glanced over at Joe. He gave her a quizzical look, and she smiled.

"I'll explain later," she whispered.

Joe leaned closer to catch her words, then nodded. He slid an arm over the back of her chair and leaned closer to her ear.

"I'm starting to think this isn't about Obadiah anymore."

His arm was warm behind her, and when
she looked over at him, he was smiling in a
way that was both friendly and rather tender.

"I hate broccoli," Lottie said loudly.

Everyone was silent, then Joe leaned back
and Hazel started to laugh. Leave it to a little
kid to break the seriousness of a conversation.

"Good thing you've got tomato soup, then,"
Joe said. "Come on. Eat up. You love tomato
soup."

"I do love it," Lottie agreed.

"Tomato soup could leave a man filled in
the most wonderful way for the rest of his
life," Eli said meaningfully. "Personally, I
don't want a lifetime of jelly doughnuts or
broccoli. I like something simple and filling
and hearty. Like this soup."

"Well…" Belinda looked both mildly confused and mollified. "I'm glad you enjoy it,
Eli."

And they all turned their attention to eating. Somehow, to Hazel at least, it just seemed
safer.

HAZEL WAS PRETTY. That was the thought that
dominated Joe's mind as he finished up his

meal. Hazel Dobbs was probably the prettiest woman he'd ever laid eyes on. That wasn't a useful thing to notice, either. But he'd also felt the way she'd leaned toward him ever so subtly when he'd whispered to her. He'd found himself leaning toward her, too. And he liked that.

That was his problem, wasn't it? There were perfectly appropriate single moms at his daughter's school who'd love nothing more than to make a family with him, but he didn't feel that tug toward them. He didn't think of them in quite the right way. And then there was Hazel—a woman he hardly knew, who seemed to draw him toward her like a metal filing to a magnet—and she was all wrong.

She was the jelly doughnut. That was an awful analogy from Eli, wasn't it? But it was the truth. Hazel was the kind of woman that made him long for more time with her, that made him watch the porch when he was working. She made him wonder what she was thinking when she got that look on her face, like when she said she'd explain about the tension at the table. And it wasn't just curiosity about gossip. He wanted to know what *she* thought.

This was very dangerous ground. And he'd

been in another awkward situation before with the woman he'd hired to work with him—that had been in front of Belinda Wickey, too. But this time, he wasn't trying to put off a woman who wanted him. He wasn't even trying all that hard not to feel something for Hazel. Maybe he was the fool this time around, and Hazel was just making use of this country quiet while he developed a seriously inappropriate crush. Maybe he had it coming after all of his evasion in romance—some payback for the hearts he'd inadvertently broken along the way. What the old woman must think of him at this point, he'd probably rather not know!

"Thank you very much for lunch," Joe said. "It's much appreciated, Belinda."

"Not at all," Belinda said with a smile. "You feel free to get back to work. I'm just glad to see you fed."

He wasn't going to be able to talk to Hazel alone again at the table—not without drawing all sorts of attention to it. So he pushed back his chair and stood up. Lottie followed him, and he felt Hazel's attention swivel as he passed behind her chair.

Was there any chance she was feeling this, too?

Yep, he was making a fool of himself. He'd

look back on this and cringe later—he was sure of it. But when he looked over at Belinda and Eli, they seemed to be distracted with each other as Eli tried to stand up to help clear the table and Belinda ordered him to sit himself back down and let his ankle heal.

And then Hazel looked over at him, and he caught her gaze for one heart-stopping moment.

No, this wasn't just him…and that made it worse. But there was nothing he could do, so Joe headed on outside, and Lottie trailed after him.

The rest of the afternoon went rather quickly, and toward four o'clock, he noticed Lottie rubbing her eyes. She'd played hard today. So he went into the truck, grabbed her blanket and laid it out in some shade.

"Why don't you lie down?" Joe said.

"I'm not tired," she said, and then her mouth opened in a jaw-cracking yawn.

"Oh, don't sleep," he said seriously. "I just thought you could lie down and see if you can spot a squirrel in that tree. You'd have to lie on your back and stay very still, and then you might see one."

"A squirrel?"

He had her interest now.

"Yep." It wasn't a lie. He'd seen one up there earlier. "But don't fall asleep. Just wait really quietly."

"Okay." She lay down, her eyes fixed on the limbs above.

That would do it. He headed back over to the garden, and when he next looked in Lottie's direction, her eyes had slipped shut, and her breaths came slow and deep. He'd pay for it tonight, that was guaranteed, but she needed the rest. All this fresh air tuckered a kid right out.

When Joe had the last of his tools loaded into his truck, Lottie was still asleep, her little arms and legs akimbo in the middle of her blanket. He slammed the tailgate shut, letting the sound echo, and Lottie's steady breathing didn't change a bit. Should he wake her up? He crossed his arms and looked at her for a moment, considering.

The front door of the house opened, and he glanced over to see Hazel coming onto the porch. When she silently met his gaze, he headed over in her direction.

"Hi," she said when he arrived, and she sank down onto the step. He sat down next to her. There wasn't a lot of space, and his grubby jeans brushed against her clean ones. He grimaced.

"Sorry," he said.

She leaned into his shoulder and gave him a nudge. "You aren't as filthy as you think."

"No?" He brushed off his jeans all the same. Her arm against his side felt nice, and he smiled over at her. "I'm trying to decide if I should wake up Lottie or not."

Her gaze slid over to where his daughter was sleeping, and he saw Hazel's expression soften. There was something about that tenderness directed at his rambunctious child that made him soften, too.

"She's been playing hard," Hazel said.

"Yeah… She's more energetic than most."

"I don't think so," Hazel replied.

"No?" He looked down at her quizzically. "At the grocery store, you should see the looks we get. And at day care, I'm constantly getting little notes home about reminders that she is not to hit others, or how she refused to use her pleases and thank-yous, or…" His blood pressure was rising just remembering the constant examples that his daughter hadn't behaved perfectly. "But she's a good kid. She's got a good heart. I hate the thought of adults making her feel like she's not good enough."

"Good," she said. "That's your job. And she

is a good kid. She's not any more energetic than other kids. Just because she's learning her manners, or even learning how to make her point by keeping her pleases and thank-yous to herself, doesn't make her bad. In fact, a four-year-old who acted with the wisdom and maturity of a kid twice or three times her age would be downright creepy."

"True," he said. "You're making me feel better."

"I'm glad," she replied. "You should feel better. Look, just some advice from some-one who's been there—ignore the judgmental looks of grocery-store people. People who are shopping for groceries are not at their best."

"I'll do that," he said.

"Everyone makes this stage feel like the defining moment of a kid's entire future," she said. "There isn't a bigger load of garbage. I watched my daughter's class from kinder-garten all the way up to high-school gradua-tion, and the guy who got valedictorian used to bite other kids and had to be taken to the hospital when he shoved a crayon so far up his nose that the teacher couldn't get it out."

Joe started to laugh.

"And there was this one girl who was so painfully awkward that I just wanted to hug her every time I saw her. She was a little shadow of a girl. She just…disappeared when she was in a room. She couldn't seem to make friendships work for years. She was lonely, and the mean girls used to pick on her. My daughter would tell me about it when she got home from school, and I used to tell my daughter to include her because I felt so bad for her. But by grade ten, she and Maddie were best friends, and she was the sweetest girl… She ended up finding her place in drama, and she made lots of friends. She had this really nice boyfriend, and it all just came together for her. But in those younger years…"

"Things shake out," Joe said.

"Things definitely shake out." Hazel looked up at him, and Joe adjusted his position so that his shoulder went behind hers. It was more comfortable…but it also brought them a little closer, and it was comforting.

"So what was the thing you were going to explain at lunch?" he asked.

"Oh, that." A grin spread over her face. "Eli is in love with Belinda."

"What?" Joe frowned. "I know he really respects her. They've been friends and neighbors for a long time. There might be a small crush in the works—"

"He told me."

Joe paused, letting that information settle. Eli was in love with Belinda…

"Why hasn't he said anything?" Joe asked.

"He's still working up his nerve. He tried to tell her when they were young, but something was already starting with her first husband. So he stepped back. And…no other woman would do."

"That's really sad."

She shrugged. "I was going to say romantic, but to each his own."

Joe chuckled. "I'm not heartless here. I mean that it's sad he met the woman who was his one and only, and he missed his shot. That's incredibly sad. And it's too bad he didn't get a second chance at love and happiness with someone else."

"He strikes me as a remarkably stubborn guy."

Joe smiled ruefully. "People have said the same about me."

Hazel chuckled. "Refusing to see the potential in the women right in front of you?"

His gaze flickered across her face, and he saw the blush rise in her cheeks.

"I didn't mean me," she added quickly. "That might have come out wrong."

Joe sucked in a breath. "The other women didn't have that special…spark, I guess. I was starting to wonder if I was expecting too much."

"Maybe you are," she said, and he could tell she was trying to joke, but she hadn't moved from that place against his shoulder, either.

"Nah," he said. "You know why?"

"Why?"

"Because I feel it with you." He almost bit back the words, but he might as well say it. "I don't know if it's mutual, but I feel that kind of ignition with you, and…I know it's possible."

She didn't answer, but she adjusted her position and turned toward him. Her expression was cautious, but he saw some vulnerability in her blue gaze, too. She could have pulled away… She might yet, if he didn't make sure she knew what he was trying to say.

"Not that I'm asking for anything," Joe clarified.

"Okay…" A smile flickered at her lips.

"I'm not." He chuckled softly. "Okay, I get how this sounded. But trust me, I know that we're heading in different directions, and that you want different things. And there's nothing wrong with that. I guess I just owe you a thank-you for proving I'm not holding out for the impossible."

"You're welcome," she said softly. "I think."

He smiled ruefully. "It's a good thing."

"You deserve the whole package, Joe," she said. "You should definitely hold out for it."

A woman who made him feel like this... The problem was, he'd been looking around for four years, ever since he became a single father, and his heart was a rather complicated organ, it seemed.

"You deserve it, too..." he said. A wisp of hair fluttered in front of her nose, and he reached up and brushed it aside. It had been a gesture without thinking, and he froze as his finger touched her cheek.

"The problem is, this kind of chemistry doesn't come along every day," she murmured.

"It doesn't." His gaze dropped down to her lips, and he knew he had to stop this. There was no future between them, and he wasn't the kind of guy who was capable of just fooling around. He had too much at stake. And he had a feeling she did, too.

Lottie moved and rolled over on the blanket. Joe saw her from the corner of his eye, and he dropped his hand.

"Daddy?" Lottie said.

"Over here, kiddo," he said.

Lottie sat up and rubbed her eyes. "I'm hungry."

"It's time for us to get home for supper." But his gaze was on Hazel. He'd said too much, hadn't he? Again!

Hazel dropped her gaze and scooted away from him—just a couple of inches, but he felt it. And she was right to do it—they now had an audience.

"I made an appointment to go for a pleasure flight tomorrow afternoon," Hazel said.

"Yeah?"

"Do you and Lottie want to come?" she asked, and her gaze met his again.

"Do we dare?" he asked. "I mean you and me...do we dare toy with this?"

Because he'd meant what he'd said, and what he was feeling for her was incredibly powerful. It would be easier if it was one-sided, but it obviously wasn't. The smartest thing to do was for both of them to take a huge step back.

"I'll stick you in the back seat," Hazel said. "Lottie can have the front."

He looked over at his daughter as she came over to where they sat.

"What do you think, Lottie?" Joe asked. "Do you want to go for an airplane ride tomorrow?"

"With you?" Lottie asked.

"Of course with me, too," Joe said. "You and I are a package, right?"

"Okay." A smile spread over Lottie's face. "A real plane ride?"

"A real plane ride," Hazel said. She pushed herself to her feet. "It's scheduled for four o'clock."

Lottie started chattering immediately, hopping excitedly from one foot to the other.

"I can make that work," Joe said.

"Good."

"Should we exchange phone numbers?" he asked. "Just in case?"

She nodded, and he took her phone from her fingers and typed his number into it. She saved it and then texted him. It was done— and somehow having her number felt like one of those victories again.

He wanted to say more, but it was probably better that he couldn't. He should be more careful than this, but how could he deny his daughter a flight? That was the excuse he was running with, at least.

"Let's get home, Lottie," Joe said. "Time to go make supper."

CHAPTER NINE

HAZEL WATCHED AS Joe's pickup truck crunched back down the gravel drive, and she tried to calm her swirling thoughts. There was definitely attraction between them, but they were both rational adults. What was attraction, anyway, besides a chemical response to each other? They could override that. Heck, it might just wind down and peter out…right?

What did she know? In the past, her being a tired mom had been enough to dissuade most men. All she'd have to say was "I'm a mom. This is complicated," and they'd see the light rather quickly.

The side door opened, and Hund came outside, sniffing around. She watched him continue his tour, nose to the ground for a moment or two, then she pulled out her cell phone.

She shot off a text to Maddie: Hi, sweetie. How's England?

Maybe she just needed to remind herself

about why keeping things uncomplicated was such a high priority.

Hazel's video chat rang, and she picked up. Maddie's face popped onto the screen.

"Hi, Mom," Maddie said. "It's not great."

"What's going on?" Hazel asked.

"Dad decided it would be nice for me and Adel to get to know each other one on one," Maddie said and she grimaced. "So I met up with her at this swanky restaurant—chosen by Dad, might I add. I didn't have a thing in my suitcase that was appropriate to wear to this place. Adel came in dressed to the nines, and she orders us this expensive little hors d'oeuvre platter, and then proceeded to tell me the limits to which they are willing to go for my education."

"What?" Hazel could feel her blood pressure start to rise.

"Wait until you hear it!" Maddie said. "I am permitted exactly four years of college, so she advised me not to waste any time figuring out what I want to do. I will not be allotted any financial support for any education beyond that. That will be my own responsibility. Also, no expensive out-of-state colleges, please, as they have other things to deal with besides me going to school."

"Sweetie, you know you aren't relying on them alone for school," Hazel said. "You know that between me and your grandparents, you'll get the education you want. And your father has stood by his word so far. I doubt this is coming from him."

"No, it's not coming from him. It's coming from *them*." Maddie's voice was tight. "And you want to know the kicker? Sophie wants to be a doctor. At the age of fourteen, no less. Of course, she'll never change her mind, but they're planning to pay *her* way."

Hazel pressed her lips together, trying not to let her anger punch through.

"Don't worry about her," Hazel said. "Like I said, Adel isn't going to limit you. I promise you that."

"I know, Mom," Maddie said. "It isn't that I'm actually worried about my future. It's that I'm being treated like some sort of freeloader. I'm his *daughter*! Do I deserve less than Sophie and Stephane?"

"Of course not."

"Yeah, well, so far I've been treated like some unwelcome guest," Maddie said. "And I'm so sick of it… Dad is happy to see me, but you can tell how uncomfortable he is when his wife and kids are around."

"Did you tell him what Adel said?" she asked.

Maddie shook her head. "No. And I'm not going to. It'll just make things more awkward. Adel wants to get rid of me, and she'll succeed."

"Is that fair to your father? Or to you?" Hazel asked. "He's always provided for you, and he's kept in touch and tried to keep a relationship with you. Is it fair to let his wife cut you off from your father?"

"What am I supposed to do?" Maddie asked. "This is his family. Apparently, I'm just some mistake from his youth. That's the story they've all heard—I can see it in their faces."

"I'll call your dad," Hazel said.

"No. Mom, this is my relationship with my father," Maddie said. "Don't call him. Don't get involved. But if I get a call from him in ten years and he wants to be at my wedding or whatever, he's going to get a no!"

"You love your father," Hazel said. "And while I know he's being an idiot right now, he does love you."

"Love is more than a monthly check, Mom," Maddie said. "It's more than a phone call and a few nice words. It's action. And it's also how you talk about someone behind their back."

"I know." Because Maddie was a good, honest young woman. And she knew she was being treated badly.

"Sweetie, just enjoy your trip. I'm sorry about your dad, but he might have to learn this one the hard way."

"Yeah, I guess so." Maddie's voice was tight with emotion. "Okay, well, Heidi and I are going on a bus tour tomorrow and it leaves early, so I'd better get going."

"Okay. I love you."

"Love you, too."

Maddie hung up first, and Hazel stared down at her phone in frustration. What was Todd even thinking? He'd been a good father. He'd had his own life, but he'd never forgotten about Maddie. What was this about? Some intense insecurity on Adel's part? Were they more broke than they appeared? Or was Todd just ready to move on with his new family, and he'd figured he'd done his due now that Maddie was past eighteen? She wished she knew.

Hund came sniffing over in her direction, and she bent down to give him a pet.

"This, too, will pass…" she murmured to the dog.

Maddie would come home, and she'd deal

with her hurt and anger, and they'd carry on with their lives.

But in the meantime, Hazel wished she could take this pain away from her daughter. She wished she could fix it and smooth things over. Because a long time ago, when Maddie had been a bouncy little girl a whole lot like Lottie, Hazel had been able to fix absolutely everything.

If only that part could stay the same.

THE NEXT AFTERNOON, Hazel watched as the Amish countryside slipped past them on their way to the hangar. Lottie chattered away in the back seat, pretending to be the characters from her favorite kids' show about the planes, and flying her toy Boeing 757 around in front of her.

Hazel hadn't slept well. She'd been thinking about Maddie's situation, and she was frustrated. Todd knew better. He'd always made sure that Maddie knew he loved her. So what had changed on this visit? Was he just intimidated by this beautiful young woman who was obviously no longer a child? Or was he caving in to his wife's insecurities? Hazel had had to visualize letting it go before she could fall asleep.

But flying always helped. There was something about getting up above the clouds that changed her perspective and filled her with hope and optimism.

They pulled into the hangar's parking lot. Leaving Joe to have a discussion with Lottie about his expectations from her during the flight, Hazel headed inside to get things lined up.

Miles accepted her payment and gave her the keys to a Cessna that had already been fueled up and was ready to go.

"There's a bit of weather west of here," Miles said. "Looks like some rain showers but no lightning or winds. Pretty gentle. They aren't expecting it to move our way. Your flight plan is due east, so you should be just fine."

Hazel looked at the weather report and nodded. "Yeah, it seems that way to me, too."

The Cessna was parked outside the back of the hangar, glinting in the sunlight. A plane this small was entirely different than the big passenger planes she'd been training with for her commercial license. Walking around the plane—feeling the ailerons and looking for any sign of damage that might spell trouble up there—filled her with a kind of nostalgia.

She'd been sixteen when she'd gone up on her first discovery flight. And nothing had ever been the same again.

She was in the middle of her preflight inspection when Joe and Lottie came up. Lottie was holding her father's hand and standing very still next to him.

"Are you ready for your plane ride?" Hazel asked with a smile.

Lottie nodded. "I'm ready. I'm going to be very, very good."

"Joe, I should mention that there is a rain shower west of here. We're flying east, so we shouldn't hit it. Even if we did, it wouldn't be a big deal. But if you aren't comfortable—"

"It's fine," Joe said. "You're the pro here. If you think it's safe, I believe you."

"Good." She smiled. "Okay, so let's go inside the plane and get comfortable," Hazel said. "Lottie. You'll be in the front seat next to me, and your dad is going to be sitting right behind you."

Hazel got Lottie in the front passenger seat first. She put her on a booster seat and buckled her in. Then she put a headset—the smallest one Miles had available—onto her head and cinched it down smaller still.

"When we're flying, you'll hear me talk

through these earphones," Hazel explained. "This is how we'll talk to each other."

"Okay…"

Joe climbed into the back seat—a large man in such a small space—looking almost as excited as Lottie was. Hazel got into the pilot's seat, adjusted her own headset and did the last of her preflight check, ending with testing the engine and revving it high. Then she looked over her shoulder at Joe and shot him a smile.

"I never did ask—how are you with flight sickness?" she asked.

"I'm a trouper." He grinned back.

"I hope so. If you need it, there's an airsickness bag tucked into the back of my seat."

"Noted."

"Okay, Lottie?" Hazel handed Lottie an open airsickness bag. "I want you to hold on to that with both hands. And if you feel sick, you do it into the bag, okay?"

"And if I don't feel sick?" Lottie asked.

"You still hold on to it."

"Sounds like you learned some of this the hard way," Joe said.

"I had a little girl of my own, remember?" She chuckled. "Okay, I'm going to need you both to stay quiet. I'm about to start talking to the air traffic controllers, okay?"

Takeoff was smooth, and Lottie gasped as the wheels left the ground. She clutched her airsickness bag in both hands, her breath coming in quick gasps.

"You okay, Lottie?" Hazel asked.

Lottie turned shining eyes to Hazel. "I'm *wonderful!*"

"You're in trouble, Joe," Hazel said with a laugh. "She loves this."

"Yeah, I had a feeling I would be..." he said, his voice coming over the headphones warm and low.

Hazel began their ascent. The little plane trembled on the updrafts, churning its way higher into the sky. Some high cloud cover had blocked the direct sunlight, but they wouldn't be flying that high, anyway. She tipped the wing a couple of times to give Lottie a view of the diminishing ground beneath them.

"That's fun!" Lottie said. "Do it again!"

"One more time, then we focus on getting higher," Hazel said, and she banked the plane again so that Lottie could see the ground.

"I can't see people," Lottie said.

"They're down there," Hazel said, straightening the plane again and continuing their climb.

"No, but I can't see. We're too high," Lottie said.

Her mother. Hazel knew exactly what Lottie was thinking about, but it wasn't her place to say anything. She looked over her shoulder at Joe and mutely met his gaze.

"Lottie, TV shows and real life are different," Joe said. "The TV show is just pretend. This is a real plane, so it'll be different than *Miley and Buster's Airport*."

Lottie remained silent.

"Is she okay up there?" Joe asked. Lottie sat still, her grip on her airsickness bag relaxing. Her lips were pressed together in a thin line.

Hazel reached over and gave Lottie's knee a pat. "Hi there."

"I wanted to look for my mom," Lottie said. "That's what I wanted to do."

"I know," Hazel said.

"Lottie, we talked about this," Joe said. "Some kids have moms, and some don't. Every family looks different, and this is our family—you and me. Okay?"

Lottie didn't answer, and when Hazel glanced over her shoulder again, Joe's jaw was tense and he was staring straight ahead. How many times had he battled this out with Lottie? Hazel knew from experience how stubborn kids this age could be.

"Do you want to know something about airplanes?" Hazel asked. Lottie didn't answer, so Hazel continued, "When I feel sad or angry or upset, and I get into a plane and fly, it's like all those upset feelings drop out the bottom of the plane, and they're gone. So you might not be able to look for your mom up here, but you know all those upset feelings you get when you think about looking for her?"

"Yeah?" Lottie said.

"Pretend they just dropped out the window." Hazel shot her a smile. "Imagine them falling away like bricks, dropping back down to the ground while you keep flying."

"Okay…" Lottie smiled then, hesitantly at first. "What if they hit someone?"

This kid was logical. Fine. No bricks.

"Maybe drop them like rubber balls, then," she said. "They'll just bounce off of some guy, and he'll be all confused."

Lottie giggled at that.

"When you're in a plane, you don't have to think about ground problems," Hazel said. "That's the rule."

"Is it really the rule?" Lottie asked.

"It really is." Hazel looked back at Joe. Had she gone too far? A smile touched one side of Joe's lips and his dark gaze caught hers, then she turned back to face forward.

"How about you, Joe?" Hazel asked. "Do you have any ground problems to let go of up here?"

"Not too many," he said. He was silent for a moment, then added, "Maybe one or two."

"Drop them like bricks!" Lottie said. Maybe they were back to bricks, after all.

"Alright," Joe said. "I mean, if those are the rules."

Ahead, the cloud cover was lower, and she saw the approaching gray smudge of storm clouds. She checked the compass. This wasn't the storm from the west. This was a new one developing.

"Okay, I'm going to turn and tip our wing so we can look down at the ground once more... Ready?"

She made a steep banking turn, looking at the land beneath them for confirmation. They were definitely heading in the right direction.

A crackly voice came over the radio. "Hey, this is Miles. We've got another storm show-ing on the radar." He gave some of the pertinent information, including the size and approximate location.

"Roger that," she said ruefully. "I've got visual confirmation. We'll get above it. Thanks, Miles. Over and out."

But that storm was brewing fast, and a couple of raindrops hit the windshield. A gust of wind buffeted them. She continued their ascent. Higher was safer. She had this under control.

JOE COULDN'T REACH his daughter over the seat—and he had a pretty strong instinct right now to put a reassuring hand on hers. Normally, he was the tough guy, the reliable one, but up in this airplane, he was downright useless. Not a great feeling, with rain starting to pelt the windows, then zip off the glass, pushed by the strength of the wind.

"Are you scared?" Lottie asked, her voice quavering.

"Me or your dad?" Hazel asked with a low laugh.

Joe wasn't about to admit to being scared. That was one parenting trick he'd learned—act like the hero even when he didn't feel like one. His daughter needed to know that her dad wasn't afraid of anything, so she could relax knowing he'd take care of it. Was it healthy? He had no idea, but he wasn't about to change it, either.

"You," Lottie said. "Are *you* scared?"

"No, I'm not scared," Hazel said. "This is my job, sweetie. I'm a pilot. I fly planes all the time."

"Oh…"

"When you're the one in the pilot's seat, and you're the one calling the shots, it's not so scary. I took classes, and I've got lots of practice. That's the secret, you know."

Good to know, because in the back seat, Joe was starting to get a little nervous. The plane trembled as wind whipped around them, and they seemed to bounce on top of it.

"That's called turbulence," Hazel said. "If the wind was water, this would be choppy water, when it's all wavy."

"And that's not scary?" Lottie demanded.

"Not when you know what it is," Hazel replied. "And I know where the air is smooth again."

"Where?" Lottie asked.

"Up there, where we're headed."

Hazel didn't seem flustered in the least, and she kept the plane headed steadily upward, even as Joe's seat bumped and trembled underneath him. He could feel the pressure of their climb tipping him back. Her voice was calm and controlled in his headset, and he found his own blood pressure lowering just listening to her.

"You see, these storms are pretty normal," Hazel said. "And they're actually quite close to the ground, too. We aren't all that high. That's why when you see them coming over the hills, they look like a gray mist. Have you ever seen that?"

"No," Lottie said.

"I have," Joe said. "It's what it looks like, Lottie."

"Well, that gray mist is rain, and it's basically just part of the cloud," Hazel went on. "So these rainstorms are really just low clouds dropping all their worries to the ground. If we were on the ground right now, it would just be regular rain falling—nothing too out of the ordinary. Just rain falling on your umbrella. Pitter patter."

"Really? The rain where the worms come out on the road?" Lottie asked.

"That's the kind."

Lottie had a passion for rescuing worms and throwing them back into the sodden grass they'd been escaping from.

"Interesting," Joe said.

Hazel glanced at him over her shoulder and her blue eyes sparkled with a smile.

"I always thought so, too. Weather intrigues me." She turned forward again. "I'm not a storm chaser or anything, but I like to understand why things happen up here."

"I suppose it's good to know in your line of work," he said.

"You bet."

"You're very reassuring," he said. "Another good thing for a pilot."

She laughed, the sound warm and close in his headset, a direct contrast to the gray mist surrounding them and the shaking and trembling of the aircraft.

"And then, just at the top of the rainstorm…" Hazel said, and suddenly they burst out of the clouds and brilliant sunlight met them in a dazzle. The sky above was blue, and when Joe leaned over to look out the window, he could see the white mounds of clouds beneath them. It was like the storm had never been, and everything was sparkling and clean up here. His heart pounded hard in his chest— relief, he realized.

"Wow…" Joe said aloud.

"It's so pretty up here!" Lottie said. "There's no rain!"

"The rain is all down below," Hazel replied. "We're above the storm now. See? I told you it would be fine."

Yeah, she had, hadn't she? She was good at this—reassuring her passengers...and calming *him*. There was something about her that inspired his trust, and right now he couldn't help but think he'd like to have her around a whole lot more often...

"This is something I told my little girl as she grew up," Hazel said, glancing over at Lottie. "You might find yourself in all sorts of storms, but when you climb up high enough, it's a whole different view from above. Every storm passes, and above every storm...is this!"

The white, billowing cloud tops felt like an entirely different world. Suddenly, Joe thought that just letting his worries fall away made a whole lot more sense.

"I'm not sure she'll understand that," Joe said. "But it's beautiful all the same."

"I had to repeat it to Maddie over and over again as she grew up," Hazel said. "And it just occurs to me now that she could probably stand to hear it again with her trip in England."

"Timeless advice," Joe said.

"It does seem to be," she said. "Sometimes we all need reminding, though."

"That's what family is for," he said. That's what a mom was for.

"Yes, it sure is…"

This was what his daughter needed—a mom with some wisdom and experience. A mom who'd remind her that the turbulence in life wasn't the end of the story, and that with some patience and skill, there were gorgeous things waiting for her. And maybe he needed this, too—a woman to remind him to put aside his worries and appreciate all the good things around him…

But how come when he imagined that kind of scene lately, the woman leaning into his shoulder and getting sleepy next to him had wavy blond hair and smelled faintly of lilacs? Hazel had proven that the kind of spark he'd been yearning for was possible…but she couldn't be the partner he needed. He knew it.

Maybe Joe would just have to remember that, with some patience, he'd get to the top of the clouds, too…eventually. Hazel was his glimpse of sunlight that would keep him moving.

She was right. From above, he could see that the storm wasn't that large, and she circled around, radioed the ground with her altitude and location, and headed back.

"Look down there," Hazel said when they'd passed the storm. "See the buggies?"

"Do we know them, Daddy?" Lottie asked.

"I don't know." He chuckled. "Maybe."

"We can tell Mr. Eli we saw him from way up here!"

Lottie was excited again, and telling Eli they saw him specifically might be a bit of an exaggeration, but he was glad to hear the happiness in his daughter's voice.

Down below, Joe could see the Amish farmland stretching out, laced together with fences and dotted with cattle. Ribbons of road woven through the hills, buggies with horses creeping along like ants. He could see the roofs of houses and barns. Ahead of them, in the mist of cloud and a retreating storm, a rainbow arced across the sky.

"See that rainbow, Lottie?" Joe asked, leaning forward.

"Can we fly over to it?" Lottie asked.

"No, it's actually refracted light that—"

Hazel began, and then she glanced back at Joe for just a second. "We can't do it because rainbows run away. They're very skittish. We'd have to sneak up on it, and this plane is just too noisy."

"Oh." Joe could see Lottie's curls go up and down as she nodded. "That's like Amber at day care. If you get too close to her, she has a tantrum. But if you sneak up on her sometimes, she lets you play beside her."

"Just like Amber," Hazel said, and Joe smiled to himself.

She had good answers for a four-year-old. Maybe she'd be friends with him, and they could talk on the phone from time to time. Having her voice in his ear like this would be a treat…and she might have some ideas to help him through all the other parenting stages awaiting him.

Because right now, he realized, the thought of her just leaving, and of him never talking to her again, hurt. Once a man had felt sunshine, it could be hard to go back.

Hazel landed the plane with hardly a bump as the wheels touched the tarmac. The ground was wet from recent rainfall, and sunlight slanted down, warming the air. Hazel pushed open a triangle of window, and that electric scent of fresh rain swept into the plane. He loved that smell—it was the smell of new growth and fresh possibilities.

"I loved that!" Lottie exclaimed. "I love it so much! Can we do it again now?"

"Not today," Hazel said with a laugh. "But I'm glad you had fun."

"Can I steer next time?" Lottie asked. "Can I make us do loop-de-loops?"

Hazel brought the plane to a stop in front of the hangar and turned off the engine. Then she leaned over and unbuckled Lottie's seat belt for her.

"No, you cannot," Joe said. "Then I'd need that motion-sickness bag. You've got to remember your poor dad in the back seat."

"Oh, yeah." Lottie turned around and peeked over the top of the seat at him. "Sorry, Daddy."

This girl would be on her way without him one of these days—launching herself fearlessly out into the world, and never once suspecting that her dad would be hiding his own fear behind his bluster.

He watched as Hazel checked a few dials and switches, pulled down a logbook and wrote in it, initialed a little box and then put it back up in a clip near the ceiling. Then she turned toward him and smiled.

"That does me good. I love a quick fly. Thanks for coming along."

Joe undid his own seat belt. "Thanks for taking us."

And if he'd been tempted to imagine Hazel doing anything with her life besides being the pilot that she was, that foolishness had been wiped from his mind.

Hazel belonged in the clouds, and no one had the right to ground her.

CHAPTER TEN

HAZEL LOOKED UP at the retreating clouds as they drove down the narrow highway. She always felt this once she came back down to the ground—a longing to be flying again already. In the back seat, Lottie was pretending that she was piloting a plane, narrating everything she did in a soft little voice that made it clear this story was for herself, not them.

"That was pretty amazing to see you in action," Joe said.

"Yeah?" She smiled. "Do you like flying?"

"I hate it." He chuckled. "Well, let me clarify that. I liked this trip with you, but getting on a plane, juggling my luggage, sitting pinned next to a stranger with no ability to stretch my legs out—not my favorite way to travel."

"Ah." She nodded. "I get that. Like I told Lottie, being the pilot is different."

He slowed as they came up behind a buggy,

then signaled as he pulled around it, giving the horse and buggy lots of space.

"You're really something else up there," Joe said.

"You mean, I'm in charge."

"Maybe." His gaze flickered toward her, and he smiled sheepishly. "I hope that didn't come across wrong. I'm just... I guess I'm really impressed."

"You can't offend me with that," she said.

"Good." He pulled back in front of the buggy again after signaling longer than usual and shoulder-checking twice. "You love it up there. I could see it."

"It's like I come alive in an airplane," she agreed. "When I started my proper flight lessons for my private license, I was nineteen and a new mom. My parents wanted me to have something just for me. Now, I get how privileged that sounds—and it is. A lot of single moms struggled more than I did financially, and I had parents who were determined to see me thrive, even with a baby girl on my hip. But having a baby, having Todd leave me, having all of my friendships change because I was a mom, and they were still teenagers having fun... Getting into a cockpit let me do something that was truly mine. And flying let me grow in a way I wouldn't have been able to on the ground."

She could still remember the things that used to hurt the most. One friend had seemed obsessed with Hazel's changed figure. After a pregnancy and a baby, she never would look like the lithe teen she used to be. There were friends who simply disappeared. Some of her aunts and uncles had voiced nasty opinions about her having a baby out of wedlock. It had been an incredibly difficult time. Add to that the heartbreak of Todd moving on with his life and leaving her behind…

"So when you said you just let your worries go up there…" Joe said, pulling her back from her thoughts.

"It started then," she agreed. "I used to care what people thought of me. There was a lot of pity. I loathed the pity. There were the questions about why I couldn't hold on to Todd… that kind of thing. But in the clouds, I left Todd, my friends and the weight of everyone's expectations behind me. I could focus on my own skill in the cockpit, and when you look at that horizon, when you realize how tiny we are compared to the world we inhabit… I don't know. It makes a difference. A teen mom becomes a fully actualized woman."

"Good for you," he said.

"You're a single dad," she said. "Maybe you get some of the same?"

"Not in the same way," he said.

"Ah." She smiled ruefully. "You're a guy, so you get patted on the back for doing the bare minimum and told what a hero you are."

He was silent for a moment, then shrugged. "A bit. I was going to deny it, but you aren't wrong."

"I'm impressed you'd admit to that," she said. "But it can't be all easy."

"It's not," he said. "I had to change my vision of my future, too. I guess I figured out who I was right here in this pickup truck. I did it through my work, through hours of creating something beautiful out of black earth and overgrown yards. But I knew that I couldn't be the carefree guy I used to be. I had to get more serious. I had to make my work count. And my Amish neighbors..."

"A link to your history?" she suggested when he didn't finish the statement.

"Yeah, definitely," he said. "But more than that. The Amish are different. They're unapologetically old-fashioned. They just embrace it. And one of the things I really liked was how it all centers around the kids out here. The moms stay home and focus on making home a little refuge away from everything else. And the dads work hard, but they also spend a lot of time at home with their families. Something about that really appeals to me. It just gets down to the basics, you know? What makes all of our hard work worth it? Our families."

She nodded. "Yep."

If that was the way he saw it, she wasn't going to argue with him. It shouldn't matter, but it *was* more complicated.

"I'm not suggesting all women should do it the Amish way," he said.

"I know." She looked over at him. "Because the kids grow up, Joe."

Shoot. She *wasn't* going to argue this. Too late.

"All too fast," he agreed.

"And then what?" she prompted. "What do the Amish do when the kids are grown?"

"Well, the kids get married and have their own kids, and you've got grandchildren, and nieces and nephews, and your grown children—it's all about family."

"I've got one daughter," Hazel said. "She doesn't have a boyfriend right now, and she's exploring her life. Part of growing up is spreading her wings. If I made absolutely everything about her, what would I have right now? Who would I be? I'd be a lonely mom, waiting for her to call me. And she'd feel obliged to help fill the void with me… It would get weird."

They were approaching the turn for Butternut Drive, and she had a feeling this memory would be tainted now—a simmering disagreement between them that shouldn't even matter. They were friendly. That was all it was supposed to be, at least.

"I know you've got dinner at the B and B if you want it," Joe said. "But I'm going to make some shoestring fries and BLTs back at our place for supper. Did you, I don't know… want to join us?"

Joe started to slow for the turn, and Hazel looked over at him in surprise. "Actually, that sounds great."

"Should we stop and let Belinda know?" he asked.

"Might be considerate," she agreed.

Joe signaled and made the turn. Maybe the evening could be salvaged yet.

JOE WASN'T EVEN sure why he'd made the sudden invitation to supper at his place. He'd just wanted to keep talking to her. He'd been hoping to stretch this out a bit. Maybe he didn't want her to think he was just an old-fashioned guy who wanted a woman in the kitchen—because that wasn't the case at all. At the very least, when Hazel left, he wanted her to remember him fairly.

But he began having immediate regrets when he realized he had no idea how he'd left the house this morning. There were definitely dishes in the sink…and how clean was the bathroom?

But it was too late now.

He parked outside the little bungalow, and he noticed how Hazel looked around, obviously curious.

"Home sweet home," he said.

"You've got a beautiful yard," she said.

There was a weeping willow, a flower garden, and of course, his lawn was immaculate, mowed in checkerboard perfection. He had a sign set up prominently in one corner, advertising his business in neat white letters against a navy blue background.

"I'd better," he said, pushing open his car door. "It's like my calling card. If I can't keep up my own yard, why would anyone hire me to keep up theirs? Let's get in and get cooking. I don't know about you, but I'm hungry."

"So am I," she said, and she pushed open her door, too.

Joe unbuckled Lottie's straps, and she bounded free, beating them to the back door. The backyard was nothing like the front. But this space wasn't about advertising—it was about feeling at home and relaxed. He had some cherry and apple trees that were currently laden with small green fruit. He had a firepit set up, too, and a few rows of strawberry plants, and raspberry and blackberry bushes that lined the back fence. If he picked the right week in August, he could feed the whole neighborhood with the food in this yard alone.

"The backyard is just for me and Lottie," he said by way of explanation.

"I like it," Hazel said. "You've got to have something just for you."

"That's what I figured," he said. "This year is the first summer she'll be old enough to pick berries or help me water the plants. I think it's good for kids to know where food comes from."

"Can we eat outside?" Lottie asked, hanging off the doorknob.

"It's a bit wet," Joe said, then paused. "But I've got dry wood in the garage. And I've got the lawn chairs in there, too, so we'd be dry enough. What do you prefer, Hazel?"

"Outside would be great," Hazel said.

Joe smacked a mosquito off his arm. "You sure?"

"Smoke helps with bugs," she said.

He shot her a grin. "I like you, Hazel."

Joe unlocked the door and they all headed inside together. The back door opened into the kitchen, his sink of dirty dishes on full display.

"Sorry about that," he said, nodding to the sink.

"You act like I didn't have a kid," she said with a smile. "I'm blind to it all. I promise."

That was a bit of a relief, and he found that he believed her. "Let me just throw some fries in the oven and get the bacon started," he said. "You can poke around in the living room if you want to."

"Can I?" She shot him a teasing grin, and he rolled his eyes.

"There's not much to see."

"It's all in the details, Joe," she said.

What details would she be seeing? A few family photos, a bin of toys, a bookshelf, a TV... He was probably pretty safe.

"Do you want to see my TV show?" Lottie asked, dancing from foot to foot.

"Sure, let's go see your show." Hazel let Lottie take her hand and drag her out of the kitchen.

For the next few minutes, Joe did the dishes, washed down the counters and got the food started. From the living room, he listened to the familiar strains of the *Miley and Buster's Airport* theme song. He did wonder what Hazel might discover about him from the details of his living room, but most of his attention was on the food. Once the bacon was done, he pulled the pan off the heat and headed outside to start the fire. He made three sandwiches—Lottie would only eat half of hers, if that—and brought the plate outside to a little picnic table under the apple tree. He brushed some leaves from the surface and put down the plate.

Some birds were hopping through the branches of the closest cherry tree. It took him a few minutes to kindle the first flames, then build the fire into a proper blaze with a few dry pieces of wood. He heard the door open behind him, and Hazel came outside.

"I pulled the fries out of the oven," she said.

"Thanks." He smiled ruefully. "I'm just getting the fire going here."

The heat pushed back the cool, moist air, and it seemed to draw Hazel closer to him.

"So what did you sleuth out about me?" he asked, poking another stick of wood into the blaze.

"Oh, not too much," she said. "I was mostly joking."

"Mostly," he said with a chuckle.

"I saw a picture of you holding Lottie when she was born, and your parents holding you when you were born." She smiled. "Lottie explained that one."

"Yeah…"

She moved a little closer to the heat, and he looked down at her for a moment.

"Can I ask you something?" he said.

"Sure."

"If you'd given a baby up for adoption, would you want to see that child again?"

Hazel turned and looked up at him. "That's hard to answer."

He nodded. "Yeah. I know I keep going over the same thing again and again. But I keep thinking about Jessica…and she didn't want to see Lottie again. She told me she thought it would be too difficult for her."

"Did you talk to her after she gave up Lottie?" Hazel asked.

He nodded. "Once. I went to see her at her home before we parted ways for good. I asked if she wanted me to send her pictures, or milestones, you know? She said no. She said it would only make it harder, and she didn't want to hear from me again."

Hazel was silent.

"So I can respect that," he said. "When Lottie's eighteen, I'll tell her more and let her navigate it on her own, but…I don't know. I'm seeing how your daughter is facing tough stuff with her biological dad, and I'm thinking eighteen might not be as mature as I was hoping."

"It's never simple," Hazel said.

"Anyway, it makes me wonder if trying to find my biological mother would be a good thing or not," he said. "If I introduce myself, what do I say? Would she want to see me? Would that blow her life apart? She's never looked for me…not that I know of, at least…"

"You're missing a step here," Hazel said quietly.

"Am I?"

She nodded. "You haven't found her yet. What if you ask around and you can't find her? Then the problem is solved for you. What if you do find her? You still have a choice about what to do with that information."

Joe nodded. "Good point."

"You still have wiggle room," she said.

He sucked in a breath. "You're right, of course."

He hadn't asked Belinda anything yet— not enough to give him actual information.

"Do you think Belinda Wickey would be discreet?" he asked.

She shrugged. "I wish I could say. I don't know her personally. She seems decent and hardworking. She really values her community. I have a feeling that just out of protecting that community, she'd be willing to keep a few secrets for you. But that's just my sense."

"And if this upsets Rebecca's world...me asking around?" he asked.

"Joe—" Hazel put a hand on his arm. "I've given birth, so I can say this with certainty. Your arrival turned her world upside down already, and giving birth to you instead of ending the pregnancy was a choice that she made. She wanted you here, and she wanted you to have a chance to live a good life. She wouldn't have gone through a pregnancy and delivery otherwise. There would have been ways...even for Amish girls."

He dropped his gaze. She was probably right. His mother could have made other choices.

"You don't need to apologize for being here, Joe," Hazel said softly. "Not even to her. Especially not to her, maybe."

Joe's throat suddenly felt tight, and he looked over at Hazel. That was it—she'd hit it on the head. He was afraid that his existence would make things worse for her, that she'd be upset to see him.

Would his birth mom be proud of him? That was the question that plagued him most. What would he see in his birth mother's eyes when she realized who he was?

"Thank you," he said, swallowing a lump in his throat. "I needed to hear that."

"You're a good guy, Joe," Hazel said.

Coming from her, the words sank a little deeper.

"I hope so," he said, then glanced toward the house. "I'll get the fries…and Lottie. Then we can eat."

She smiled. "Okay."

Was he going to do this? Was he going to sit down with Belinda and tell her exactly why he was looking for Rebecca Lehmann? He'd moved to the area with one plan in the back of his mind, and he'd just sat on it, afraid to do anything else.

But maybe Hazel was right—maybe it was time to stop feeling like bad news and look for his biological mother for his own reasons. She'd given him life—and maybe all he'd do was thank her for that choice.

Rebecca didn't owe him anything else, but it would be nice to say he appreciated her gift of life to her personally.

CHAPTER ELEVEN

JOE WENT INTO the house, called Lottie to turn off the TV and herded her outside. He served the food, and they all ate. It was simple fare, but it hit the spot. Lottie ended up with ketchup on her cheeks from her fries, and she chattered about flying in the clouds. Hazel told her about air lift under the wings, and about how she was going to be working a job where she got to fly passengers all over the state. She even showed her some pictures from her phone of planes and flight controls.

Did Lottie know how lucky she was to be sitting around a firepit with this particular pilot? Probably not. Kids never knew how good they had it. But he did. Somehow, having Hazel perched on a lawn chair next to him with the faint smoke from the fire wafting around them, this was the most relaxed he'd felt in a long while.

When they had finished eating, Joe couldn't put off driving Hazel back any longer. Lottie's bedtime was coming up fast. So he loaded his daughter into the back seat, and drove Hazel back to the B&B.

"Thank you for—for everything today," Joe said.

"I enjoyed it, too," she said, and for a moment, her clear blue gaze met his, and he felt like his breath got stuck in his throat. Then she turned toward the back seat.

"I hope you have a good sleep, Lottie," Hazel said. "Fly planes in your dreams."

"Do you fly planes in *your* dreams?" Lottie asked breathlessly.

"Every night!" she said.

Hazel shot him one last smile, and then hopped out of the cab. Joe watched as she headed over to the side door. Light shone from the window, then the door opened, with Belinda outlined in a frame of light.

Joe put the truck in Reverse. He was about to start backing up when his phone pinged, and he glanced down at it. It was a message from the day care.

"Hey, look at that, Lottie," Joe said. "You won't have to come to work with me tomorrow."

"Is day care open again?" Lottie asked.

"It'll be open again tomorrow morning," Joe said.

"I can see my friends!" Lottie said. "And I can tell them I went up in a plane!"

Joe backed out the truck and turned around to pull up the drive. Maybe this timing was serendipitous. He was going to tell Belinda a rather personal story tomorrow, and it was one he didn't want his daughter to hear.

Not yet.

THE NEXT MORNING, Joe dropped off Lottie at day care. Lottie was thrilled to be back with her friends, and she trotted inside without so much as a look back, already chattering at her teacher, Miss Pinch, about how she went up in a plane. The last thing he heard as he walked out was "Really? Wow, Lottie. That's quite the week you had…"

He was headed back toward his truck when a woman's voice stopped him. "Joe!"

He turned. It was Michelle's mom, Lucy. He pasted a cordial smile on his face.

"Hi," he said.

"What a week, huh?" Lucy said. "What did you do? I had to use up the last of my vacation days. I wish I could do this sort of thing more often. I love being at home with my daughter."

"Yeah?" he said.

"I really do! Honestly, if I could just be a stay-at-home mom, I'd be in heaven. But I've got a mortgage to pay."

"I hear you." If only he could feel more for Lucy than he did. She was pretty, a good mom and seemed to want the same things he did. The only thing missing was the spark.

"I was going to call you up and plan a playdate for the girls, but I realized I don't have your number." She smiled. Had she just asked him for his number?

"As it turned out, I took her to work with me," he said, breezing past the implied request. "I've been tiring her out pretty well."

"Michelle was bored to tears, so I took her to the city and we went to the zoo one day. It would have been fun to do that together."

Joe pushed a hand through his hair and squinted down at the woman. She was pleasant enough. She was even attractive. She had a nice way of dressing, and her makeup was impeccable. But he just didn't feel more. And when he thought about getting the girls together and cozying up with Lucy, he just felt tired. The woman he wanted to spend time with, he had—sitting around a bonfire with

Hazel for an hour had been just about perfection.

"Well, I work a lot, so I didn't have the time. But I'm glad you made the most of it. Sounds like you and Michelle enjoyed yourselves." Joe made a point of checking his watch. "I'd better get going."

Lucy pressed her lips together, then nodded, taking a step back. "You bet. See you later."

Joe hopped into his truck. Would she get the hint? Or would he have to say something outright? He didn't want to hurt her feelings, but he just wasn't interested.

He pulled out of the day-care parking lot and headed back out of town. If he hadn't met Hazel, he might have started to cave in with Lucy. She was nice and very determined. It was flattering. But deep inside, he knew he needed more than that, and now that he'd experienced the kind of connection he'd been looking for, he felt the bitter irony of the situation.

That kind of attraction was rare, and Hazel wasn't eager to be the doting mom of a four-year-old. She wasn't going to be volunteering at a PTA meeting or making cupcakes—she had her career waiting for her, and that was nonnegotiable. How long was he going to have to wait to find the right combination?

Joe felt a little melancholy as he drove down the highway to Butternut Drive, but he pushed aside the feeling. He knew what he needed to do this morning, and Hazel had helped him reach that certainty. He needed some answers, even if they were from a distance.

When he pulled into the drive and parked, he found Belinda just returning from Eli's property, a basket of eggs balanced under one arm and a hen tucked under the other. Joe watched her as she walked across the scrub grass between the two properties.

"This hen kept following me," Belinda said. "Eli has been missing his chickens, and this chicken seems to be missing human contact."

Joe grinned. "Eli is winning you over, isn't he?"

Belinda looked ready to make some retort, then she just shook her head. "Eli is Eli, Joe. He has his ways, and at this late stage of life, no one is going to change him. And that man truly and honestly misses his poultry."

Just then, Eli came thumping out the front door onto the porch, and he propped himself up on his crutch. His face lit up at the sight of the bird under Belinda's arm.

"Belinda, could I talk to you about something?" Joe asked.

"*Yah*, sure." She looked at him curiously.

"It might take a minute," he admitted.

"Then I'll be right back." She brought both the eggs and the chicken over to the porch, and Eli took the basket of eggs from her and put it aside, then accepted the bird. Eli's entire demeanor changed, and it was like the man softened from his head to his toes. He stroked the hen gently.

"*Danke*, Belinda," Eli said. His words were loud enough to just make it to where Joe was standing, and Joe could see the tremble in the old man's chin.

"*Yah, yah*, Eli," Belinda said. She stood there awkwardly for a moment, and then turned and came back to where Joe was.

"He loves those chickens," she said, shaking her head. "And his housekeeping skills might leave much to be desired, but the chickens themselves are well cared for."

Joe watched as Eli sank into the swing, the chicken on his lap.

"What can I do for you, Joe?" Belinda asked. "Is it about my guest?"

"Hazel?" he asked.

She gave him a knowing smile, her blue eyes glittering behind her glasses. "*Yah*, Hazel. I'm not blind yet, young man. I am a matchmaker, you know."

"No, it's not Hazel," he said. Even though she was on his mind a lot lately. He glanced toward the house—was she inside?

"Oh." Belinda looked a little disappointed. "What is it, then?"

"It's about something more delicate," he said. "First, I'd need your word that you'd keep my secrets to the best of your ability."

"To the best of my ability," she confirmed. "As far as my conscience will allow. You have my word on that."

"Okay, well…" Joe nodded in the direction of the stable, and they walked slowly away from the porch, where he might be overheard.

Then Joe laid out his story. It was simple enough—an Amish teenager had given birth and given up her baby. An *Englisher* couple who hadn't been able to conceive had adopted that baby and loved him dearly. He told what he knew—names, dates and approximate ages. When he stopped speaking, they stood in silence for a few beats.

"Rebecca Lehmann," she said quietly.

"Are there any Rebecca Lehmanns in this area who'd be the right age?" he asked.

"*Yah*, there is one," she said.

"Only one?" His pulse sped up. "I mean, it's a common name. It might not mean a thing—"

"I knew her in her teens," Belinda said, and she turned sad eyes onto him. "I remember when she got pregnant by an *Englisher* boy, and he disappeared. Not that her parents wanted her to run off with him. Far from it. They asked my advice."

"And you said…" His voice sounded strange in his own ears.

"I said that they had a choice before them. They could keep the baby and raise it in their home, but Becky would likely never marry. Not in our community, at least."

"Or…she could give the baby up," he concluded.

"*Yah.*" Belinda nodded. "And they made their decision as a family. I wasn't a part of that. The next time I saw Becky, she'd already delivered, and she was heartbroken. The baby had been given up for adoption."

What were the chances? "What was her mother's name?" he asked.

"Verna."

It was her. He sucked in a wavering breath. "Is she married now? Does she have a family?"

"*Yah*. She married a nice boy from another community. She's now Rebecca Weitz. They settled here, and they have nine *kinner* together."

Nine half siblings. All Amish. He scrubbed a hand through his hair.

"Do you think she'd want to see me?" he asked.

"Oh, dear boy," Belinda said, tears in her eyes. "I told you a story about a man who wanted to raise horses, didn't I?"

"Yeah," he said. "And no one would help him."

"Do you understand the meaning behind the story?" she asked.

"Why don't you tell me," Joe replied. It would be easier that way. He wasn't Amish, and he wouldn't jump to the same conclusions.

"Well, when the man came home and he told his wife that his plans had been foiled yet again, she told him that he shouldn't worry, because they would certainly eat that winter," Belinda said. "You see, our plans seldom work out the way we hope, but if we stop to look at what we have in our hands, we often-times have enough to make a very good life."

Joe stayed silent, and when Belinda looked at him expectantly, he said, "Meaning...I shouldn't talk to her?"

"Meaning," Belinda said, "it is important to keep the right perspective. You were raised by loving parents. You were supported and encouraged. Your daughter has loving grand-parents. When you look at what you have in your hands, you have everything you need for a good and satisfying life."

"I know," he said. "This isn't about fulfilling a fantasy. I guess I just wanted to meet her—to see the woman I came from. That's all. I won't cause her trouble. If she asks me to leave, I'll leave."

"But will you be okay if she doesn't react the way you're imagining she will?" Belinda asked.

"Me?" He forced a smile. "I'm a grown man."

"Grown does not mean invulnerable, Joe," she said, putting a motherly hand on his arm.

"I'll..." He swallowed. "I think I'll be al-right. I can talk it over with my mom—the one who chose me and raised me. I've got her blessing for this, so I'm not all by myself. I promise you that."

"Good." Belinda nodded.

"Will you tell me where I can find her?" he asked.

"She and her husband run a mini-golf place just outside of town," Belinda said. "They have a corn maze in the fall and sledding hills they open to the public in the winter… But this time of year it's mini golf."

"Okay." He frowned. "Wait…Lehmann's Family Fun Farm?"

"That's the one."

He'd driven past it often enough, and the realization that that Lehmann business had been the right one all along was almost jarring.

"Thank you," he said. "I appreciate it, Belinda."

Belinda patted his arm tenderly. "Would you like some pie, dear?"

She was trying to comfort him prematurely, but he didn't want it. He needed to process all of this, and he didn't do that with pie. He might be the biological son of an Amish woman, but he'd been raised *Englisher*. He shook his head.

"I'll just get to work," he said. "But thank you for the information. I truly appreciate it."

HAZEL STOOD IN the back of the bed-and-breakfast property, beyond the pump, the garden and the fruit trees. There was an old weather-beaten fence, one rail half-fallen, and beyond that fence was something she could only describe as a deep puddle. She could tell that it wasn't always there, and the grass around it looked marshy, but in the center swam a duck with a little trail of four yellow ducklings paddling behind her.

The duck quacked, and the ducklings peeped in response. Hazel had already looked at the scene through her cell-phone camera, and it was the kind of moment that simply couldn't be captured that way. Everything looked smaller, flatter, and the peacefulness of the moment just wouldn't translate. So she pocketed her phone and leaned against the fence post, drinking in the scene the way she was probably intended to—in the moment.

But there was still a part of her that wished she could share this with Maddie. She had her freedom all lined up—her opportunity to finally live the life she'd been aching for—and all she could think was that Maddie would appreciate some adorable ducklings. Maddie, who was enjoying England right now: seeing the sights, sending pictures of sheep farms and weaving looms and the remnants of a mournful old castle that probably held more ghosts than any of them could guess...

Maddie was experiencing life, and ducklings weren't going to measure up to those adventures, were they? But ten years ago, Maddie would have been enthralled with a little line of peeping balls of yellow fluff, and Hazel suddenly missed those younger years so deeply that her heart almost seemed to stop in her chest.

Motherhood changed everything.

Hazel heard footsteps behind her, and she turned to see Joe approaching. He had on work jeans slung low on his hips and a white T-shirt, but everything was still clean. He obviously hadn't started working yet.

"Found you," he said, and something in his deep voice made goose bumps run up her arms.

"Hi," she said.

"Lottie's day care is open again."

"I'm sure that's a bit of a relief."

He nodded and pushed his hands into his pockets. "What's over there?"

"Ducklings."

He came over to her side and leaned against a firm portion of fence next to her. His gaze trailed over the scene, but he still looked sober.

"They're pretty newly hatched," he said.

"Yeah?"

He nodded. "They grow fast. By the end of August, they'll look like mature ducks and be ready to fly south."

"Neat," she said. "I'll bet Lottie would love these."

"Yeah…" He smiled then, but his eyes were still somber.

"Joe, are you okay?" she asked.

"I'm fine…" He turned toward her and heaved a sigh. "Mostly. I know where my mother is."

Hazel stared at him, his words catching up with her heartbeat. "You talked to Belinda?"

"Yeah. I thought she might need time to ask around, or maybe have to scratch her head a bit, but she knew exactly who I was talking about. The names, ages—everything matched up."

"Is she local?" Hazel asked.

"Yep. And I know who she is and where to find her."

"That's…huge," she said.

"It is." He turned back toward the temporary pond and leaned his elbows on the fence. For a moment, she stood motionless, but then she slid a hand through the crook of his arm, resting her fingers on his warm biceps. He leaned toward her, shifting his weight onto one leg, and she rested her cheek against his shoulder. His warm, rough hand slid over her fingers, and they stood that way for a couple of minutes, just leaning into each other.

He needed her strength—she could feel that coming through him with every tremble of his pulse. She kept expecting him to pull back, but he didn't. And she was glad.

"What are you going to do?" Hazel whispered at last.

"I'm not sure yet," he replied. "I thought I'd go over there and introduce myself, but the more I think about that, the less I like the idea. I don't think our first reactions are always the ones we'd choose…if that makes sense."

"That makes perfect sense," she said. "Are you going to ask someone to talk to her first?

Maybe let her know you're looking for her and see what she says?"

"Nope," he said. "I want to just go over there and visit the place. I want to show up as a regular old tourist and see if I can spot her."

"Oh…that would work, I suppose. Would you say anything?"

He shook his head. "No, I won't. But I do want to see her. I want to see what she looks like—maybe I want to see if she looks happy. I suppose she will be. Belinda says she and her husband have nine kids."

"Nine!"

Had they made up for the baby boy she'd given up? Had they filled up her heart and soothed away that pain? She looked up at Joe, and his gaze was still locked on the ducks in the pond, his eyes sad.

"At least you know where she is now," Hazel said. "Now you can proceed however you want—or not! There's no pressure for you to do anything at all."

"I want to see her," he said, and his voice firmed. "Definitely." Then he looked down at her, his warm, brown gaze moving over her face. "But a guy driving up and playing mini golf by himself and staring at the owner—that might seem weird."

Hazel chuckled, and the seriousness of the moment broke. "It would, quite honestly. They own a mini-golf place?"

"Yeah, among other things." He laughed softly. "I need someone to go with me...maybe play the part of my girlfriend. We could be a couple playing mini golf together. That wouldn't be weird."

No, it would be quite wonderful, actually. Wandering through a mini-golf course with him, joking, talking, maybe holding hands...

"I bet you could make Michelle's mom's day by asking her out to mini golf," Hazel teased. And she was teasing...but it was a possibility for him. There were women who'd be happy to step in.

Joe rolled his eyes. "Har, har. My life is complicated enough right now. I was thinking of you."

"Because I'm less complicated?" She wasn't sticking around; she wouldn't be expecting anything from him. Michelle's mom would certainly get her hopes up.

"Because I'd rather be with you. Simple as that." His smile dropped away, and he met her gaze. "If things are going to be complicated anyway, I'd rather have you around than anyone else."

"Oh…" The breath seeped out of her. The feeling was entirely mutual, but it was so dangerous. She wasn't staying here. She wasn't what he needed, and she couldn't give up her career opportunities. This was supposed to be a working vacation before she finally launched herself into her dream job. And here she was getting entangled with a man who wanted a stay-at-home mom for his child! This wasn't wise.

"I don't know how you feel about walking around a mini-golf course with me, but if it wouldn't be too miserable on your vacation…?" He didn't finish the thought, but he raised his eyebrows.

This was where Hazel should say no. She should back out and let him find someone more appropriate. She had her own work she needed to review—and there was quite a bit of material left to cover. This was about her future, too—about her fresh start. He had to have friends here, someone who'd be able to understand and not take advantage. It didn't have to be Michelle's mom. She opened her mouth intending to have something appropriate come out, but instead she just said the truth.

"It wouldn't be miserable at all." She swallowed. "I'd probably enjoy that more than I should. I joke about Michelle's mom, but the truth is, I don't blame her a bit, Joe. You're easy to fall for."

"I'm going to take that as a compliment," he said.

"It is."

"But what you mean is, you don't think I can behave myself," he said with a sudden sparkle in his eyes.

"I didn't say that!" She laughed.

"Well, I'll have you know that I'm a perfect gentleman. I'll hold your hand if you let me. But that'll mostly just be moral support for me because it would be kind of huge to see my mom… Other than that, I'll leave your reputation unsullied."

Did he really think that would make it easier? Holding his hand, leaning into his strong shoulder, pretending to be more to him than she had any right to… He reached out and touched her cheek gently, his dark gaze softening even further, then dropped his hand.

"Would you come with me, Hazel?" he

asked. All teasing was gone from his voice, and he seemed to be holding his breath.

"Yeah, I'll come," she said.

"Thanks." A smile touched his lips. "I really appreciate it."

"When do you want to go?" she asked.

"I have about four or five hours left before I'm done here for the week," he replied. "Would this afternoon work for you?"

"Sure. Just let me know when you want to leave." She'd use that time to pore over her books and get as much covered as possible.

"Well, I'd better get to work, then," he said, hooking a thumb over his shoulder. She smiled and nodded in response, and watched as he walked away.

He was so tall and strong, but under all of that male strength was a very tender heart. He needed a friend right now—maybe more than a friend. But her true, deep and honest friendship was all that she could offer.

And if she wasn't careful, she'd find herself falling headlong in love with this man, and all of her determination to stop her heart at the line of friendship would be for naught.

She exhaled a shaky breath.

Keep it together, Hazel, she told herself. *You're the one in the pilot's seat.*

But somehow, when it was her emotional world at stake and not her physical safety, that rule didn't work as well. In a few days, she'd be back to her regular life. Maybe then her balance would return.

CHAPTER TWELVE

HAZEL SAT IN a rocking chair by the kitchen window, her protocols book open in her lap, but today she was having trouble focusing. It was because of Joe, of course. He was going to lay eyes on his biological mother, and she was going to be his moral support for it. She was still chastising herself for agreeing to it. Not that she didn't want to be there, because she did, but because she wouldn't be here much longer than that.

He needed more than she was offering.

She'd tried reading up in her room, but it was getting hot up there, and the porch had attracted a couple of wasps. So she'd moved into the kitchen, mostly because the kitchen table would give her enough space to spread out her books. Belinda and Eli were there, though, and she wondered how much review she'd actually get done.

Amish country quiet was more of a theory than a reality, it seemed. There was more drama unfolding in this old B&B than in her whole apartment building, she was willing to bet.

"He's going to be here any minute," Belinda said as she washed off the counter with strong swipes. "And you need to talk to him, Eli."

"I don't think I'm the one to do that," Eli replied. "You're the matchmaker."

"But you're a man."

"There are plenty other men you could round up for your uses," Eli retorted.

"None in my kitchen right now."

Hazel smothered a smile and put her bookmark into her book. Who was she kidding? She wasn't going to review much of anything until the older folks had sorted out their issue.

"Hazel, you agree with me, don't you?" Belinda asked, turning to her. "Eli needs to be the one to talk to Obadiah. There are times that a young man needs to hear male wisdom. Especially when he's stopped listening to his own matchmaker."

"Well, I—" Hazel began.

"He knows what he wants! What am I supposed to tell him?" Eli interjected.

"That I have two very nice girls who'd be more than willing to talk about a future with him," Belinda said. "Two! And they are both sweet, and good cooks, and come from decent families. If he wants a wife, he needs to be reasonable."

"If he won't listen to you, I doubt he'll listen to me," Eli said. "We men are a stubborn lot. He'll have to learn on his own, Belinda. And that's my male wisdom right there."

"Male wisdom…" Belinda muttered, and Hazel chuckled.

"He might have a point," Hazel said. "You can give the most solid advice to a person, but they have to see the wisdom in it themselves. Maybe Obadiah needs to learn the hard way. Maybe he needs to see Miriam marry another man before he moves on to a girl who's interested."

"Ah, but that is a bad idea," Belinda replied, shaking her head. "Would you like to be the woman a man moved on to after he couldn't have his first choice? Women have some pride, too."

"Pride goeth before a fall…" Eli murmured.

"That is not even relevant right now, Eli!" Belinda said irritably, then she sighed and shut her eyes. When she opened them again, she said, "Eli, I'm sorry to have snapped. I seem to do that a lot lately, and I don't mean to. But it's like you're being willfully blind to what I'm trying to do here."

"I'm not blind to it," Eli replied.

"Then talk to him, Eli," Belinda pleaded. "You are the right man to do it. He needs to hear what could happen to him if he doesn't get reasonable now."

"What could happen to him?" Eli's voice rose slightly in pitch, and Hazel could feel the tension in the room suddenly thicken.

"Eli…" Belinda said quietly. "You know what I mean. Do you want your lot for him? Do you want Obadiah to be well-nigh eighty years old and never married because he was too stubborn to see where happiness for him lay?"

"So you think it's over for me, do you?" Eli demanded.

"It's pretty close, Eli," she said, then her face softened. "Oh, Eli. You aren't the only one who got old. What, do you think I'm about to go find a new husband at my age? We're old people! And our job is to pass along our wisdom to the young ones. That's how this works."

"I'm not so old as you think," he muttered.

Belinda looked over at Hazel, her face pink with exasperation.

"And what do you think, Hazel?" Belinda asked. "Am I alone in wanting this young man to be reasonable?"

Hazel let out a slow breath. Who was she to give advice? She hadn't found her Mr. Wonderful yet, and right now, she was dangerously close to falling for a man who'd never be her match, either. She looked out the window just in time to see Joe walk to the back of his truck and lower the tailgate. He somehow managed to look even better with some dirt on his hands and a streak down his white T-shirt.

A buggy turned in the drive, and Joe's attention was pulled over his shoulder as he seemed to hear it.

"I think you're right, Belinda," Hazel said. "Being reasonable saves on heartbreak."

It certainly would for her.

Eli cast her a sad look. Had she just betrayed the old guy? She felt a pang of guilt.

"Not that it's the right answer for everyone, Eli," Hazel added. "Just in this situation... you know?"

And perhaps for her own situation, too. Eli shook his head and looked away from her.

"Now, Eli, don't be like that just because she agrees with me," Belinda said. "Obadiah is a good man, and he deserves a wife and home of his own. I want to see him living his years fruitfully, not waiting for something that will never be."

They heard the buggy then, and Belinda gave a decisive nod.

"If you won't talk to him, it'll have to be me," Belinda said. "Are you certain you won't help me, Eli?"

"I will not," Eli said, lifting his chin.

"Fine. Thank you for your honesty."

Eli took his crutch and pushed himself up. "I will help him with the horse, though."

"Eli, you are supposed to be healing!"

But Eli didn't listen. He hopped to the mud-room and disappeared inside. A moment later, the door banged shut.

"That man..." Belinda muttered.

Should she say anything at all? Belinda certainly should know by now how Eli felt. She was a matchmaker. Wasn't she supposed to be attuned to these things? She shouldn't say a word. She should keep out of it. But before she could stop herself, she said, "I think he might be in love with you."

"What? Eli?" Belinda batted a hand through the air. "Oh, no, dear. You have to understand our ways. I'm just his neighbor."

Yeah. Well, some things were universal, and Eli had confirmed his feelings for her.

"And if I was right?" Hazel asked. "If he were in love with you?"

"Well, that would complicate everything, wouldn't it?" Belinda said. "I'd have to stop being so familiar with him, lest I lead him on. But trust me, we're old friends. We might bicker like a married couple, but we are far from it. I'm sorry if I've made you uncomfortable at all. I can be a little bad with boundaries, my son tells me. I'd be a much better hostess if I just shut my mouth and served you pie."

"Not at all!" Hazel said. "This is part of your charm. With no internet, we've got to have something, right?"

Belinda smiled ruefully. "The bishop will not allow Wi-Fi. I do apologize for that, but this is how we live. This is what makes us special."

"I know," Hazel said.

"There are perks to having less distraction. We can focus on human relationships—real, in-the-flesh ones. I understand that people talk to each other online, but what about the people standing right in front of us?"

As if on cue, Joe passed through Hazel's

field of view again, a shovel over one shoulder as he headed back toward his truck. His gaze moved toward the window, and when he spotted her, a smile turned up one side of his mouth, and her breath caught. She sucked in a deep, purposeful breath.

"Sometimes, we avoid the very people who are right in front of us, wanting to be noticed," Belinda went on. "Sometimes, we can miss out on a very promising relationship, all because we were distracted and didn't notice the treasure before us."

Hazel turned back. "But what if that treasure is too complicated?"

"It happens..." Belinda said. "I truly am a proponent of realistic expectations. The happiest couples I've seen in my life have been those who watered the grass they were standing on. They saw what was theirs, and they put their energy into growing it. No pining after anyone else. No wondering what might have been. No longing for something that belongs to someone else. Just gratefulness for what they worked for, and a determination to make the best of it."

It sounded very reasonable...and satisfying. She'd do well to take that sound Amish advice. Boots sounded on the steps, and the door opened. Obadiah came in through the mudroom first, and he gave Belinda a respectful nod. Eli followed him inside, hopping along with his crutch.

"Eli said that you had something to talk to me about," Obadiah said.

"*Yah*, I do," Belinda said, and her gaze moved over to Eli, who leaned against the wall.

"And he, uh, said I ought to listen well and take to heart what you have to say." Obadiah licked his lips and twisted the rim of his straw hat in his hands.

Belinda shot Hazel a look of surprise. It looked like Eli had come through, after all.

"I'll just go for a walk…" Hazel murmured, and as she came to the mudroom, Eli caught her eye.

"You're backing her up," Hazel said softly.

Eli shrugged. "Don't want the young fellow to turn out like me, now, do I?"

Eli pressed his lips together, then dropped his gaze. He'd loved one woman his whole life…he just hadn't married her. And he was the example of a life to avoid. She wanted to say something, to hug him, do something, but one *Englisher* woman couldn't fix anything here.

"He could do worse, Eli," Hazel murmured.

The old man didn't answer, and Hazel headed out the door. As the screen door bounced shut behind her, she heard the language change to Pennsylvania Dutch inside as Belinda began to speak.

Who knew? Maybe the old matchmaker would talk some sense into Obadiah after all, and he'd get a lovely wife and let go of his crush on Miriam. Eli was now supporting Belinda's advice, and there were some good options waiting for the guy if he wanted to get married and move on with that part of his life.

Although Eli's sad, crinkled eyes had lodged themselves in her memory. The man had a loyal heart—that could not be argued. It just hadn't panned out for him…

But why did the thought of Obadiah being reasonable and adjusting his expectations leave Hazel feeling just a little bit sad? It would be nice if somewhere, illogical, irrational love could get a win.

Joe finished up his work and surveyed the vegetable garden—rows of small tomato plants that he'd bought from a greenhouse, and mounds of moist, black earth waiting for seeds to sprout carrots, cabbage and lettuce. It felt good to be finished. The main work here at the B&B was done, at least, and the rest would just be upkeep.

Obadiah's buggy sat with the horse still hitched up, but was sheltered in the shade of a tall tree. Joe tossed some tools into the bed of his pickup. But his mind wasn't on the job well done... He rubbed some dried dirt from his hands and glanced up as Hazel came out the side door of the house.

"Hi," Hazel said. She looked deflated.

"You okay?" he asked.

"I'm fine." She nodded toward the garden. "It looks really good."

"I'm pretty much done here," he said. "I'll need to give Belinda the tour, though, and get her okay with it all."

"Oh...as in done the whole job." Hazel met his gaze. "As in...not coming back to the B and B after this."

"Probably not," he said. "Why, you think you'll miss me?"

He shot her a grin, and he was gratified to see her cheeks pinken. She shrugged and dropped her gaze. He headed over to the steps, and after a moment, she followed him.

"What if I did?" she said.

"I'd be glad," he said. "It's good to be missed."

"I guess it was coming, wasn't it?" She looked up at him.

"Yeah, but…we can still see each other," he said. "It's not like I'm disappearing. You have my number."

"True." She looked away from him, out at the yard. "We just had a great excuse to see each other this way. And it isn't like I'm not leaving in a few days, too."

It was a detail he didn't want to think about right now. Whatever this was between them hadn't been planned, and while it might evaporate in a few days' time, he'd have to deal with that when it happened. Today, he had her here with him.

"We had an excuse to see each other the last few days," Joe said. "So maybe now we admit we like it, and we make it a choice."

She looked up at him, a cautious expression in her blue eyes. "That's dangerous ground, Joe."

"Choosing to be friends?" he said. "It's not so scary."

She shrugged faintly as if not entirely convinced. This wasn't exactly friendship, and he knew it. But it wasn't anything more than friendship, either. Whatever this was tugging them together, it was hard to define.

"I can handle it," Joe said. "Can you?"

"Probably." Her eyes sparkled then, and he felt a wave of relief to see it.

"Good. Besides, you're coming along to get a look at my biological mom, aren't you? If that's not friendship, I don't know what is."

"That's true," she said. "So that's what this is? Just two buddies?"

"Nope," he said. "Calling you a buddy feels wrong." He eyed her for a moment. "I'm willing to leave it a mystery, as long as I can see you again."

She smiled at that. "Deal."

"I need to get Belinda to take a look at things, but I don't feel like I should disturb whatever is happening in there," he said.

"That…" She nodded. "They're telling Obadiah about two new options—single women who'd love to go out with him. I think the point is to send him in the direction of interested women."

"Not a bad idea…for someone else." He shot her a grin. "I've got to sympathize with the guy, though. If I had an Amish matchmaker, she'd tell me to stop my bellyaching and have me married to Michelle's mom within a month. Someone else being interested isn't always the promise of happiness people think."

"Maybe you'd be like Miriam, and Michelle's mom would be sent off to someone more receptive," Hazel said with a chuckle. "You never know."

The side door opened, and Obadiah came outside. He headed straight for his buggy. Belinda and Eli followed, and from their vantage point on the step, all they could see were the old people's backs. Belinda raised her hand in a wave, and Obadiah turned his buggy around and the horse trotted off down the drive. From what Joe could see, Obadiah seemed like he was okay. Maybe he was just ignoring that store of solid Amish advice that had just been unloaded onto him. Or maybe he'd seen the light.

Joe couldn't help but wonder what had happened in there. But Amish business tended to stay private. And he should be grateful for that because he had his own business he wanted to keep discreet. Belinda and Eli stood there side by side, and if he didn't know better, he'd think they were an old married couple saying farewell to a guest. They had that look about them—that almost visible tie that came from sixty or seventy years of knowing each other. Wasn't that what Joe wanted to find one of these days? Someone who'd build that kind of tie with him?

Except Eli and Belinda were no example of romantic happiness. They weren't romantic anything. Joe was about to stand up and get Belinda's attention when she turned to Eli, not seeing them on the step.

"Thank you for that, Eli," Belinda said. "I appreciate it."

"You appreciate what?" Eli sounded irritable. "That I told Obadiah that he'll end up being a miserable, lonely old man if he follows his heart?"

"He needed to be told, Eli," Belinda said. "Someone had to do it. If everyone just kept telling him what he wanted to hear, it wouldn't be good for him. He's better off facing facts."

"I'm sure." Eli sounded bitter.

Joe looked over at Hazel, and she raised her eyebrows. Should they say something now, or…

"Eli…you know the situation," Belinda said. "He's stubborn and about as mule-headed as my Eeyore."

"Maybe he is," Eli said. "Maybe he isn't. That's not what upsets me. I really don't have any kind of burden on my heart for young Obadiah."

"You should!" she retorted. "He's a member of our community, and—"

"You told Obadiah that I lived a long, lonely life," Eli said, cutting her off.

"Did I?"

"*Yah*, you did. You told him that my entire life has been a sad and pathetic one."

"I didn't say pathetic!" she retorted.

"It was implied, Belinda."

"Well...you can't say you don't regret your choices now, can you? You could have gotten married, had some children and you'd have great-great-grandbabies by now, if you had. You miss having a woman around. You know it. You're in my kitchen often enough."

"Ah." Eli's voice was shaking now.

"What do you mean, *ah*?"

"I mean *ah*!" Eli pulled off his hat and thwacked it against his leg. "It's good to see how you see me!"

"How I see you? It's how the whole community sees you!"

"What would you even know about my life, Belinda?" Eli demanded. "Did you visit my home? Did you come sit in my kitchen? Did you spend any time at all in the home that my brother and I built together?"

"I visited—"

"Long enough to turn up your nose and tell me I was living in a barn," he said. "Not long enough to actually sit down and drink a cup of tea."

"It would hardly be sanitary..." Her words were almost too quiet to hear.

"I clean my dishes, woman."

Belinda seemed speechless, and when Joe's gaze flickered toward Hazel, she grimaced. They shouldn't be listening to this, but it wasn't like they had much choice, and it sounded like this was a long time coming.

"But since you seem so comfortable speaking for me, maybe you should hear what I actually think about my life," Eli went on. "I've enjoyed my years. Sure there have been hard times, and I'll admit to a few lonely times, too, but it wasn't all difficulty. I built up this farm with my brother. I had fun. I did work that I loved. And I might not have been to any woman's taste, but I wouldn't count my life wasted. I was a good neighbor to you, Belinda Wickey. I was a good neighbor to your dearly departed husband, too. For a good sixty years we've lived side by side, helping each other in hard times and looking out for each other. And you repay me by embarrassing me in front of some young pup who can't seem to get the attention of the woman he wants?" His voice was rising now. "Who cares?" The old man threw his hands up, lost his grip on his crutch and caught it before it fell. "Why is it the end of the world if Obadiah stays single awhile?"

"Because he asked for my help as a matchmaker," Belinda said weakly.

"And making sure Obadiah is properly married to a woman who will have him is more important than our friendship?" Eli was visibly shaking. "You'd insult me and use me as an example of some kind of loser because he won't do what you want him to do? Why not leave him to his own devices? Why not tell him you can't help him because he won't cooperate and let him be? Either he'd go find a woman who liked him more, or he'd keep pining, but it's hardly your business!"

"I don't think you're a loser."

"That's a lie, woman," Eli said gruffly. "And you know it. But I'll tell you this. I've been a loyal friend to you for all these years, and you've repaid me badly, Belinda Wickey. Very badly."

Eli started hobbling off, and Belinda planted her hands on her hips.

"Hund!" he called, and from seemingly out of nowhere, the black dog came loping up to Eli's side.

"Where do you think you're going, Eli?" Belinda called.

"Home!" he bellowed over his shoulder. "I'll be just fine. Where's my hen?"

"She's in the old puppy pen," Belinda replied. "She's got food and water in there."

Eli changed direction and hobbled toward the backyard, Hund trotting along beside him. Belinda stood immobile, and for a moment, Joe wasn't sure if she'd erupt in rage or what...but then her shoulders slumped. Shoot. Was Belinda going to cry? His own heart squeezed in response.

Joe looked over at Hazel and her gaze was locked on the old woman. She reached over and grabbed Joe's hand, giving it a squeeze. They couldn't say anything now or even retreat. They were trapped there until Belinda noticed them, and they'd seen far more than they should have.

Belinda slowly turned, and when she spotted Joe and Hazel sitting there, tears rose in her eyes, and she put a hand over her mouth.

"Oh, Belinda," Hazel said, getting up and going over to her. "It's okay."

"No, it isn't, but it's my mess to fix. I'm sorry you saw that," Belinda said. "Don't you worry about me. Maybe it's just a lesson that we Amish are as flawed as anyone else."

"If you go talk to him, maybe—" Hazel began.

Eli came back around the corner then, hobbling along, leaning on his crutch and putting a little weight on his bad foot.

"I can't get the hen with a crutch, so I'll trust you to take care of her until I can come back," Eli said loudly. "Hund, let's go!"

Eli was losing some of his upper hand in this dramatic exit with all the talking, but the old man turned and continued limping off toward his own property, the dog running ahead and coming back, then running ahead again.

"I'll bring the hen over later, Eli!" Belinda called.

"I will come for her myself!" Eli shouted. "I wouldn't want to put you out!"

"Eli, there's no shame in accepting help!" Belinda called back.

"I do not need it!"

Yep, that upper hand was fast slipping away, and Joe smothered a smile.

"I can give you a quick tour of the work I did," Joe said, speaking up for the first time.

"What's that?" Belinda looked over at him as if she'd just remembered he was there. "Oh, Joe, I'm sorry. I'm not in the mood to look it all over. I do trust you. I've seen you working, and I've been watching your progress. Can I just pay you?"

"Uh…" Joe shrugged. "I suppose so. Sure."

"Is the price the same as what you quoted me?" she asked.

"Yes, ma'am."

She nodded, looking tired. "Then I'll go get my checkbook."

A job complete. He wished he felt better about it—not just his work, but about how he was leaving things. This wasn't his business, and he knew it. Belinda and Eli would sort themselves out, and if they couldn't, the bishop would pay them each a visit and help them make peace. They certainly weren't alone, but he felt like he was a part of the community, too. Maybe on the outside, maybe just as an *Englisher*, but he cared.

"Thank you," he said when she came back, a check neatly written out to his business for the full amount.

"No, thank you, Joe. I truly appreciate your work," she said.

"Belinda, if I can help with anything—" he began.

"No, no, Joe," she said. "I'll sort it out somehow. I'm embarrassed you saw us at our worst today. The truth is, I hurt Eli's feelings, and I fear I was in the wrong. I have used him as an example of consequences to avoid, and I didn't even think he'd disagree with me. But he was a good neighbor to us…to me. A frustrating man, and a constant challenge to my way of thinking, but the very best neighbor a woman could ask for, all the same. I'll have to tell him that." She winced. "I hate admitting when I'm wrong, Joe. But I don't see any way around it."

CHAPTER THIRTEEN

HAZEL CLICKED HER seat belt into place as Joe pulled the truck around to head up the drive. Behind them, all was calm again. A breeze rustled through the treetops, and Eli's hen clucked from the backyard. And yet, Hazel could still feel the sadness here. A friendship had broken today. Something had changed… and maybe it had to. Eli couldn't go on loving Belinda and having her live right next door and be mildly annoyed with his existence. Someone was bound to get hurt.

Was Hazel playing a similar game here with Joe, toying with emotions they were smarter to avoid?

"I always thought the Amish had it all figured out," Hazel said softly. "Or at least mostly figured out."

"Not so much," Joe replied, and Hazel looked over at him, catching a smile that tickled the corners of his lips.

"No, I suppose not," she said. "But that's

part of why I chose a vacation out here. I like to think of the Amish communities as above our petty squabbles, you know? It would be nice if living an old-fashioned life was enough to smooth things out."

"Well, as someone who moved out here partly for the peace and quiet, I can tell you that it does help," he said.

"Yeah?"

He nodded. "There's drama, but…less of it. I don't think anyone can avoid conflict forever. And the Amish do try, but anytime you get two people together, there's going to be something." He cast her a wry smile. "Tension…or some unexpected connection."

It was hard to stop those things from happening, and maybe they were the best parts of life. The goodbyes were the hard part. And at least for Hazel and Joe, they wouldn't see any more of each other. She'd go to the city, and he'd continue here. But for the Belindas and Elis of the world, they couldn't heal in the same way. They had to go on seeing each other, facing each other, dredging up those feelings again and again, even if it was one-sided.

Joe stopped at the intersection where Butternut Drive met the highway and signaled his turn.

"I appreciate you coming along with me," Joe said. "I don't want to seem like some guy out there to stare at a woman. It would come off wrong. And then I'd have to explain myself, and I'm not sure I want to do that yet."

"I know," she said. "It's fine."

"And some people will probably know me. I mean, not this family, in particular, but this is a pretty small community. So we'll just be a couple going out on a date," he said.

"Just two ordinary people." She smiled, hoping to get him to relax, but it didn't seem to help too much. She reached out and touched his leg, and he put his warm hand on top of hers.

"Maybe you could be the one to ask questions—you know, just be chatty and curious," he said.

"I can do that."

"Okay..." He nodded. "Okay."

"This is nerve-wracking for you," she said.

He glanced over at her, then flicked his gaze back to the road. "Definitely. I've been wondering about her for my entire life. I've been wondering why she gave me up. She could have raised me. Yeah, her life would have been harder, but she could have."

Hazel didn't answer. She didn't feel like he needed one from her. The only answers that mattered would come from Rebecca Lehmann.

"Eventually, I think Lottie will meet her mom, too," he went on. "I wonder if I'll have been enough for Lottie over the years."

"Definitely," Hazel said. "Were your parents enough for you? Of course. They raised you, loved you, encouraged you…but being enough doesn't mean being everything."

Joe gave her fingers a squeeze. "That's… very true. It's hard to admit to not being your kid's everything, though."

"Joe, she'll grow up," Hazel said. "And she'll need more people than just parents. She'll need friends, teachers, aunts and uncles, grandparents, and eventually, she'll need a family of her own. We're their whole world for a very short time, and then their needs grow."

"So I should get used to it?" he asked.

"You might want to." She laughed softly. "Joe, I raised my daughter alone. I raised her well, loved her, prioritized her…but that doesn't mean she doesn't have to sort things out with her father. It just means she's got the backbone to do it because I helped to give her that. You are absolutely enough. I promise you that."

But Hazel understood that feeling—wanting to be everything when she couldn't be. It was the same helpless feeling of knowing her daughter was struggling with her relationship with Todd and his family, and not being able to do anything about it. It was the same feeling as wanting to fully support this man next to her, to be a real partner to him, and knowing it wasn't her place.

They carried on down the highway, and she saw the sign for Lehmann's Family Fun Farm as they came close to the town limits. There was a turnoff, and a few signs pointing the way down a side road until they came upon an Amish farm with a large sign out front announcing mini golf, farm tours and crafts for sale. There were a couple of vehicles parked out front already, and some families were on the mini-golf course.

"Here we are," Joe said.

She looked over at him. "You ready?"

"Yep." He pressed his lips together, paused for a beat, then opened his door. "Ready as I'll ever be."

When Hazel got out of the vehicle, Joe came around and waited for her. There was a large covered tent in the front yard with some folding tables underneath it. From what Hazel could see, there were some fabric crafts for sale there. They ambled in that direction. A teenage girl stood behind one of the tables, and she smiled at them.

"Good afternoon!" she called.

"Hi!" Hazel said.

The girl didn't say anything else, but Hazel led the way to look at some of the items. Joe trailed behind her.

"Do you make these yourself?" Hazel asked.

"*Yah*, a few. My *mamm* and my sisters did most of it, though. They're better at it than me."

"Are you the family that owns the farm?" Hazel asked.

"*Yah*, that's us."

A sister. Hazel glanced back at Joe, and he looked a little pale.

"We have some woodworking, too, that my *daet* and brothers do. But they didn't put it out today," the girl went on.

"How many kids in your family?" Hazel asked.

"I'm sixth of nine," she said.

"That's a big family," Hazel said, shooting the girl a smile. "I'm an only child, if you can believe that. So is Joe, actually."

"I can't imagine that," the girl said, shaking her head. "It must be boring. No one to talk to or play with."

"You make do," Hazel said.

She wanted to keep the girl talking, if she could. More talking was more information for Joe. This was definitely his half sister.

"We've got mini golf, too," the girl said.

"Is it popular?" Hazel asked.

"*Yah*, normally. People like it. We only set up two weeks ago. It was too rainy before that."

"It doesn't work to golf in the rain," Hazel said with a smile.

"Are you guys related to the other Lehmanns around here?" Joe asked suddenly. "Like Lehmann's Electronics, or Lehmann's Crafts?"

"Um...not Lehmann's Electronics," she said. "But I think we're related to the owner of Lehmann's Crafts, and one of the guys at Lehmann's Plumbing, too. My cousin Mark Yoder works there with his sister's husband, who's a Lehmann. Mark got married recently, and I got to be in the wedding. It was actually really special because he fell in love with his wife, and she—" she lowered her voice "—gave up a big inheritance to marry him."

"Oh, yeah?"

"*Yah*. She should have married a farmer to inherit her *daet*'s farm. But she wanted Mark. So there you go."

"Amazing."

"*Yah*, our family goes way back here. But I'm not really a Lehmann, either. That's my grandparents' name. I'm a Weitz."

"Oh, okay…" Joe nodded.

"Your mom must stay pretty busy?" Hazel said.

"*Yah*, I guess. We're all pretty busy."

Hazel picked up some pot holders and a hand towel that would hang off a stove handle.

"I'll get these, please," Hazel said.

"Sure." The girl grabbed a small, thin plastic bag and put the items inside, then she went over to her money box. "They're five dollars each, so that's fifteen dollars."

Hazel pulled out her wallet and paid. A younger boy came running up from the house and he shot them a shy smile, then said something in Pennsylvania Dutch.

"Right now?" the girl asked.

"Yah."

"Okay. You take over, then." The girl smiled at Hazel. "I've got to go help my sister with something."

"No problem," Hazel said. "We'll just take a walk around."

Hazel hooked an arm through Joe's and guided him back out to the sunlight, her bag swinging at her side.

"I think those are your siblings," she said softly.

"I think so, too," he murmured. "But I can't very well sit down and talk to them. I'm a man—that comes off weird."

"I know. Maybe let me do the chatting, then."

A young Amish man with a cleanly shaven face stood in front of the mini golf. There was a little hut and a covered stand that held golf clubs. Beyond that was an array of colorful mini-golf holes with hills and bridges, and little mini Amish scenes to golf through.

"I recognize him from Miriam's place," Hazel said.

"Oh, yeah..." Joe perked up a bit then. "He went home with a kitten."

"They all did, in his defense," she chuckled.

"So he's one of the men who are Obadiah's

competition," Joe said. "This really is a small community, isn't it?"

They walked up to the little covered stand where they'd pay.

"Hi," Joe said. "How much to golf?"

"Five dollars each," the young man said.

"We think we recognize you from the other day," Joe said. "You were at the Yoder farm, weren't you? And you ended up with a kitten?"

The man's face reddened. "*Yah*, I did go home with a kitten..."

"How is it settling in?" Hazel asked.

"It's being spoiled rotten by my little sisters and brothers," he said. "So you want to play?"

"I do," Hazel said, and she looked up at Joe questioningly.

"Yeah, sure," Joe said. He dug out his wallet and handed over two fives. "This should be fun. What else do you guys have out here?"

"Well, there's the craft tent, and there's some goats behind the house you can pet if you want," he said. "And my *mamm* sells jam and preserves, if that interests you."

His mother...

"Jam," Hazel said quickly. "Yes, that does. We'll definitely stop for jam today."

She looked up at Joe again, wondering what

he'd want to do, but he grabbed two clubs and handed her one.

"First we golf," he said quietly.

She nodded. "Fair enough."

Maybe he wasn't ready to jump right into the jam purchasing. Besides, this was his brother—his younger brother, who had a crush on Miriam Yoder.

Joe put a hand on the small of her back and guided her toward the first hole.

"You need some balls!" the Amish man called.

Joe turned and Hazel watched as the young man lobbed two golf balls toward them, one at a time. Joe caught them both and put one on the plastic turf.

"That would be my brother," he murmured.

"It seems that way," she agreed. "Did you want to talk to him?"

"You go first," he said, instead of answering.

Hazel took the first putt. She was pretty good at mini golf. It was all about hand-eye coordination, and she had that in spades with her job. That was a trade secret—never golf against a pilot or a surgeon. They'd wipe the turf with you.

Joe went next, and they finished the hole,

Hazel completing it in three strokes. Joe took five. He looked down at the score sheet and the nub of pencil.

"You don't need to keep score," she said.

"Why not?"

"Because I'll beat you, and you'll feel bad about that, and you've got enough on your mind right now without losing at mini golf to me." She shot him a smile.

He chuckled. "You think ahead."

"I always do."

"I can handle losing to you," he said. "I'm keeping score."

Behind them at the farmhouse, the front door opened and a middle-aged woman came outside, put a brick in front of the screen door and started setting up some jars on a shelf beside the door. She was slim and tall, and from here seemed to have brown hair with some gray streaks. She wore black running shoes with a plum-colored cape dress, and a white *kapp* over her hair. Her apron was gray, though—probably a work apron meant for some serious business. Hazel reached out and caught Joe's hand as he filled in the little squares with their strokes.

"Joe," she said.

"Hmm?" He looked up, and then he turned,

following her gaze toward the house. He froze. She felt his arm suddenly tense, and the air seemed to whoosh out of him.

Joe felt his chest tighten. The woman on the porch was far enough away that he couldn't hear what she'd said to a preteen girl behind her. The girl came out a moment later with more jars.

Just a simple family moment—nothing surprising there. Except that the slim older woman was his biological mother. Funny, he'd never imagined her looking quite like this. In his mind, she'd stayed a perpetually frightened sixteen-year-old.

"Do you want to go over there?"

He tore his gaze from the scene and looked down at Hazel. She was watching him, sympathy in her blue gaze.

"Not yet," he said. "We're just a couple playing golf, remember? Let's finish up and then go over."

"Okay."

He picked up his golf club and turned back to the game at hand. Suddenly, all nine holes seemed like they'd take an eternity. Was he acting too rashly having come over here? Maybe he shouldn't have done this...

"Let's play the same ball," Hazel said.

"What?" He swallowed and realized he hadn't moved yet.

"We can play the same ball," she repeated. "Teamwork. I hit it, then you hit it. Back and forth until we're done. What do you say?"

His heartbeat, which seemed to have stalled in his chest, had finally caught back up with the rest of him, and he nodded. "Uh…yeah. That would be nice."

No competition, after all. He did like that better.

"Good." She smiled. "Come on. It won't take too long."

Somehow, this was easier to handle because even when his shots were terrible, Hazel's were perfect. Every time. She would have beat him miserably, wouldn't she? But her skilled putting put the ball in the hole within three or four shots, and they moved forward together.

"You're good at this," he said, watching her line up a putt.

"Told you." She chuckled. With a hollow-sounding tap, the ball rolled steadily toward the hole. It missed by half an inch and stopped six inches away. Almost.

"I like this better with you on my team," he said.

She smiled, crossed her arms and nodded toward the ball. He tapped it into the hole, then bent down to retrieve it. His gaze moved toward the house again—the middle-aged woman was still arranging jars.

His mother...and this green, well-maintained farm was her life. These kids—the adult children and the younger ones—were hers. She'd likely made that jam. Why did that put a lump in his throat? It was a beautiful life, and he wanted good things for her. It was just a little hard to see that he hadn't been part of it.

Hazel led him through the last two holes. The ninth, she played alone, and then kicked the ball the last three inches into the hole at the end.

"Good game," she said, and they handed their clubs and the two balls back to the young man.

"Thanks a lot," Joe said, and he almost sounded normal, even to himself.

"Let's get that jam," Hazel said softly, and she slipped her hand into his. He closed his fingers around hers, and he felt like he was holding on for dear life. He hoped she didn't mind.

The woman was still on the porch. She

turned as they came across the grass toward her, and she gave them a friendly smile.

"Hello," she called. "Welcome to our farm."

"Hi," Hazel said, equal cheer in her voice. "This is a beautiful place. So you're the owners?"

"Yes, my parents actually own it, and my husband and I run it," she replied.

"A real family affair," Hazel said.

"*Yah*, that's how we do things," the woman replied. "It's the Amish way."

"My name is Hazel." She squeezed Joe's hand. "This is Joe."

"Nice to meet you. I'm Rebecca."

His heart gave a little lurch at the confirmation. This *was* her—the woman who'd given him up. But her life looked quite idyllic now. Joe glanced around the porch. There was a pair of worn leather shoes beside the door. And he could see in the sitting-room window, where an old man was seated on a rocking chair, his head tipped back and an open book turned facedown on his knee. He was asleep. Was that Joe's grandfather?

His adoptive grandparents had died when he was young. It would be quite extraordinary to suddenly have some living grandparents.

"I saw the jam," Hazel said quickly.

"Yes, my daughters and I make it together," she said. "I've got five different flavors right now."

For a couple of minutes, Hazel discussed jam, and he listened to them talk. Hazel bought two jars.

"That's great you make it all with your kids," Hazel said. "I have a nineteen-year-old daughter, and I'm realizing now how fast that time together flies."

"*Yah, yah*, it really does," she agreed. "I have nine *kinner* of my own. They grow so fast."

"That's a lot of kids," Joe said.

"It's the perfect number of kids," she said, looking up with a smile. "I'd even have welcomed more, if they had come along. We love big families out here."

But would she welcome him? He wasn't a "kid." She was talking about babies, and he knew it, but there was a part of his heart that seemed to be holding its breath all the same.

"Do most people have big families?" Hazel asked. "Joe and I both each have one child, so we're used to something different."

"Only one?" Rebecca didn't seem to quite understand that concept. "Well, our community, like other Amish communities, believes in large families. But I think we have the most children, at least around here. There is one other family with eight, and the rest have fewer. But my older sister, who moved out to Indiana, has fourteen."

"Fourteen!" Joe hadn't meant to say that out loud.

"*Yah*, fourteen," Rebecca said, shooting him a smile. She seemed to like having shocked him.

"That's quite the spread," Hazel said. "How big is the gap in your family?"

"My oldest son—" there was a slight hitch in her voice "—is twenty-five. He's married with little ones of his own. And my youngest just turned nine."

"That's a lot of work for you," Joe said.

Rebecca's gaze returned to Joe, and she didn't seem to know what to make of him because she frowned slightly. Did she think he was criticizing? Disagreeing?

"The bigger *kinner* help with the younger ones," Rebecca said, "and by the time the older ones get married, they know all about diapers and potty training and everything else. It's good training for family life."

Joe nodded. He wasn't quite sure what else to say to that. How many children she had and how she ran her home wasn't his business. To her, he was just a man she'd never met with a chatty girlfriend.

"So how long have you run this place with your husband?" Hazel asked.

"Oh, ever since we got married. My parents were ready to step back, and for us Amish, we have our parents live with us in their old age, so they moved out to a *dawdie* house in the back, and my husband and I turned the farm into what it is today."

"So this tourist location was an idea you and your husband had," Hazel said.

"*Yah*... Well...it was my idea." Color crept into Rebecca's cheeks. "I shouldn't say that. It sounds prideful."

"If it's true, it's true," Joe said. Let her take some credit if she wanted to.

"I thought it would work, and my husband gave it some thought," Rebecca said. "We started out with the corn maze in the fall, and everyone liked it so much that a couple of years later we added in some sleigh rides in winter, and then some maple-syrup-candy making in the snow. We even sell crafts at the craft fair every year. It's starting tomorrow at the exhibition grounds."

"And it grew from there," Hazel said.

"Much like the children do," Rebecca said, and then she laughed at her own little joke. "You turn around and suddenly your business is bigger than you remembered. A little addition here and a little addition there… The mini golf was our last addition. And that was… Let me see…Noah was fifteen—I remember because he was working on building his buggy, and he had to pause in that to help his *daet*… That was ten years ago."

"Noah is your oldest son?" Joe asked.

"Yah." She smiled. "He's a big help to us."

She looked toward the tent with the crafts inside. Another couple had arrived and were looking over the tables, and Rebecca's attention was turning to the new customers. This was it. This was his last chance to say anything, if he was going to.

But then a man came around the side of the house—he was tall, strong and very fit for his age. He looked like he was in his mid-fifties. His beard was long and gray, but his shoulders were wide, and his hands looked work-toughened.

"This is my husband, Menno, now," Rebecca said.

"Hello," he said with a smile. "Can I help you with anything?"

"We were just asking questions about your farm," Joe said.

"We're happy to answer them," Menno said. "Becky, the girls ran into trouble in the kitchen."

"Oh!" Rebecca shot her husband a smile. "I'd better go see to it, then."

She disappeared into the house, the screen door bouncing shut, and Joe watched her go. He caught Menno watching him, and he felt some heat come to his face.

"My wife is a busy woman," Menno said pointedly.

"Yeah…" This looked bad, didn't it? "I, um, I thought I knew her. That's all. I guess I don't."

But his mother knew his name. Would she have told her husband that?

"What's your name?" Menno asked.

"Joseph Carter."

Menno's face suddenly paled. He knew that name, obviously. The Amish man squinted slightly, looking at him more closely. Then he crossed his arms.

"Well, it's very nice to meet you, Joseph," Menno said, his tone less friendly than the words. "I hope you have a good day."

"Thank you."

For a moment, he and Menno just looked at each other, and the silent message was clear.

Menno was staring him down, his lips pressed together and his eyes flinty. Joe gave Hazel's hand a squeeze, and he led the way down the steps and back toward his vehicle. Hazel had to almost jog to keep up with his long strides, but Joe was done. He needed to get back and pull his feelings together.

"Joe, slow down," Hazel said.

He obeyed her instruction, and he realized he hadn't let go of her hand, either. He released her then and rubbed a hand through his hair.

"Do you want to go back and talk to him?" she asked. "I'm pretty sure he recognized you."

"It's my name. My parents told my biological mother what they were naming me," Joe said, and his throat was tight.

And Menno had made it pretty clear he wanted Joe to clear out, too. Joe just shook his head and opened the passenger-side door for Hazel. She eyed him for a moment, then got up into the seat. He closed the door and strode around the front of the truck to the driver's side, but as he walked, he looked back toward the house.

Menno stood there, as if on guard, legs akimbo, but his expression had changed. He looked conflicted now, less certain of himself. When he saw Joe's scrutiny, he unfolded his arms, and they hung limply at his sides.

Menno was trying to protect his wife from the shock of seeing him. It would seem that Joe wasn't good news, after all.

Joe hopped up into the driver's seat and turned the key. His mother had a good life—kids, grandkids and a husband who obviously loved her deeply. She'd given up Joe, but she'd gotten the life she'd wanted in exchange. Who was he to mess with that?

CHAPTER FOURTEEN

HAZEL STAYED SILENT as Joe turned the truck and headed up the drive toward the road. He drove with one hand on the steering wheel, the muscles on his forearm taut, his jaw clenched. He was holding it all inside—she could see the strain.

"Are you okay?" she asked quietly.

"Yeah." He reached over and took her hand, and his touch was surprisingly gentle. "Sorry. I don't mean to be like this."

"Like what?" she said. "Human? You just met your biological mother and some of her family. Some of *your* family. That's huge."

"Yep."

Maybe he didn't want to talk about it. She looked down at his broad, strong hand over hers. He released her hand when he got to the first turn, and he leaned forward to check both ways before he turned onto the next road.

"Do you want to stop somewhere and just... breathe?" she asked.

"Would you mind?" He looked over at her, his dark gaze swimming with emotion.

"Of course not."

They were on a gravel road, and she could see the zip of cars on the highway ahead, but he pulled over to the side of the road and stopped. For a moment, he sat there, both hands on the steering wheel.

"She didn't know me," he said, and he dropped his hands to his lap. "I know that's ridiculous, but it's what I can't stop thinking. You know how if you were suddenly separated from your daughter, you'd look for her in every face for the rest of your life?"

"Yeah," she said.

"And you think that you'd know her again if you saw her ten years from now, or twenty, right? You'd recognize her, somehow." He sighed. "And I'm not saying this is rational, but somehow I hoped she'd recognize me."

"Oh, Joe..." Hazel reached out and took his hand, tugging it over to her lap.

"I was a newborn when she saw me last." He turned toward her and laced his fingers through hers. "And I think of Lottie as a newborn. Would I know her at four if the last I saw her was that squished-up little face?" He shook his head. "And I'm expecting Rebecca to see me at thirty-seven and have a miraculous spark of recognition."

"Motherhood isn't miraculous," Hazel said softly. "It's not some magical connection. It's work. It's feeding them, and changing them, and learning their quirks. It's late nights and early mornings, and bad dreams and encouraging speeches. It's day-in-and-day-out work for eighteen years, and then remembering it all and replaying it in your head for the next fifty or sixty. It's not magic."

"I know..."

"And you know who'd know your face anywhere?" she asked. "The mom who raised you. She'd pick you out of a crowd. She'd know the back of your head. She'd recognize you immediately even after ten years. You do have that, you know. It's just with the mother who put in that time with you."

"There's no magic to it..." He sighed.

"No," she said. "I'm sorry, but there isn't. There's hard work, and long days, and short years. That connection is earned."

"I feel a bit ridiculous," he said. "I had planned to be a little more mature and pulled together."

Hazel squeezed his hand. "Will you go back one of these days?"

"I don't know…" He sighed. "Maybe not. Menno didn't seem happy to see me. I'm not sure I'd be welcome."

"You could always send in someone else— Belinda, maybe? Someone to pave the way."

"I could." He sighed. "But I'm not sure it's a good idea. Belinda told me this story about a man who wanted to raise horses. He went around to everyone, asking for help with his goal. They gave what they had with really good intentions, wanting to help him out. But what he needed were some horses to start with, and that's the one thing he didn't get. What they gave provided for his family, gave him a way to feed them, but it didn't give him what he'd wanted…" He sighed again. "Sometimes it's better to be thankful for what you've got and stop pestering people about the horses, you know?"

Hazel frowned. "Did Belinda not want you to introduce yourself?"

"Not exactly. She just…feared I'd be disappointed, I suppose. She wanted me to be thankful for what I had."

Hazel nodded. Not terrible advice. But Joe had just met his biological mother, and she could tell that this wasn't going to just go away for him.

Joe looked at his watch. "I need to pick up my daughter."

"Of course," Hazel said.

Joe put the truck back into gear and pulled his hand free. Her fingers felt cold where his had been, and she closed her hand into a fist in her lap.

She wanted to comfort Joe, to somehow make this better. But she couldn't. And she'd be wise to remember that story about the horses, too. She had a job waiting for her and a daughter who needed her. Now was not the time to start longing for more.

THAT EVENING, Joe stood in the kitchen, listening to the soft ticking of the clock. Lottie had tired herself out at day care that day. In fact, Miss Pinch had even given Joe a report that Lottie had been so excited about her airplane ride that she'd been awake all naptime and chattered about it, keeping the other kids around her awake, too. That was considered bad behavior in day care, and Lottie had received a pink sticky note, describing her infraction.

"She was telling the kids that her mother left her, and she wants to find her," Miss Pinch had said quietly. "She was telling a very animated story about how she wanted to fly close to the ground to see her mother, but instead she'd gone on top of the clouds. I sense…she's working through some things."

That was an understatement. He'd thanked Miss Pinch for letting him know, and they'd headed home. Lottie hated getting pink sticky notes. She writhed with shame every time Miss Pinch handed one over, and Lottie got a lot of pink sticky notes. She was the kind of girl who just couldn't fall in line and hold the rope, or lie down and be quiet for naptime, or refrain from sharing her lunch crackers with the boy who had a gluten intolerance. But on their way home, they discussed the importance of following the rules all the same.

"Sometimes it upsets people to hear about your mom leaving," he said. "You can talk to me about it anytime at all, but sometimes, we have to be careful about who we tell our big stories to, kiddo."

But that wasn't the only paper he was given. The day care had made some handprint art that was being shown at the craft fair that week, and it struck him that Lottie had been trying to tell him about it in her own way. When he showed her the paper and asked her about the handprint art, Lottie got excited. She desperately wanted to go see her very own handprint on display.

Except, Rebecca's family was going to be at the craft show. Would it come off as weird if he saw them there? Would Menno think he'd been following them, causing trouble?

Whatever Menno thought, Joe had his own daughter's hopes to manage.

"We'll go tomorrow evening," he promised Lottie. "We'll find your handprint on display, okay? I can't wait."

After everything his daughter was dealing with, he couldn't put it off. And now, Lottie had fallen asleep early, utterly exhausted from her day, leaving Joe with his thoughts.

Joe hadn't expected seeing his biological mother to hit him quite this hard. He'd thought he had his expectations under control. And the worst part was that protective stance Rebecca's husband had taken with him…as if he'd planned to harm her, or upset her, or… He sighed.

"She's my mom," he said aloud.

She was, and she wasn't. She was the woman who'd given birth to him, but not the one who'd raised him. Maybe Hazel was right—he did have a mom who'd pick him out of a crowd or recognize the back of his head, and that connection was earned. She'd put in the time, the heart, the energy, the love. Would Jessica recognize Lottie? He doubted it. So why did he have this unexplainable hope that Rebecca would sense something in him?

His phone rang, and he looked down to see that it was his dad's cell number. He picked up the call.

"Hi, Dad."

"Hi, son, how are you doing? Is my grand-daughter in bed already?"

"Afraid so. She's tuckered out."

"Must have been a good day." Joe could hear the smile in his father's voice. "But I'm glad she's asleep. I wanted to talk to you."

"Yeah? What's going on?"

"That's what I wanted to find out," his father said. "How's it going over there? Your mom said you were thinking of finding Rebecca. I just wanted to see how you're doing with all that. It's pretty heavy, and I…I guess I was worried about you."

"I'm fine," Joe said. He wasn't even sure where to start.

"I know you are," his father replied quietly. "You're a good, strong man. You'll always be fine in the end, but maybe just humor your old dad here and let me in on what you're thinking."

Joe exhaled a slow breath. He hadn't been planning to talk to his parents about it just yet, not while he still felt all tangled up. But his dad always had been the one to knock down his walls and get him to open up.

"I found Rebecca, actually. I saw her." The story tumbled out of him matter-of-factly, and briefer than he felt it should be. It had been a monumental event, and yet it seemed to spill out rather quickly. He'd seen her. She didn't recognize him. The end.

"But her husband knew your name," his father clarified when he was done talking.

"Yeah. And he made it pretty clear he didn't want me around."

"I'm going to be blunt here," his father said. "But what do you care what this man wants? He loves his wife, sure, but his wife has some history that doesn't include him."

"Maybe he doesn't like that."

"A man had better get used to it," he replied dryly. "Every woman had a life before she met her husband. She didn't pop into being because she got married. Me included, might I add. Your mom had gotten a degree in music theory and was ready to buy her first home on her own when I met her. Did I get to be all jealous because she'd dated other guys before me? Absolutely not. I got to be darn grateful that she picked me when she could have had any other."

"Well, maybe these two aren't quite as secure as you and Mom," he replied.

"Maybe not, but don't let that be your problem. This is your community now, right?"

"Yep. It is."

"Then you'll run into these people. You don't have to say anything to Rebecca ever if you don't want to, but you are their neighbor."

He had an image in his mind of Rebecca with her kids, her jam, her sprawling land…

"She got the life she wanted, Dad. I'd say it worked well for her."

"Everybody puts their best face forward, son. Everybody. We smile. We sometimes pretend that we're happier than we really are. We plaster over any heartache, and we give people what they want to see. It's human. Just because Rebecca smiles and loves her family doesn't mean there isn't a part of her heart that will always ache a little bit. Women, I've learned, smile through a lot of heartache. Your mom, when we were trying to have a baby, had so much hidden pain. But then she'd go out there and teach music lessons with a smile on her face, and she'd buy birthday gifts for her sister's kids, and she'd hide that hurt inside of her. I know how much a woman can plaster over. Just because she has a good life doesn't mean she won't want to meet you. And the fact that her husband knows about you means that you won't break up her marriage. You might have been a surprise, but you aren't a shock, if you know what I mean."

"You don't think I should give up?" Joe asked.

"I don't think you should let her husband chase you off," his father replied. "That's my thought. This is your biological mother, and she hasn't told you she doesn't want to talk to you. Someone else was speaking for her, presumably without her even knowing who you were. That's not fair. She deserves a chance to choose if she wants to talk to you, too."

"That's true..." he murmured.

He'd known that this would be complicated, but he'd have to be discreet about it, too. It might take more time. He might need to develop a keen interest in pot holders for a few months before he found the right moment to say something.

"Dad, I just want to tell you that no matter how well this goes with Rebecca, or how badly, which seems more likely right now, you and Mom will always be my parents. I'm not trying to replace you or—"

"I know, I know," his father said quietly. "We love you, too, son. Your mother and I both know that you are a good man with a big heart, and it is plenty big enough to hold all of us. I am confident of that."

They talked a little longer about Lottie and her plane flight, and her drama at day care. Joe's dad always made him feel a bit better about parenting. He just laughed and said, "That girl is a leader, not a follower. I wouldn't worry too much, Joe."

By the time he hung up, he felt a lot better. He stood there, his phone in his hand and his mind spinning forward. There was one person he really wanted to talk to. He dialed Hazel's number, and she picked up after a couple of rings.

"Hi, Joe." Her voice was warm, and he found himself smiling.

"Hi. I was wondering if you might like to go to a craft fair tomorrow evening."

"The one Rebecca mentioned?"

"Yeah." He paused. "The thing is, Lottie's day care has a display there this week, and she's just dying to see her handiwork hung up for all to see."

"Very exciting stuff," Hazel said, and he could sense her smile.

"This isn't about Rebecca. Not really."

"Okay."

"I mean, we might see her, but—" He sighed. "This is a big deal to Lottie. And I want to see it, too. So what do you think? Do you want to come along?"

"Sure." She didn't even hesitate. "It would be nice to see you again before I go back home to Pittsburgh."

Home. Right. Her time was very limited, too, and then she'd be two hundred and fifty miles due west. His heart sank just a little.

"When do you leave?" he asked.

"Day after tomorrow."

So soon… "Yeah, I want to see you, too."

And he meant it, deep down on a gut level, probably more earnestly than she even realized. Why was it that when he found a woman who slipped under his defenses like this, she was on her way out?

"So…you'll pick me up?" she asked.

"Yeah. Tomorrow around six, say?"

"Sounds good. I'll be ready."

And having her come along really did soothe

his nerves. Whatever Hazel was becoming to him, she was bypassing all the superficial layers and getting right to the core of him. When she went home again, he'd have to find a way to see her.

CHAPTER FIFTEEN

"SOMETIMES, PEOPLE WANDER away and they get lost," Lottie said as they walked into the main craft pavilion. The interior felt dim after the bright sunlight outside, and the hum of voices and the smell of fried hand pies, french fries and burgers filled the air. Joe tightened his grip on his daughter's hand.

Hazel walked on the other side of Lottie, and she looked over at Joe with a rueful smile. One of the things he loved about Hazel was her ability to see the humor in Lottie's antics. There was no judgment from Hazel.

"Sometimes, they don't hold the rope," Lottie went on, "and then they see something fun like a dog or a dandelion or something, and then the class goes on without them, and they get lost that way."

"That's why you have to hold the rope," Joe said seriously.

"Miss Pinch says I'm a runner, and she makes me hold her hand," Lottie replied.

Joe chuckled. "Miss Pinch is a wise woman. Lottie, you have to stay close. No wandering off, okay?"

"I don't wander off," Lottie said, sounding mildly offended. "Miss Pinch hasn't forgiven me from one time. One time, Daddy!"

Yeah, that one time had traumatized the entire day care. Lottie had wandered off and it took an hour, the police department and five years off the end of Joe's life to locate her.

"That sounds like a story," Hazel said.

"That story makes my daddy mad," Lottie said. "And then he gives me a long talking-to."

Joe rolled his eyes. Yeah, he did tend to give her the don't-ever-run-off-like-that-again speech every time she brought it up—mostly because she always sounded a little too satisfied with herself and retold the tale with the nostalgic passion of a high-school football star.

"But I think that my mommy might have done that, Daddy," Lottie said, tugging at his hand. "Grown-ups don't have ropes to hold. That's the problem."

Oh, grown-ups did have tethers that kept them right there next to their kids. They had heartstrings and promises. He looked over at Hazel, and tears suddenly misted her eyes.

Yeah, he felt like that a lot lately with his daughter. She was yearning for something he couldn't provide. She wanted her mother, and Jessica wasn't coming back.

"I don't need a rope," Joe said, forcing a smile. "I have you!"

"I'm not a rope!" Lottie laughed.

"Yes, you are. Look at you!" He squeezed down her arm, and she wriggled and squealed at the tickle. The logic never mattered, but distracting her from questions she wasn't ready to hear the answers to was important. How was he supposed to tell her that her mother wasn't lost but had simply left? But when Jessica had let Joe take his daughter, she'd given him the greatest gift possible— the opportunity to be the dad who raised Lottie. She could have had the baby and given her up to someone across the country. She could have kept Lottie herself and never told Joe a thing. But she didn't—she'd made the agonizing choice to give Lottie to him, and in that heartbreaking decision, Jessica had given Joe his world. Try and explain that emotional tangle to a four-year-old who wanted nothing more than to find her mom.

"Do you have a mommy, Hazel?" Lottie

asked. She slipped her hand out of Joe's grasp and skipped along between them.

"I do have a mom," Hazel said.

"And a daddy?" Lottie asked.

"And a dad, too. Yes." Hazel looked up, scanning the pavilion. "I wonder where your handprints are, Lottie."

Good. Hazel was going to help him distract Lottie. Joe looked down at the map. "Past the petting zoo and just to the left of the mini doughnuts."

"Oh, yeah!" Lottie said. "Let's find my handprints!"

Joe caught Lottie's hand, and she held on to him for a couple of minutes, and then she tugged free again. On his other side, he caught Hazel's hand, too. This felt good—almost like a family, he realized. Hazel leaned into his arm, and he memorized the feeling of her warmth against him. Hazel was comforting in a way he'd never found before in all his years of looking, and she was going to ruin him for anyone else.

They ambled down a wide aisle. There were booths on either side with crafting supplies, small businesses that sold their own handiwork. Lottie was drawn to a build-your-own-teddy-bear booth, but it was expensive, and he had to call her away from it.

"But I want a bear," Lottie said hopefully.

"Lottie, you can't have everything," he said. "I'll get you some mini doughnuts. How about that?"

"Can I have a bear instead of doughnuts?" she asked.

"No."

"Okay, I'll have doughnuts."

Hazel laughed softly. "I love watching her do that cost-benefit analysis in her head. She's a shrewd one."

"I'm a shrew," Lottie said.

"No, you're shrewd," Hazel said. "Different thing. One is a little furry mouselike animal, and the other one means you're very smart."

"Am I smart?" Lottie asked, and he could see her almost holding her breath.

"Very," Hazel said.

Lottie walked a little way ahead of them, her shoulders back. That one honest compliment from Hazel seemed to have built the girl up. Did Hazel know how powerful her words were?

"Are you sure you can't put off your shiny new job for another week?" he asked. He was halfway joking, but there was a small part of him that wished she could do just that.

"I don't dare," she said quietly. "There's competition for the position."

"Yeah…" He squeezed her hand. "I'm going to miss you." She was silent, and he looked down at her. "I mean it. I know it might be crazy and fast, but…I'm really going to miss you."

"It's too late for us to start this over and spend less time together, isn't it?" she said sadly.

"Do you want to?" he asked.

She shook her head. "That's the problem. I wasn't supposed to have a vacation fling. I'm not that kind of woman."

"This isn't a fling," he said.

"Then what is it?" she asked.

"It's ill-timed, and maybe it's star-crossed, but it's real." And he meant it. What he was feeling was far from a crush, far from a fling. What he was feeling was strong enough to rock him if he let it, and he was just barely in control of it as it was. But when he wanted someone by his side for moral support, it was this beautiful pilot he hardly knew. And he wasn't normally like that.

"I'll miss you, too," she said, and he thought he heard a catch in her voice.

Lottie trotted ahead and suddenly beelined over to another craft table that had a colorful quilt done up in rainbow colors on display. This one was being manned by an Amish family, and it was only when Lottie leaned up against the table that the woman turned, and he recognized Rebecca.

"Is that a special blanket?" Lottie asked.

"*Yah*, it's called a quilt. Do you like it?" Rebecca asked.

"I like the colors. It's pretty."

"Thank you. I made it myself."

"All by yourself?" Lottie sounded amazed, and when Joe and Hazel reached her, Rebecca was looking at Lottie with a peculiar expression on her face.

"Is this your daughter?" Rebecca asked, looking up. She smiled. "You're the young couple from yesterday."

"Yes, this is my daughter," Joe said.

"She's the spitting image of my oldest granddaughter," Rebecca said. "If you put her in a cape dress, she could be her twin."

"Really?" Joe's pulse sped up. DNA could be that way—cousins looking like siblings.

"Maybe it's my imagination," she murmured.

Hazel gave his hand a squeeze, and he looked down at her. She smiled faintly, then tugged her hand out of his grasp and moved down the table. She picked up the corner of the rainbow-colored quilt. She was giving him some time.

"Can I get you anything today?" Rebecca asked. "These dolls are very popular. Our little girls play with them."

Rebecca gestured to a basket filled with little cloth dolls with blank faces. They wore dresses in the same colors as Rebecca and her daughter, and each had a little black bonnet.

"We're here to see my handprint art!" Lottie said. "My day care is famous now. We have art on the wall."

Rebecca chuckled. "That's wonderful."

"Will my mommy see it, maybe?" Lottie asked, looking up at Joe. "Maybe? Just maybe?"

Motherhood wasn't magic—wasn't that what Hazel had told him? But his daughter was hoping for a little magic.

"Maybe I can spot it," he said. "Let me see your hand…"

He made a big show of inspecting her palm. "Yep…I might be able to spot it. We'll see."

Lottie started to giggle again because of his

mock earnestness, and as he met his daughter's sparkling gaze, his heart gave a tumble. What he wouldn't do for this kid…

The Amish girl who'd served them at the farm came up next to Rebecca and said something softly in Pennsylvania Dutch.

"She says your daughter looks like Suzannah, my granddaughter," Rebecca said. "I'm not the only one who thinks it."

"*Yah*, she does," the girl said shyly.

"Do you have Amish in your family?" Rebecca asked, fixing Joe with a curious look.

"Uh—" He swallowed. "Yeah, there's some."

"That would do it," Rebecca said. "We have a lot of family connections, and you can get a certain look that's very common. Who are you related to? What family?"

Did he want to do this right now? He swallowed. "I, uh…I've been told we have Lehmanns."

She didn't look phased by that. "Oh, *yah*. We have literally thousands of Lehmanns in this area alone. I know of two different couples who married, and both had the last name Lehmann, but they came from different family lines, so they weren't related to each other… Not close enough to matter, at least.

So it's very common. There's the Lehmanns with two *n*'s, and the Lehmans with one. And then there's the Lehmans who came from Switzerland, and the Lehmanns from Germany. And we've even got a Lehmann branch that came from the Russian Mennonites and converted a hundred years ago. So we've got lots of Amish Lehmanns, and then there's lots of *Englisher* Lehmanns. Are you a Lehmann, too, by any chance?"

"No—" He shook his head. "I didn't realize there were so many."

"Oh, *yah*. We're everywhere." She smiled. "Now, my husband's family is more direct. The Weitzes are all pretty much the same family."

Joe picked up a doll wearing a pink dress. It was about the size of some of Lottie's other dolls, and he wondered if he bought one if she'd play with it. Maybe she would, and when all of this shook out, he could tell her that her grandmother had made it.

Or was he jumping too far ahead there?

"I make those myself," Rebecca said.

"I'll take one," he said. "I bet Lottie would like it. Wouldn't you—"

He turned and looked to where his daughter had been standing, but she was gone. He blinked, and his heart hammered to a stop. He looked around, taking a full circle. Normally, he spotted her pretty quickly, but this time, he didn't.

"Lottie?" he said.

Hazel looked up then, too, and she also spun in a quick circle.

"Lottie?" He raised his voice, more command in his tone now. If she was within hearing distance, he wanted her to jump and get back over here. But there was nothing.

The murmur of the people passing through the pavilion suddenly felt overwhelmingly loud, and he scrubbed a hand through his hair.

She was a runner, alright. For crying out loud. Why hadn't he kept a better eye on her?

"If she comes back here, can you put a hand on her and keep her here?" Joe asked Rebecca.

"*Yah*, of course!"

"Hazel, I'm going toward the art display. Maybe she was trying to find it. You go that way, toward the food. We meet back here."

Hazel nodded, her face pale, but he could see the mom in her gathering her focus. Without another word, Joe headed off toward the art display. When he found his daughter, she was going to get the lecture of a lifetime!

HAZEL WOVE THROUGH some booths, poking her head into each one as she passed. Maddie had done this a couple of times when she was a preschooler, and Hazel had learned that little kids liked to go look at things they normally weren't allowed to touch when they had some moments of stolen freedom. She could only hope that was what had happened, because the other possibilities closed off her throat.

She sucked in a deep breath and scanned the crowd. People milled around, women pushing strollers, men carrying tired toddlers on their shoulders. It was mostly young families and older people. One older couple had a stroller, too, but an elderly poodle with milky eyes was inside.

Hazel looked down one aisle, glancing into booths and hurrying on past. How far could one little girl have gotten?

And then she spotted a pink striped shirt and blond curls, and relief flooded through her. Lottie stood in a booth that seemed to be selling card-crafting material, and a woman in a security uniform squatted down in front of her.

"Are you alone?" the security guard asked.

Lottie hiccupped but didn't answer.

"Where is your mommy?" the security guard said.

"I don't know!" Lottie wailed, and Hazel's heart nearly broke in two.

Where was her mommy, indeed? That was the question weighing on that little heart, and no one had an answer for her. No one could tell her the truth that was too big and heavy for a tiny girl to bear.

"Lottie!" Hazel said, and Lottie whirled around. Her eyes widened, and her mouth turned into a square as she started to sob a different kind of cry and ran full speed into Hazel's legs. She wrapped her arms around Hazel's thighs and wept into her jeans.

"Come here," Hazel said, bending down and catching her under her arms. She lifted her up and held her close as Lottie wrapped her legs around Hazel's waist.

"Thank you!" Hazel said to the security guard, and the woman smiled and nodded.

Hazel looked like Lottie's mom—she knew it. Anyone seeing her would think that, and she realized in a rush that she wished she could be Lottie's answer, her comfort, her distraction from bigger things. She wished she could go back in time and be the young mom again with boundless energy and an entire future ahead of her. But she wasn't that young mom anymore. She was a mom who'd done all of this already and who finally had her chance at the next stage.

Time had marched on...and Lottie needed a mom fully devoted to her, just like Maddie had gotten. She needed a mom she could count on, one to help her stop looking for the mom who hadn't kept her. Lottie and Joe both needed that, and she felt a wave of sadness that it couldn't be her.

"Let's find your dad, okay?" Hazel said into Lottie's hair. "He's worried sick, sweetie."

She fished her phone out of her pocket and sent an awkwardly typed text to Joe: I found her. Then she tucked her phone back into her pocket and carried Lottie back in the direction from which she'd come. Lottie wouldn't have let Hazel put her down if she'd tried.

"I just wanted to see the handprints!" Lottie wailed into Hazel's ear. "I wanted to see them, and I couldn't find them, and my daddy was gone, and I couldn't find the handprints!"

"I know, I know," Hazel murmured. "But we found you now, and it'll be okay."

Lottie's wails started to subside, and when Hazel turned the corner, she saw Joe standing there, his phone in his hand and a look of relief on his face—he seemed to have gotten her text.

"There he is," Hazel said, and she bent to put Lottie down, but Lottie didn't let go. She straightened, then tried again, and Lottie reluctantly unwound her legs and arms from around Hazel. When she turned and saw Joe, she ran for her father.

Joe bent down and scooped her up into his arms. Hazel took her time walking up, letting him give his daughter a big hug.

"Okay, we need to talk, young lady," Joe said, and went over to a bench. He sat Lottie down and squatted in front of her. "When we are out, you do not just take off like that. I don't care what you wanted to do or what you wanted to look at. You stay right by my side and pretend you're tied to me with a very short string. Do you have any idea how dangerous it is to just wander off?"

This was a lecture Hazel knew by heart; she'd given it often enough to Maddie at the same age. She stood back, giving Joe some parenting privacy. These times between a parent and a child built their relationship. There really was no magic in being a parent. They messed things up as often as they got it right, but enough love seemed to smooth it over. And all these times of panic, fear, relief, learning, growing and figuring things out together were the threads that wrapped around them again and again and again, until it was like a rope.

The very rope Lottie didn't hold on to very well. Good thing her dad did!

These parenting moments when strangers gave the side-eye and judged a child's behavior were the very moments that mattered most. How many times had Hazel been in the exact same position? A perfectly behaved child made the parent look good. But a little runaway rascal? That was the kind of life experience that taught a girl just how much she was loved. That was formative.

Hazel looked down at her phone. She'd missed a text from Maddie, and she felt a yearning for her own daughter. When Maddie got back to American soil, she was getting a big hug. Hazel opened the text.

Hi, Mom. I did something big.

Hazel blinked. Uh-oh. Maddie was a patient, thoughtful young woman, but when she decided to let loose…

She typed, What's going on? How big? Should I be worried?

There'd better not be a new European fiancé or something!

No worries, Maddie typed. Dad and his family took me out for dinner. Adel was being insufferable. Dad was letting it go. So I told him off.

Right there in the restaurant? Hazel could just see it—Todd and his prim and svelte wife being told off by the American daughter who'd had enough. Todd had always been there for Maddie financially, but the day-in-day-out stuff was where a relationship was built. He'd missed out on the most important part of it.

What did you say? Hazel asked.

I told him to quit blaming me for being his firstborn, and that if he and Adel have such a shaky marriage that I'm a threat for just existing, they should get some marriage counseling and leave me alone. Oh, and I told him that Adel doesn't want him to help pay for my college education, so they could start there.

Hazel laughed out loud. Nicely done!

Thanks. Adel is furious. Dad said I was rude. The waiter gave me a piece of cake and told me it was on the house. I told Dad to call you. I'm leaving for my castle tour first thing in the morning.

And that was how a Dobbs girl took care of business! Hazel hadn't felt this proud in a very long time. Good for her. Maddie had said what she needed to say. And it would mean more coming from Maddie herself, instead of from Hazel in the background.

Have a wonderful time, Hazel texted back. Good for you. You have my full support. If he calls me, I have a few things to say to him, too.

Just beyond Joe and Lottie's earnest discussion on the bench, Hazel spotted the handprint artwork hanging on the wall. They'd found it, after all. It was a large canvas with children's handprints making a colorful display in primary colors. At the bottom, she saw the painted words *Miss Pinch's Day Care, Danke, Pennsylvania*, and the year.

Hazel's phone rang, and she saw Todd's number from England. Great. So he was calling already.

"Hi, Todd," she said cheerily.

"Hazel." That acquired English accent sounded ridiculous on him. "Madison is upset, and I was hoping you could talk to her. She's not getting along with Adel, and I wish she'd try harder. This hasn't been an easy visit for any of us, and Adel has taken it hardest of all."

Yeah, that wasn't the approach to take. Poor, poor Adel. Adel knew Todd had a daughter when she married him. Maddie was not going to be erased or shoved aside.

"I have spoken with Maddie," Hazel said. "And from what I understand, you didn't get your family ready to meet our daughter. Your kids don't know how to deal with it—and that's not their fault. They're kids. They need help with that. As for Adel, that's your marriage, and if you haven't made your wife feel secure in your love for her, then that's on you. Don't you dare blame Madison for your failure to get your family ready to meet your oldest child!"

There was silence on the other end. She'd probably gone too far, but Hazel knew exactly who to blame here. And while it might be easier to blame Adel for being spoiled and high-handed, Adel wasn't the main problem.

Todd needed to fix this. He still hadn't said anything.

"Anything else?" Hazel asked curtly.

"No, that's it," Todd replied, his tone equally terse.

But fighting with Todd wasn't the answer, either. Whether they liked it or not, they were Maddie's parents. They'd brought her into this world, after all.

"Todd, I don't mean to fight with you," she said, softening her tone. "I know this is complicated. I do. None of it is easy. But the years are flying by, and you don't want to leave this as your daughter's last memory of her visit with you. She'll hold a grudge, and you'll regret it. You've worked too hard to keep a relationship with her over the years to waste it like that. I know Maddie. She's got a huge heart, and you've got until tomorrow morning before she leaves on her tour."

"Should I go talk to her?" he asked uncertainly. "I don't really know her like you do—"

"Yes, you fool, go talk to your daughter!" Hazel said, and she couldn't help but laugh. "Talk to her. Tell her you love her. Tell her you're terrible at this, but you want to do better. Tell her you're proud of her, and that your love for her isn't based on your family. She

needs to hear all of it. You're still her dad,
Todd. Act like it."

"Yeah. Okay."

"And I say that with the best of intentions.
You've done well by Madison, Todd. You really have."

"Thanks, Hazel."

"I mean, this trip, you might have mucked
it up, but…"

"Yeah, yeah…" But there was a smile in his
voice. "I'll go find her."

"I'm glad. Good luck."

As Hazel hung up the phone, she looked up
to see that Joe had just noticed the handprint
art on the wall, too. The lecture was over,
and Joe and Lottie were standing there, hand
in hand, their heads cocked at the very same
angle as they looked up at the wall. It was
just like the hangar, father and daughter experiencing it all together. They were alike—
the same stance, the same fire and energy…

Hazel didn't want to interrupt this, either.

"Do you know what handprint is mine?"
Lottie asked.

There was no way to tell. There were no
names—just colorful fingers and palms. What
would he say?

"Oh, yeah, I can see yours." Joe pointed. "That one. And that one, there. And that one."

"Really?" Lottie looked impressed. "Those are mine?"

"Yeah. I can tell."

"How?" The logic was coming out in this kid. She looked down at her own hand, her fingers splayed.

"I'd know your handprints anywhere," Joe said. "I'm your dad. I look with my heart."

Lottie smiled at that, beaming up at her father adoringly, and tears rose in Hazel's eyes. Yep, that was how parenting worked—there wasn't any magic but a heart full of love and a whole lot of invested time. Joe turned then, and saw Hazel.

"Everything okay?" he asked. She blinked and pulled a hand through her hair.

"Yep, it's fine. I see you found the special piece of art."

She joined Joe, and he caught her hand in his warm grip, tugging her in next to him.

"Found it," he said. "Isn't it great?"

And then all three of them stood there in a line, looking up at the colorful handprints. Why was she imagining more days like this, more time spent with the two of them, more prizes like a canvas of children's fingerprints on a pavilion wall?

She blinked back that mist of tears that kept threatening. Because she wanted that—and she wanted her flying career, too. She wanted dinner out with her grown daughter, and regional flights, and an Airbus cockpit. But she also wanted Joe—his warm hand, his strong arm, his tender heart and his sweet little girl, who reminded her of those long days and short years of being a young mom. And suddenly, a thought struck her that squeezed the breath out of her lungs.

She'd fallen for him, hadn't she?

Oh, shoot. She'd fallen for both of them!

CHAPTER SIXTEEN

IN DANKE, there were several popular restaurants—a few Amish places and then the regular pizza places and burger joints. Restaurants serving traditional Amish food had parking lots filled with cars and pickup trucks. The pizza joint had more buggies there than automobiles. The reason was simple—Amish people didn't need to eat out to get traditional Amish food. But pizza and burgers? That was worth a restaurant trip.

Joe pulled into the pizza place and parked about a yard from a horse and buggy.

"Can I pet him, Daddy?" Lottie pleaded as he undid her seat belt and wriggled out.

"Nope," he said. "Same rules as the donkey."

"He'd bite my hand off?" Lottie asked solemnly.

"Yes. Maybe not your whole hand, but you need all ten fingers for later, too."

Hazel chuckled, and he shot her a grin. He

liked having her laugh at his dad jokes. Getting a laugh from Lottie felt like a win, but getting one from Hazel touched a different part of his heart. It felt the way holding her hand felt—like shared warmth.

He led the way inside the busy restaurant. There was a free table at the back, and the hostess led them over to it and gave them glasses of water to start.

"We're pretty busy. If you know what you want to order, I can get it started now," the waitress said.

"Do you like pepperoni?" Joe asked.

Hazel nodded. "My favorite."

"Good. Ours, too. We'll have a pepperoni pizza, please."

"What size?" the waitress asked. "Small, medium, or family-sized?"

He looked over at Hazel, and suddenly it was like the whole room dimmed, and it was only her. He'd always ordered medium when it was just him and Lottie. It was enough pizza for the meal and some leftovers. Lottie loved leftover pizza.

"Family-sized," he said. Not because they needed that much pizza, but because it felt right in another way.

"Great!" The waitress smiled, and she hurried away.

Coloring pages kept Lottie busy.

"You seemed a bit upset earlier, on the phone," he said. "I don't mean to pry, and if it really isn't my business—"

"It was Todd," she said. "Maddie's dad."

"Oh…" He hated that he felt a protective urge toward her at the mention of her ex. Todd wasn't his business, but he was starting to feel like her feelings might be. "Is everything okay?"

"Maddie told him off." A smile sparkled in her eyes. "Quite eloquently, actually. His family has been giving her a really hard time, and you know, I don't even blame them."

He was letting his family pick on his daughter, though, and that didn't sit right with him.

"I might," he said.

"Well…I think the onus was on Todd to prepare them to meet her. His kids are young teens—they're not going to navigate that well on their own—and his wife was obviously feeling threatened."

"By you?" he asked.

"Why me?" she asked with a smile. "Am I kind of scary or something?"

"Because you're gorgeous, and smart, and

successful. I could see her being intimidated," he replied.

"Sweet as that is, no. I think she's more intimidated by the fact that he had another child."

She talked on about the dynamic—he'd heard it before, but she seemed to need to talk it out. None of these relationships were easy.

Joe couldn't help but think of Rebecca. Would she be able to tell her children that she'd had a baby in her youth? Would she be willing to wade into those messy, truthful, hard discussions? Would they even have a chance to blend?

Some families were blended because the parents of a child split up. But what did it look like when the child had been given up? Jessica would very likely never be in the picture again—he didn't expect there would be any blending whatsoever with Lottie's mom. Why was he expecting more from Rebecca and her family?

"What are you thinking?" Hazel asked.

He smiled faintly. "Things not meant for small ears."

She nodded. She'd understand that all too well. It was tough being a parent. When he wished he could talk and get some emotional support, he couldn't do it. Being a dad meant bearing it alone lest his daughter learn too much too quickly.

Soon enough the pizza arrived, and they turned their attention to eating. When the meal was done, he paid the bill and they headed back out to the truck.

"Do you want to take a drive?" Joe asked Hazel after he'd buckled his daughter in. He wasn't ready to drop off Hazel yet and say goodbye, and he wasn't sure he'd have another excuse to see her, either.

"Sure."

Besides, a busy day, a full tummy and a drive in the truck was just the trick to get Lottie to fall asleep, and that felt like his best chance at getting Hazel alone. Or as alone as they could get.

As he pulled out of the parking lot, another buggy turned in, and he nodded to the driver—a middle-aged woman with several other women in the buggy with her. It looked like an Amish girls' night out. He started down the road about five miles an hour under the speed limit, and he noticed when Hazel's shoulders relaxed and she leaned back into the seat.

In the back seat, Lottie was making airplane sounds and flying her metal airplane around. He looked at her in the rearview mirror and smiled. Who would he be without his daughter? He'd be freer, probably have more money in the bank, but he wouldn't be half the man he'd grown into. Lottie had changed him in a thousand ways for the better.

Hazel looked down at her phone, then she chuckled.

"Maddie just said she talked to her dad, and he apologized. There's something about him sending her money for a car when she gets home."

"Good," Joe said. "I'm glad he's coming to his senses."

"Me, too."

They fell into silence, and he turned onto another gravel road, driving up past some Amish homes and picturesque barns. Cattle stepped through lush grass, grazing contentedly as the sun bathed them in long, golden rays.

"I never get tired of this area," he said quietly.

"It is beautiful," she agreed.

"Makes me wonder if this life is in my blood somehow," he said.

"It might be."

He reached over and took her hand. Then he

remembered his daughter was in the back seat, and he glanced in the mirror at her. Her head was tipped to the side, and she was asleep. At last…

"Do you ever think about a slower pace?" he asked, easing up on the gas even further as he drank in the view. "Taking some time off, maybe? Sticking closer to home?"

"I did that already," she said softly. "When Maddie was growing up."

"I know, but…you were a single mom then," he said. "What if you had a guy who'd make things easier for you?"

He looked over at her, a quick, uncertain glance. Her face had grown pink, and she caught his eye.

"What are you asking?" she asked.

"I don't know…" And he honestly didn't! He hadn't thought any of this through, but the idea of her just leaving felt incredibly wrong, too. "I guess I really like having you around, and I'm trying to find a way to do more of this."

She was silent, but her grip tightened on his hand, so he knew he hadn't offended her.

"I mean, look at this place," he said. They'd just slowly crested a hill, and Amish country tumbled out below them—winding roads, cattle dotting the pastureland and a single black buggy working its way up the hill toward them.

"It's paradise," she said quietly.

"I know," he said. "Life is slower here. And… Look, you know I'm a package deal. I'm a dad—nothing changes that. But I really think we have something special. It's nothing I've felt before, at least."

"It is definitely special," she said, and her voice suddenly sounded thick.

"I'm talking before I've thought anything through," he said, "but I don't think I have much time here to figure it all out before you go. The thing is, I think you're amazing, and there's a connection here that sprang up really fast. And you've pretty much ruined me for Michelle's mom."

Hazel laughed softly. "I owe her an apology."

"You don't need to," he said. "Just…tell me this isn't over."

"You'll change your mind about that," Hazel said. "You'll realize that I'm not the kind of woman you need once you get some space to think."

"I have nothing but space to think," he retorted. "Do you see all these wide, open spaces? It's just me and my thoughts, and this feeling inside of me that if I let you go, I'll regret it for the rest of my life."

He pulled to a stop at the side of the road, and the horse and buggy rattled past them. He looked into the back seat once more at his sleeping daughter, then turned to Hazel.

"Are you feeling any of this?" he whispered.

She nodded. "I am, but—"

There it was, the *but*... He wasn't ready to hear it yet, and he wasn't quite sure how to put it off, so he leaned over, slipped a hand behind her neck and tugged her closer until his lips hovered next to hers.

"Hold that thought," he murmured, and he leaned into a kiss.

HAZEL SUCKED IN a breath of surprise as Joe's lips covered hers...but maybe she shouldn't be surprised, she realized in a thought rattling just outside the soft glow of that kiss. She'd been wanting this for some time, too... There were reasons not to do this...weren't there? Except right now with his strong fingers tucked behind her neck and the faint tickle of his stubble against her face, she couldn't remember why.

He pulled back, and she kept her eyes shut for a moment longer.

"I wanted to do that," he breathed.

"Me, too…"

She opened her eyes, and his dark, warm gaze moved over her face. His hand moved down her shoulder and arm, settling on her wrist in a tender, protective grip.

"I'm just going to be a hundred percent honest here," he murmured. "I don't think I'll ever meet someone quite like you again."

"I honestly hope you don't." She smiled faintly. "That's selfish of me, I know."

"Are you really okay just walking away?" he whispered.

Was she? Could she hop into a cab and head back to her life and just put this man behind her? Or would she be thinking about him day and night, wondering what he was thinking, or how Lottie was doing, or…wondering if he was thinking about her…

"No," she admitted. "I'll be thinking about you. Constantly."

"You opened my eyes to what I want," he said.

"That's not true." She put her hand up against his chest. His heartbeat pattered against her fingertips. "Partly true, but not the whole picture. You still know what you need—a stay-at-home wife and mother for Lottie. A woman who will be there, putting in those long hours and making the three of you a family. Maybe you'll want more kids. But me? I've got an adult daughter and a career I've worked fifteen years to build. We fell for each other, but it wasn't smart!"

"We might have to agree to disagree, there," he said with a rueful smile. "Falling in love with a woman is never an actual choice."

She froze, her breath caught in her chest. "What?"

Color touched his cheeks. "I said that out loud, did I?"

"You did…"

"How else do you explain it?" he asked, searching her face. "I think about you all the time, I try to find excuses to spend time with you. When something massive happens in my life, I'm not looking for my parents or close friends to talk about it, I'm looking for you. You tell me about your ex, and all I can think is that I want to be the guy who does better by you—who makes him look like a distant bad choice by comparison."

"Joe, you already outshine him."

"Good. I want to. And it's the truth. Maybe

it's fast, and not too wise of me, but I'm..."
He smiled hesitantly. "I'm in love with you."

It explained a lot of what she was feeling, too, and his words sank under all the logical reasoning she'd been mentally collecting. He loved her... When was the last time she'd heard a man say that? And when was the last time her heart had yearned back in response.

"I love you, too," she said softly. It was both crazy and true.

Joe leaned in, and this time, she closed the distance between them. She kissed him with all the pent-up longing inside of her that she'd been afraid to admit she had. But he was right—they'd fallen for each other. She pulled back first, and he reached up and touched her cheek tenderly.

"That's a good thing," he whispered.

Lottie was snoring softly, and they both looked over at her. Her cheeks were flushed, and her toy plane was lying in her lap. She'd had a long day, gotten lost, questioned everything about her mother and now had fallen asleep in the safety of her father's truck.

"But I'm not what you need," Hazel murmured. It hurt to say it, and her voice shook a little. She wished it hadn't—that she could sound confident in this.

"You could be," he said.

"I'm a career pilot, Joe…" She turned back to face him.

"What if you did sightseeing tours around here?" he asked. "You could build up your own business. People love those scenic flights, and you're amazing up there."

"I told you before that flying a Cessna and an Airbus are as different as a bike and a semitruck," she said sadly. "It's like taking all of your skills and giving you a flower pot. You might grow a gorgeous flower, but you'd always know you were capable of an entire garden, an entire yard… I've worked for the Airbus. I've worked so hard, and every hard day where everything was going wrong, and my daughter was tired and cranky, and I felt bored and boring, I would stand by the window, look up at the clouds and think, 'It'll be okay. My turn is coming.'" She swallowed against a lump in her throat.

"And your turn is here," he said.

She nodded. "I can't just let it slip through my fingers. The competition to get that job was fierce, and if I put it off, I might never get a chance to work a regional airline again. And—" this was the part that would hurt him

"—I'm not sure I'd forgive myself for giving it up."

He nodded.

"Unless you could see a way to loving a regional pilot..." she added.

"Loving you? Easy." But his eyes stayed sad. "It's just that Lottie has been through a lot. She needs stability. She needs someone who stands by her and loves her and is there for all the daily parenting stuff that I miss because I'm working. I need her to stop looking for her birth mom like she's in a desert searching for water. She needs a mom at home with her. She *needs* it."

"I know..." Hazel had seen that hole in Lottie's heart, and it was the exact size and shape of a devoted mother. She needed a mom who'd put her first in her bad days and her good days. She needed someone to love her as ferociously as her dad did. Lottie needed a reason to stop her search.

"You have to put her first," Hazel breathed. "That's what dads do."

"Yeah."

She met his gaze, and she felt tears rising inside of her. This was what she'd been trying to avoid.

"For what it's worth, I'll miss you like crazy," she whispered around a tight throat.

"Me, too." His chin quivered.

"Do you think we could be friends?" she asked.

He shook his head. "Not feeling the way I do. I'm in too deep for that."

And so was she, but she was mentally scrambling for a way to put off this goodbye. Joe put the truck into gear and they pulled forward, back onto the gravel road. They didn't say anything—the only sound in the vehicle was that of the soft snores from Lottie in the back seat. He reached over and grabbed Hazel's hand. She twined her fingers with his, her chest feeling heavy.

The drive back to Butternut Bed and Breakfast was a short one on the back roads. And when Joe pulled into the drive, Hazel looked down at their hands. If only this didn't have to end, but it did. It was the right thing to do.

From the back seat, the snoring stopped, and Lottie said blearily, "Daddy? Are we home?"

"Not yet, Lottie," he said, and he met Hazel's gaze.

There was nothing more to say, and rehashing it would only confuse a sweet little girl.

"Thank you," she said, tears in her voice. And she meant it as a thank-you for everything—for the time he'd spent with her, for trusting her with his little girl's hopes and dreams, and for loving her even when it made no sense.

But she couldn't explain, so she released his hand and hopped out of the truck.

A vacation fling didn't even begin to cover what they'd experienced, and she'd need to be alone to sort it all out in her head. She walked briskly to the side door, and when she turned, Joe was looking at her, his gaze full of sad longing. Then he looked away, and the truck went into Reverse.

As Hazel opened the side door, she was met with the sound of a chicken's clucks. She went through the mudroom and into the kitchen, where Belinda was standing with her arms crossed, looking down at a hen in a wire cage sitting on a towel in the middle of her table.

"Hello, dear," Belinda said, looking up. "Did you have a nice time?"

"Yeah." She couldn't exactly explain what had happened, nor did she want to.

"I've got to bring Eli his hen back," she said. "There was a coyote circling outside, and if anything happened to his hen, it would break that man's heart."

"So you brought her in," Hazel said with a misty smile.

"*Yah*. I did…" Belinda shook her head. "And what's more shocking still, when I bring this hen over to him, I'm going to bring back his mending, and I'm going to do it for him."

"That's shocking?" Hazel asked.

"It is for me. I've been making him sew up his own torn shirts," Belinda said.

"What's changed?" Hazel asked.

Belinda blinked a couple of times, sucked in a breath, then shrugged. "I don't know. I suppose I noticed something. That man has been doing more for me all these years than a neighbor rightfully needs to do. And I've taken it for granted. And…" Belinda looked up at Hazel with a bewildered look on her face. "I'll deny this if you breathe a word to anyone in this community, but…I want to do his mending for him."

Hazel smiled in spite of herself. "I'm sure he'll appreciate it."

"I'm sure he'll gloat," Belinda muttered. "But it is what it is."

She picked up the mesh cage and nodded toward the door. "Would you mind opening that for me?"

Hazel did as she asked, and Belinda carried the cage outside, then navigated carefully down the steps. Watching the old woman walk across the scrub grass, she felt her own resilience start to waver.

If only everything was as simple as a man with chickens and an old lady who fought her affection for him…

She went up the stairs and into her room. She shut the door, locked it, then lay down on the bed. It smelled faintly of violets, and for a moment or two, she just lay there. She'd admitted that she loved Joe tonight, and she'd walked away…

That was when the tears started. Hearts were never simple, were they?

CHAPTER SEVENTEEN

JOE WAS LYING in his bed that night, listening to the sound of the fridge humming from the kitchen. He hadn't even gotten Lottie into her pajamas. He'd just carried her into her room and laid her in her bed. Lottie would be annoyed the next morning to wake up in her regular clothes, but he hadn't had the emotional energy to wake her.

His heart felt sodden and heavy, and as he watched the shadows on the wall, he thought about Hazel, and he knew beyond a doubt that he'd never feel this again. Maybe he'd find a good woman whom he cared for, but he'd know what this kind of connection felt like. Hazel was special…and out of reach. But still, she was a once-in-a-lifetime kind of woman.

He slept fitfully that night. It was hot, and he couldn't get a breeze in through his window. He woke up early and got Lottie's breakfast onto the table—a bowl of instant oatmeal and a piece of buttered toast—and then went to wake her up.

"Rise and shine, sleepyhead," he said, and Lottie opened her eyes and squinted at him.

"I'm tired, Daddy."

"You have day care," he said.

"Can we stay home?"

"Not today, kiddo," he said. "I have to visit somebody."

"Who?"

"A lady named Rebecca."

"Oh… Okay." Lottie had already lost interest, and she got up, tugging at her pink striped shirt irritably.

"Here, let's choose some new clothes, and then we'll go wash your face…"

And so would begin another day, except this one was starting with a little less caution. He'd already had his heart broken, and he could tiptoe around Rebecca and her family, building up the courage to introduce himself, or he could just go talk to her.

She'd either be willing to talk, or she wouldn't be.

And then he could move forward. Joe didn't have any extra energy for waiting around. Sometimes a man just had to face the stuff that hurt.

WHEN HE PULLED into Lehmann's Family Fun Farm, he noted it was busier today than before. A couple of families were mini golfing, and there were several cars parked along the drive. Some older women strolled under the tent, looking at the crafts, and the old man—his biological grandfather?—was seated on the porch next to the shelf of jam jars. The whole family had pulled together, it seemed, and the place was operating like a well-oiled machine.

Joe hopped out of his truck and paused for a moment to look around. He didn't want to cause any commotion or even reveal who he was to anyone else. Where was he most likely to find her?

He headed in the direction of the house—some young men were minding the rest of the activities, but when he got within a few yards of the side door, it opened, and Menno was there, his arms crossed over his chest.

"Good day," Menno said. "Can I help you?"

"Hi." Joe stopped. "I was hoping to speak with your wife."

"She's busy," Menno said.

"Uh—" Was her husband going to be a continual guard? "I'm not here to cause trouble. I don't even want anything from her, but

I got the impression you recognized my name before."

"*Yah*, I did."

"So you know who I am," he said.

"*Yah*."

This wasn't going to be easy, was it? Joe sighed. "Look, Menno, is it? I just want to talk to her. That's it. I've been looking for her, and I found her. I know you don't want me to cause any trouble, and I promise that I won't, but I think she deserves a chance to meet me, too."

"She doesn't want to," Menno replied.

"She's a mother," Joe said. "She might care about her oldest son. Just a guess."

There was movement behind Menno, and he stepped aside reluctantly. Rebecca came onto the step, and she frowned, looking at him more closely.

"You're the man from before. The one with the little girl who looks so much like Suzannah—the child who ran away at the pavilion."

"Yep, that's me," he said.

"Who did you say you were?" she asked.

"My name is Joseph Carter."

The color drained from her face, and she put a hand on the railing to steady herself.

"You'd better go," Menno said curtly.

"No!" Rebecca reached out toward him as if she could stop him from where she stood, then she looked back at her husband pleadingly. "I want to talk to him, Menno."

"The girls are inside," Menno said.

"We'll walk, then," Rebecca said. "Menno…"

Her husband nodded, and Rebecca came down the steps and stopped in front of Joe. She put a hand on his arm, as if feeling to see if he was real, and then peered up into his face.

"I was adopted as a newborn," Joe said softly. "And my parents told me that my birth mother was Rebecca Lehmann. Her mother was named Verna. They told Rebecca what they named me before they said goodbye to her for the last time—"

Tears welled up in Rebecca's eyes, and her lips wobbled. "Joseph…my baby."

"Not quite a baby anymore," he said with a rueful smile. "I'm thirty-seven."

"Walk with me," she said briskly, looking over her shoulder. "I have children who would be very upset to learn this. I'm sorry—I don't mean to hurt your feelings, but—"

"It's okay," he said, and he fell into step beside her. She led the way behind the house and past a little fenced-in corral of goats. No one was out there with the animals, and she slowed to a stop.

"How did you find me?" she asked.

"I asked around," he said. "I talked to Belinda Wickey. She knows who you are to me, but she said she knew about your pregnancy at the time, so..."

Rebecca nodded. "There were a few who knew and kept the secret, but I have daughters. You have one, too, so maybe you understand. I've raised them to make better choices than I did, but it would change the way they saw me if they knew. Especially at this age. Maybe when they're older and safely married." She rubbed at a red spot on her apron.

"I don't want to cause you any trouble," Joe said. "I just wanted to meet you."

Rebecca nodded. "My husband is a good man. I know you might question that right now, but he knew about you when he married me, and he's spent the last twenty-nine years keeping this very secret to protect my reputation. That's a hard habit to break."

"It's okay," Joe said.

"Tell me about you!" she said. "You have a little girl..."

"Yeah," he said. "I made a mistake, too, getting involved with Lottie's mother. We weren't a good match, but when we found out she was pregnant, she agreed to let me raise our daughter. I had to promise to wait until Lottie was eighteen to tell her anything, though. And I mean to keep that promise."

"But you're raising her," Rebecca said. "That's a good thing."

"She's a great kid," he replied.

"And the family who adopted you?" she asked, and he saw a glimmer of worry in her eyes. "Were they good to you?"

"They're great," he said. "I'm their only child. My father is an accountant, and my mother is a music teacher. They raised me well—lots of love and support. They know I was looking for you, and they have no problem with it."

"Good..." She nodded slowly. "When I met them the first time, I really thought they were good people. There was an Amish family from Florida who might have taken you, but there was something about your mom and dad—it was the way they held hands. They were tender and kind. I wanted those hands to hold you." She blinked back some tears.

"Why did you give me up?" he asked quietly.

Rebecca looked around the farm, and for a

few beats she didn't say anything. Then she said, "For this."

He wasn't sure how to answer that. For land? A farm?

"For marriage, and family, and in-laws, and…children." She winced. "I'm sorry, again! I know how that sounds."

"You wanted lots of children and a husband, not to be the single mother of one," he said, and the words came out gruffly.

"I was sixteen," she whispered. "I know I was old enough to know better, and to make better choices, but I was terrified, Joseph. My parents painted a picture for me of loneliness and judgment from the community. But if we hid it and I went to have you in Scranton, then I could come back and still have a life."

"But Menno knew," he said. "It wouldn't have stopped you from marrying him, would it?"

"I told him the day before our wedding. Honestly, I wasn't sure if he'd even marry me, but I couldn't keep that secret. He forgave me for holding it back, and he promised that no one would ever know, because people would judge. We'd have our own family, and… Oh, Joseph. I know how this must hurt."

But it didn't. Not like he'd expected it to.

Her story was such an honest one—a scared sixteen-year-old girl who didn't know how to handle it all.

"I always wondered why," he said.

"I loved you," Rebecca said earnestly. "I really did. I wanted you to have a beautiful life—one you'd never have had with me. I hoped you'd grow up loved and treasured, and with parents who were old enough to properly raise you." She shrugged. "I look back, and I realize I could have kept you. I think Menno would have married me all the same. We could have gone to a faraway community— maybe in Hawaii or something! Somewhere far enough away that no one would question dates or ages, or anything like that. At my age, with grown children of my own, I see things differently. I see other options. But back then, I didn't have the same perspective. I was just a girl who was ashamed of herself."

She'd had to forgive herself for having been young. He understood that all too well.

"I understand," he said, reaching out and taking her hand. "I didn't come here to make you feel bad about yourself or the life you built. I'm happy to see you happy."

"I prayed for you," she added. "Even last night, I mentioned you in my prayers. I pray for all my children, including you, but I can't pray for you out loud, if you understand. I stop and stay silent for a moment and pray for you in my heart. Then I say 'Amen.'"

"Your prayers were answered, Rebecca," he said. "I've had a really good life with a loving family. I wanted to thank you for that."

"Oh…" She smiled weakly. "Joseph, of course, I wanted you to be loved and cherished! But you were going to be someone else's gift."

"I live in Danke," he said. "If you ever wanted to visit—maybe meet your granddaughter— you could."

"I'd like that," she said. "And, Joseph, I will tell my children about you eventually. I will."

"It's okay to take your time," he said. "There's no rush."

"And the woman with you?" she asked. "Your girlfriend, right? Is it serious?"

"Uh—" His heart gave a squeeze. "We want different things, I'm afraid. I've got this stubborn conservative streak in me, and I guess it's because of my Amish blood. My daughter has been struggling with her mother leaving when she was born, and she needs a mother who will be at home with her."

Rebecca nodded. "Hmm."

"I thought you might understand the need for a present mother," he said. "It's what you did for your kids, right?"

He wanted to be reassured here that he was on the right path, that the pain he felt wasn't wasted.

"You two looked happy," she said quietly.

"We were, but—" Did he want to explain all of this?

"You don't owe me any explanations," she said. "And I am the woman who gave up her child in order to have a proper, conservative, Amish life, so I'm not one to talk. But can I tell you something I've learned over the years that might be helpful to you?"

"Sure," he said.

"Even the proper, conservative, Amish life isn't perfect," she said. "Sometimes my husband and I argue. We hide it the best we can, but it happens. It happens in every marriage! My oldest son was arrested for public intoxication last year. That was embarrassing. My middle girl won't even speak to us right now because we forbade her from dating an *Englisher* boy she's convinced she loves. My old father started gambling at the age of seventy-two, and we only recently figured out it's because of dementia. Life isn't perfect—it just keeps coming. And as the years roll on, the thing you think is too much to bear ends up being just one thing in a line of many things that weren't perfect. But do you know what holds a family together?"

Joe looked at her in silence.

"Love," she said. "That's it. There's no big secret. And there is no way to have a perfect family with no troubles. They don't exist. Some just hide it better than others."

She looked over toward the house, and Joe followed her gaze. Menno was on the porch, watching them. Someone called to him, and he headed toward the mini golf, but he looked back in their direction one last time.

"And you see that man?" Rebecca asked with a fond smile. "I'm going to argue with him later. Not because I want to, but because seeing you is going to bring up our own insecurities in our relationship, and no one knows how to talk about seeing the son again who you gave up for adoption. And Menno will be grumpy, and he'll stomp off to take care of the animals, and he'll skip supper. But when he comes back again after all that, we'll talk it through more calmly."

"How do you know?" Joe asked.

"It's been twenty-nine years of marriage,"

she said. "I know. The point is, we're not perfect, but we love each other. I love that man with all my heart, and he loves me, too. Even if you find someone who ticks off all those items on your list, like my Menno does, you still won't be perfect."

"Hazel's a pilot," he said in rush. "She loves her career. She's worked hard for it. It would keep her away from home for days at a time sometimes."

Rebecca just nodded.

"Isn't that a problem?" he persisted.

"If you loved each other enough," she said, "you'd figure it out. I wish I had more wisdom for you, but truly, all I know is that nothing is perfect, but sometimes a person is perfect for you."

She made it sound so simple, even manageable... She nodded in the direction of the mini golf. Menno was looking toward them again, and Rebecca smiled.

"I love that man," she said. "Do you love Hazel?"

"More than I even realized," he said.

"Tell me how it goes," she said, then looked up at him uncertainly. "If you want to, I mean. If you feel comfortable. If... I don't suppose I can ask for that, can I?"

Rebecca just stood there, tears shining in her eyes and her cheeks pink with embarrassment. He'd been wondering about her for a lifetime, and he'd found her. Who cared what she was owed or what she deserved? His heart didn't come with those limitations attached. He'd been raised better than that. Joe bent down and wrapped his arms around her, holding her close. Rebecca leaned into his chest and tipped her head against his cheek. He felt her shaky breath as she exhaled.

"You could ask for the world, Mom," he whispered with tears in his voice.

When he released her, she put a hand on his cheek. "I'm going to find a way to tell my kids, Joseph. Just give me time, okay?"

"You got it."

She could take all the time she needed. That wasn't the rush. But right now, he needed to find Hazel. Their conversation wasn't quite over yet...

EEYORE THE DONKEY was missing again. When Hazel woke up that morning, there was a whole hubbub outside about how the gate was open and the donkey was gone. Eli insisted he hadn't touched the gate, and Belinda had to grudgingly admit that the donkey was smarter than all of them combined because he seemed to come and go at will.

Eli went out in the buggy looking for the donkey, and he invited Hazel along, but she didn't have the heart for it. As Eli's buggy rolled up the drive and disappeared down the road, Hazel decided to take one last walk before she left Danke.

She wasn't sure why she was staying any longer, to be honest. She should go home—get her head on straight. But leaving also meant leaving Joe and Lottie behind, and that was hurting more than she'd anticipated.

But being a mom to a young daughter again wasn't the life she'd planned so carefully. And she'd finally achieved the career goal of her dreams, just in time to fall in love with a single dad. It wasn't her dream to leave her heart behind in Danke, either.

"Sometimes Eeyore just comes back on his own," Belinda said, coming out of the house with a handful of carrots. "I'll leave these for him. If he's close enough to see them—" She waved the carrots over her head. "If you wanted a carrot, Eeyore!"

Hazel smiled. "Does that work?"

"He's a character, that donkey," Belinda said. "You'd be surprised."

"I think I'll just take a walk," Hazel said. "If I see him, I'll come back and tell you."

"Thank you, dear," Belinda said. "It's appreciated."

Hazel headed up the drive, and she felt the sadness from yesterday sinking back down onto her shoulders. She loved Joe, and she wasn't what he needed. That was the problem. He needed a different kind of woman. He needed the woman she'd been fifteen years ago, not the woman she was now. And it was the woman she was now who loved him.

The day was warm, but a cool breeze kept her comfortable. Her mind was occupied with her own heartbreak as she ambled along, and she was mildly surprised to find herself at the highway. She stopped and looked around. Ahead of her, on the gravel road opposite, she saw an Amish woman walking toward the highway, too, Eeyore being led along. Was that Miriam? It looked like her.

Hazel waited while Miriam led the donkey across the highway. She smiled at Hazel.

"Look who I found," Miriam said.

Hazel nodded. "He caused a whole ruckus running away this morning."

Eeyore plodded along slowly, hardly seeming interested in returning home. He nuzzled at Hazel.

"Being all sweet now that he's been caught," Miriam said. "Are you heading back?"

"I can if it's easier," Hazel said.

"It might be," Miriam replied. She looked over her shoulder, and Hazel saw the mild worry in the young woman's eyes.

"Everything okay?" Hazel asked.

"I'm just leaving some visitors behind." She sighed.

"Did you want to get back to them? I can go call Belinda—"

"No, no. I'm actually glad to get away."

"The men who are interested in you," Hazel said, guessing.

Miriam nodded. "They are all nice. But…I feel in my heart that there is something not right about each of them. They're nice. They're very interested. They are talking to my family and trying to win my favor, but…"

Hazel understood that all too well.

"I was rather pretty once upon a time," Hazel said.

"You're still pretty," Miriam said with a low laugh.

"Thank you. But I mean…I was prettier. I drew attention. I had a lot of male interest.

And there was one boy who liked me just as much as the others, but he was smoother than they were. His family had money, and he asked me out to nice restaurants and bought me gifts. He was kind and respectful, and he could make me blush and giggle…and I chose him."

"That sounds good?" Miriam eyed her uncertainly.

"I fell in love with him," Hazel said. "I really did. I believed every sweet thing he said, never once thinking he might not stand by his flowery speeches. His name was Todd. I believed him when he said he loved me. I suppose he did love me, but when it came right down to it, he couldn't marry me. I found that out when I got pregnant, and he left the country."

"Oh, no!" Miriam said, grimacing.

"It was twenty years ago," Hazel said. "But I chose wrong. I've had a long time to look at where I could have done things differently. But I'm grateful for my daughter. She's wonderful, and I'm so glad I'm her mom."

"What warning signs did you miss?" Miriam asked, frowning. Was this story hitting home for her?

"The signs I missed? Character. Todd was

sweet, he was fun and he knew how to make me feel special. But relationship success comes down to the boring things, like work ethic, and honesty, and just a general stick-to-itiveness. I was looking at the wrong things. The boring stuff—the stuff your mother tells you matters—really is the most important part."

Miriam nodded slowly.

"Now, I'm not saying I know the guy personally," Hazel went on, "but I happen to know that there's a young man who is head over heels in love with you. But you find him boring."

"Obadiah?" she asked with a frown.

"That's the one." Hazel shrugged. "I don't know him. And spark matters! It really does. But if you're looking for a man who's willing to take on the world to get a chance with you—that's him. And when I asked your local matchmaker about him, she said he's stable, and determined, and focused on doing things the right way. She thinks he should be happy with a girl more on his level. Less pretty, I think was the point. But he wants you."

"I hardly noticed him, honestly," Miriam said. "Belinda mentioned him, and I thought it was a joke."

"I don't think Belinda jokes about matrimony," Hazel said. "It might not hurt to look at Obadiah a little closer. He might not look like it, but he's got the heart of a warrior."

"Not us Amish…"

"Okay, the heart of a bull?" Hazel said, trying again. "There's more than meets the eye. That's what I'm saying."

"Is that your advice from experience?" Miriam asked.

"It sure is," Hazel said. "If I were your age and had it to do again, I'd at least consider him. Keep in mind that the guys who flirt really well and make you giggle? It's a learned skill. They can do it because they have lots of practice. The guys who have no game at all? Those are the real treasures. I know our cultures are different, but some things—like men, and love, and passion—are universal."

Miriam blushed. "*Danke*. Thank you."

"You're very welcome."

They reached the drive for Butternut Bed and Breakfast, and they turned in, Eeyore plodding cooperatively behind them. Belinda was waiting on the step, her hands on her hips.

The really good guys were hard to come by. They blended into the background sometimes. They could be shy or just not have the words when other guys swept in with every line imaginable. They could be single dads, sometimes, focused on their growing daughters.

Overhead a small plane buzzed across the clear blue sky, and Hazel looked up at it. It was no Airbus, but it was still flying… What if she could stay and continue loving Joe and Lottie, and show that little girl that moms could stick around? Would that be selling out on her own dreams, or would it be a simple change of course toward a different dream she hadn't dared to hope for yet?

CHAPTER EIGHTEEN

JOE DIALED HAZEL'S NUMBER, put the phone on speaker and tossed it on the seat beside him. Then he put the truck in Reverse and pulled out of Lehmann's Family Fun Farm. His mind was spinning, but Rebecca had made an excellent point. No family setup was perfect, and "perfect" probably wasn't even possible, not with human beings in the mix. But he knew one thing for sure—he didn't want to let Hazel go.

Hazel picked up on the second ring.

"Joe?" she said.

"Hi…" He felt a wave of relief at the sound of her voice. "It's good to hear your voice."

"Same." He heard the smile in her voice. "I miss you."

"Me, too. More than you probably know."

"We aren't making this any easier, are we?" she asked.

"No…and maybe we don't need to. That's the thing. We love each other, right? Let's talk.

I've been to see my birth mom, and I had a pretty big epiphany."

"Oh?"

"Where are you right now?"

"Like, this second?" she asked with a low laugh.

"This very second. Where are you?"

"I'm at the hangar," she said. "I'm looking at some planes."

Of course she would be.

"Can I come see you?" he asked. "I need to talk to you in person."

"Sure," she said.

"Give me fifteen minutes," he said. "Don't leave, okay?"

"I'll be here."

"I love you, Hazel," he said. "I really do."

He hung up the call and signaled onto the highway. That was fifteen minutes for him to come up with some way to tell her that he wanted to marry her. Yep, it was crazy—it even sounded that way rattling around inside of his head—but it was also true. Now that he'd found her, he didn't want to spend one more day without her. And he thought he had a solution.

HAZEL LOOKED OVER the specs for the Cessna once more. Miles stood back, his arms crossed over his chest. He'd been watching her think this over for a good twenty minutes already.

"Do you want a few minutes on your own?" he asked. "It's a big decision. Like I said, I'd be happy to work with you to start up a sight-seeing business here."

"I appreciate that," she said.

"And there's plenty of people who ask about something like that, so I think you'd be booked up pretty fast."

"Yeah…" She walked around the outside of the plane and ran her finger over a small scratch in the paint of the fuselage. The plane was in good shape, and it would carry three passengers at a time. Considering the cost of fuel, insurance, maintenance and her need to make a living off of a small business, she could probably find a price for tours that would make this feasible…

"Maybe I'll just—" Miles hooked his thumb over his shoulder. "And you can think it over and let me know when you're done out here?"

"Sure, Miles. Thanks."

The old man hobbled back into the hangar, where his coffee was waiting for him. Being an Amish-country tour guide wasn't her dream job, but it would keep her flying, and that little detail was one she couldn't bend on. She was a pilot to the core, and she couldn't let go of that part of herself, even if she was willing to be flexible on where she flew and what uniform she wore.

The smart, midnight blue pantsuit with the silver wings stitched across the left breast pocket would be for someone else.

That still stung, but a life with Joe would make up for it. She might have some explaining to do to Maddie, though! She hadn't even hinted to her daughter yet about what she was planning. That was a face-to-face conversation… Or at the very least, that was a conversation for after she sorted out the details.

She looked over her shoulder toward the parking lot. Her heartbeat sped up when she recognized Joe's red pickup truck pulling in. She put the page of specs back on the plane seat and shut the door, then she headed over in his direction. Overhead, a small plane buzzed upward, taking off into the midmorning.

Maybe later on she'd take a celebratory flight. Maybe Joe would come with her…

"Hi," Joe said as he reached her, and then he pulled her straight into his arms and kissed her.

"Hi…" she said when he finally pulled back, and she blinked up at him.

"So…I tried to come up with a little speech, but I don't have one," he said. "Here's the thing. I love you. I've been looking long enough to know that what we have doesn't come around too often—once in a lifetime, if you're lucky. And I don't want to let you go. You're a pilot. You know what you love to do, and I don't want to be the guy to hold you back, either."

"So you came out here to kiss me and remind me why we won't work?" she asked, her throat growing tight.

"No, I came out here to tell you that I've been really foolish. I had this idea in my head of what would make the perfect family scene, and that doesn't work. Heck, if I wanted that, Michelle's mom would be willing to be the stay-at-home mom. What I want is a life with a feisty pilot who loves me."

Hazel smiled past the mist in her eyes. "About that. I'm looking at a Cessna. I figure I could buy it and start a flight sightseeing business out here, just like you suggested. I didn't know I wanted a life with you when I made all my plans, Joe. Now that I know I want to be with you and Lottie, I'm just going to have to adjust."

Joe shook his head. "No. Not a chance. You worked fifteen years to get that job offer, and you wanted it so badly you could taste it. You're good at what you do, and they picked the right woman for the job. How much would it keep you away?"

"Sometimes three or four days at a time. But not always. It depends on the schedule."

Joe nodded. "Okay."

"Okay, what?" she asked hesitantly.

"Okay. I can deal with that. Just come home to me, okay? Come home to me and Lottie. Because we'll need you, too."

"Are you sure?" Hazel asked.

"I'm positive. The thing is, do I want my daughter giving up the success she worked for in order to please some guy, no matter how heart-stoppingly handsome he happens to be?" He shot her a grin.

"My guess is no," she said.

"I also don't want to explain to Maddie why I held her mom back," he said. "Perfect comes in many shapes and sizes. Let's make ours together."

She nodded, and she stood up onto her tip-toes to kiss him once more.

"Oh, and—" Joe pulled back. "The most important part of this is that I want to marry you. I want to belong to each other and come home to each other. And if you'll let me be all old-fashioned in one more thing, I really want you to be Mrs. Carter."

Hazel nodded. "Yes, I will marry you, Joe."

"That's all I wanted," he said, wrapping his arms around her. "Man, I really should have planned a speech. This story isn't going to tell well, is it?"

"It's going to be just fine," she said.

Because the end of the story of how they met was going to be how they got engaged in front of the airplane hangar, and how they realized that life together was everything that they needed. And somehow in his arms, her heart was soaring in the same way it did when she was up there in the clouds with a propeller keeping her aloft…

EPILOGUE

HAZEL AND JOE planned a big church wedding. At first Hazel thought she just wanted something small to make it legal, but then her mother had reminded her of her grandma's veil, and she'd known that there was no other way to do this. If she was getting married, it was going to be a big, floofy, traditional wedding, complete with Grandma's veil.

They got married on the Thanksgiving long weekend because that was when Maddie was free from school to be there. Hazel had one bridesmaid—her daughter—and Joe had his cousin as the sole groomsman. And Lottie was the flower girl, of course. They had several Amish guests at the wedding— Belinda Wickey and Eli Lapp sat together on the groom's side. Eli had been excited to "eat wedding food," as he'd put it. Belinda was just thrilled to be included. Rebecca and Menno also attended together. They hadn't fully explained things to their children yet, but Re-

becca had insisted that they go to her oldest
son's wedding, and Menno had asked Joe to
forgive him for his earlier surly protective-
ness. He'd even passed along some marriage
advice, which Joe had told Hazel last night:
*You choose the person you marry, and you
keep on choosing them, even if things don't
go like you expect. Sometimes a marriage
takes many sets of vows. Just keep promising and meaning it.*

Hazel had thought it was particularly beautiful.

Joe's adoptive parents were there, too. They
were very involved in pulling off the wedding, helping with details like finding the
men's corsages when they went missing and
rounding up a stick of deodorant when Joe
realized he'd forgotten his. They were going
to be lovely in-laws—Hazel could tell.

Her side of the pews was filled with her
parents, her uncles and aunts, cousins and
friends… She'd even invited a couple of fellow pilots from the regional airline she now
flew for. Sometimes she still felt like she
needed to pinch herself to see if she was
dreaming. She'd gotten everything—the man
of her dreams, a beautiful little stepdaughter

and the job she'd longed for all these years, flying passengers around the state.

That November morning, instead of putting together a Thanksgiving feast, Hazel stood at the closed church doors in a white tulle wedding dress, listening to the murmur of voices from the sanctuary and the soft organ music. Joe was in there waiting for her, and Hazel's stomach gave a tumble.

This was it!

"You look beautiful, Mom," Maddie said, adjusting the veil. Maddie looked effortlessly beautiful in her rose satin dress, and Hazel's heart swelled with love.

Lottie stood silently, her eyes wide and her little mouth pressed shut. Hazel bent down in front of her and tried to coax a smile out of her.

"You look so pretty, too, Lottie," Hazel said.

Lottie didn't answer, but her lips trembled. This was one of those big moments where a little girl would have big feelings. And there had been enough of those moments for Lottie where they couldn't properly explain things to her because it would be too much, but maybe it was time that Hazel did.

"Lottie, can we talk for a minute?" Hazel asked.

Lottie nodded.

"Your dad and I decided to get married, and I thought you liked that," Hazel said.

"I do," Lottie whispered.

"Well, here's the thing," Hazel said. "I know we talked about all of this before, but maybe I could say it again for you, just so you'll remember it. I chose your dad because I love him, but you're a part of this, too. I'm choosing you, as well. I'm choosing to be your mom, and to take care of you, and love you, and be superproud of you. Did you know that?"

Lottie nodded her head. This wasn't going to be enough. This child needed more than they'd told her earlier.

"Sweetie, I know you've been asking about your birth mom a lot," Hazel said. "I don't have answers there, but I can offer you this. Sometimes we get lucky enough to choose our family. And when I look at all the choices out there, I choose you."

"Me?" she whispered.

"Yep. I have a daughter already, and I'm choosing one more. Remember, I'm the pilot!" Hazel said with a hopeful smile. "I decide where that plane goes, and I fly that plane right back to you every time!"

"Do you promise?" Lottie whispered.

"Cross my heart… I'll love you, Lottie. I'll be the best mom I can for you. Would you let me?"

Lottie looked over at Maddie, who had tears brimming in her eyes. "I get Maddie, too, right?"

"Of course!" Maddie said, and she wiped a tear from her cheek. "We're a package deal. All of us."

"What do you say?" Hazel asked softly. "Will you choose us back, Lottie?"

Lottie nodded. "Okay. You can call me Lottie, and I'll call you Mommy."

Hazel pulled Lottie into her arms, and Maddie put her arms around them both. Just then, the organ music changed to that familiar prelude to the wedding march, and Maddie released them.

"Quick. No tears!" Maddie said, wiping her cheek again. "We're going in, Lottie!"

Lottie squirmed to the ground and Maddie handed her a basket of flower petals. Maddie looked down at the little girl, and Lottie looked up at Maddie with big, adoring eyes.

"I can't wait to have a sister, Lottie," Maddie said softly.

And then the doors were flung open, and

Hazel looked up to see Joe standing at the front of the church, and his gaze locked on hers. Her heart skipped a beat in response.

Yes, this was it. They were making a family today—two lonely hearts and the beautiful girls who'd now be sisters. Lottie started forward, and then Maddie followed behind, and as Hazel took her first step down the aisle, she knew this was right.

Marrying Joe was more than coming home—it was like a takeoff. Because this marriage was going to be an adventure together—one she couldn't wait to start.

* * * * *

Don't miss the next book in Patricia Johns's The Butternut Amish B&B miniseries, coming November 2023 from Harlequin Heartwarming

THE NORA ROBERTS COLLECTION

40% OFF!

Get to the heart of happily-ever-after in these Nora Roberts classics! Immerse yourself in the beauty of love by picking up this incredible collection written by, legendary author, Nora Roberts!

YES! Please send me the **Nora Roberts Collection**. Each book in this collection is 40% off the retail price! There are a total of 4 shipments in this collection. The shipments are yours for the low, members-only discount price of $23.96 U.S./$31.16 CDN. each, plus $1.99 U.S./$4.99 CDN. for shipping and handling. If I do not cancel, I will continue to receive four books a month for three more months. I'll pay just $23.96 U.S./$31.16 CDN., plus $1.99 U.S./$4.99 CDN. for shipping and handling per shipment.* I can always return a shipment and cancel at any time.

☐ 274 2595 ☐ 474 2595

Name (please print)

Address _____ Apt. #

City _____ State/Province _____ Zip/Postal Code

Mail to the **Harlequin Reader Service:**
IN U.S.A.: P.O. Box 1341, Buffalo, NY 14240-8531
IN CANADA: P.O. Box 603, Fort Erie, Ontario L2A 5X3

HARLEQUIN
PLUS

Try the best multimedia
subscription service for romance
readers like you!

Read, Watch and Play.

Experience the easiest way to get
the romance content you crave.

Start your **FREE TRIAL** at
www.harlequinplus.com/freetrial.